A
Dead-End
Job

Justin Alcala

THE PARLIAMENT HOUSE

9781953539922

Edited by Mary Westveer, Wyn Davis, and Alyssa Barber

The Parliament House

www.parliamenthousepress.com

Cover Design by Shayne Leighton

To my wife Mallory, who doesn't think I'm funny but supports the fact that I think I'm hilarious. The fake encouragement is noted.

To my children, Lily and Ronan, who promote me from "Creepy Writer-Man-Child" to "Creepy Writer-Daddy-Man-Child." Also, no, I do not condone PROFESSIONAL CONTRACT KILLER as your college major.

To Sara Schuh Jodon of Add an Eye Editing Services. Did you know you're really smart?

For Fred and Mary Schuh. Could there be cooler in-laws?

To all that we've lost during this pandemic, especially Carlos Sanchez, Nick Sebek and Colin Mayo. If you've had someone torn from your life, I'm truly sorry. This is for them as well.

PROLOGUE

CHICAGO'S CHIEF PUBLIC HEALTH INSPECTOR FOUND DEAD IN HOME

"Damn it," Death spat, scratching another name onto his legal pad. The list was growing longer. Death picked up his steaming mug that read "*I drink coffee for your safety*" and sipped it before clicking the "next story" tab. He'd only been in his apartment's kitchen turned home office for ten minutes and already he was at wits' end, the top of his stylus pen half-chewed. Death, The Grim Reaper, Charon, whatever you wanted to call him, the title demanded respect. Afterall, he had held his position before men wore pants. Yet never in his career had someone been so tenacious as to start killing mortals before their expiration date. Death didn't even know how it could happen. He picked up his smart phone, using his stylus to dial the numbers on the touch interface.

"Yeah, Jumbo, it's Death. How long until you get into the office?" Death leaned back in his chair and took another sip from his cup. "Well, I can assure you that you'll get here safely." Death sighed. "I'm sorry. It's just been a tough morning already. Whoever this person is, they're still getting past our system. None of these names from last night were in the program." Death slung his boney feet on an empty duct taped kitchen chair. "Alright," he groaned into the receiver. "I'll reboot while I wait. See you soon."

Death pocketed his phone. He pressed up from his seat, knees popping, and shuffled to the server room. The room doubled as the gallery for his collectible action figures. He removed a thick brass key, the bow at the end shaped like a waving *Hello Kitty,* from his sleeve and pushed it into the lock. After several spins, the mechanism clicked open, and Death pushed inside. Death gave a thumbs up to his prized 1982 Masters of the Universe Skeletor toy, which was still in its original package, before heading to the server's reset button and pressing it. The hum of electric computer fans quieted before starting up again. Death watched the monitor's *reload* bar fill up. Once completed another screen arose. The title read, *Deaths for Today.* Death compared the names and times before checking the total number.

Good morning.

151,613 deaths programmed for today.

It's currently seventy-eight degrees with a high of eighty-two.

Everything looked exactly as it did last night.

Death shook his head. "How the hell did that Chief Health Inspector die without being loaded into the program?" he asked aloud. Death clicked the refresh button several times, but the number didn't change. "Jesus," he mumbled. He shook his hooded head. "Nah, he's too busy right now." Death went through the protocol that Jumbo had taught him. He checked the wires for loose connections, examined the server's blinking blue lights, and ran the virus program. It was all exhausting. Finally, out of desperation, he used a can of aerosol to blow the dust out of the keyboard.

Ding. The bell from Death's apartment door rang.

Death picked up the hem of his drab cloak and hurried out of the room. He closed the door and locked it behind him before hurrying to the apartment's entrance. He looked through the peek hole but could only see the peeling yellow walls and ugly brown carpet from the hallway.

"Friend or foe?" he called out.

"Neither," said a nasally voice. "It's your I.T. guy."

"Jumbo," Death said in relief. He unlatched the lock on the front door and opened it. Sitting in an electronic wheelchair was a small man with dark skin, black framed glasses, and long bleached hair drawn up in beads. His thin arms perched on his chair's rests, and his crooked legs relaxed on the feet holders.

"You look different," Death greeted. "Did you do something with your hair?"

"I grew," Jumbo said drily as he pushed the controls of the chair and drove inside. Death closed the front door and then followed. On the back of Jumbo's wheelchair was a sticker that read "*Stop checking out my wheelchair-butt.*"

"Let me guess," Jumbo said as he cruised through the hallway, "you even tried dusting out the keyboard again?"

"I'm telling you, it's worked before."

"Sure," said Jumbo as he drove to the server room door and tested the handle. "Man, you're still locking this thing?"

"Do you know how many action figures are in there?" Death asked as he removed his *Hello Kitty* key and unlocked the server room door. "Well, I do. It's nearly five-thousand dollars worth." Death put the key back in his sleeve before pushing open the door. Jumbo pursed his lips as he drove inside, rolling to the main server. He reached out for the mouse, and after several clicks, opened up a black screen with white letters. Death watched as Jumbo did his work. "Besides," Death continued as Jumbo read lines of code, "All of this is a little too suspicious. I can't help but feel as if someone is pulling the wool over my eyes."

"You don't have eyes, dude." Jumbo winced at a flashing system menu.

"It's a metaphor."

"Well," Jumbo said and shrugged, "you're right. There's nothing wrong with this program."

"Jumbo, you're killing me. Aren't you supposed to know what's going on?"

"Dude, I don't know what you want me to tell you? I checked the code. Everything looks legit."

"When you wrote up this program, you said that it was flawless."

"It *is* flawless, man."

"Why is it that people that I haven't loaded die? There was that factory landlord, the Health Inspector."

"What's one or two people?"

"It's over a dozen now."

"The point is, think about where you were ten years ago? Do you remember?"

"Well, yeah." Death started rubbing the back of his neck. "But—"

"But nothing, man. Ten years ago, you were peeled to your phone from dawn to dusk making death-calls. You'd go moonlighting to put an end to those that cheated you. You know, the *Unmentionables*."

"They're called that so we don't bring them up."

Jumbo shook his head. "Now look at you. All you have to do is load up the names and the program takes care of the rest. That leaves you nearly the rest of your day to clean up the noncompliant undead, and then focus on your toy collection."

"You always ridicule the collection." Death pushed down on his temples and massaged them. "I don't know; I just can't relax when someone is killing on my behalf. I look like I don't have any control of my domain."

"Death, you're stressed. I mean face it, you're a workaholic."

"No, I'm not."

"You totally are. Even now, with hundreds of thousands of deaths, you're having an anxiety attack over a tiny anomaly. We deal in millions of deaths a year. Hiccups are going to happen every once in a while."

"Maybe you're right."

"Of course, I'm right." Jumbo drove his wheelchair closer to Death, reaching to pat the angel on the shoulder. Midway through his ride, Jumbo's wheel jammed between the toy shelf and swivel chair. Jumbo struggled to free himself, fighting with his chair's joystick. "You know what you need, man?" he asked through gritted teeth, his eyes focusing on his tire jam.

Death hung his head low. "What?"

"A vacation."

"Ha."

"No seriously." Jumbo freed himself. "You've been talking about it for months."

"Yeah, but I was joking."

"What's to stop you?"

"Seriously, Jumbo?" Death trudged out of the server room. He stopped at the threshold and waited for Jumbo to follow. Jumbo pushed his controller and wheeled out of the server room and into the kitchen. Death closed the door and locked it up again. "Who's going to kill one-hundred-and-sixty thousand people a day?"

"Death, we just covered this. That program runs itself. Every morning it loads names based off of region, age, hazards, and one-hundred-and-seventy-two other base factors. Once it does, you just need to click the get started button."

"Yeah, and who is going to do that?"

"Let me do it. I'm fighting with my roommate anyway. I might need a break."

"You mean your mom?"

"She's still my roommate. Anyhow, I could use a week away. I'll crash here while you're in Bermuda, Spain, or wherever."

"What about the Unmentionables?"

"The people that cheated death?"

Death looked around his apartment as if someone might be listening. "Well," he whispered, "yeah."

"Haven't you been looking to take on an intern for a while?"

"It never works out. I've tried several over the centuries. They always end up being lunatics."

"That's because you're too picky."

"No, I'm not."

"Look at you," Jumbo wheeled around Death's kitchen and living room. "You've fired every assistant you've ever had besides me, and let me tell you, it's been no picnic. You don't date because you say the girls don't get you, and you have no friends."

"Ouch, that's harsh."

"Sorry man, but some tough love might help for once. Death, you prefer the company of action figures over people who can walk and talk. Think about it, boss man, you're the epitome of an introverted, self-righteous, workaholic."

Death stood still for a moment. He looked around at the pictures hanging on his walls. They were filled with smiley interracial friends and happy couples he'd never met. All of them came with the frame. Death needed to be honest with himself. He'd been so engrossed in work for the last two millennium that he hadn't taken any time off for himself.

"Okay, but I'll need to personally train the intern before I go." Jumbo gave a slow clap. "Finally."

"I'll need *your* help finding the best candidates."

"Well, I can't exactly go on LinkedIn."

"Are you going to help me or not?"

"Take it easy." Jumbo held up his hands. "I have an idea."

"And what's that?"

"It's just a matter of research." Jumbo looked at Death's laptop on the kitchen table. He drove his wheelchair in front of it and minimized the current window.

"Jumbo," Death moaned as he followed, "what are you doing?"

"I'm accessing the shared drive." Jumbo clicked into several folders until a gridded list opened. He clicked a bar on the menu labeled *sort by fate*. Several hundred names in red letters came up, along with a description of their age, profession, and forecasted death. "*Voila*," Jumbo said as he highlighted the names with his cursor.

"What am I looking at?"

"This is a list of several thousand people who will die today and go straight to Hell." Jumbo clicked the *magnify* button to zoom in on the screen. "They will not pass go. They will not collect two-hundred dollars."

"And?"

"*And* I'm sure that each and every one of them would gladly choose to serve as your intern instead of suffer in the fiery pits."

"Why would I want one of these jerks as my intern?"

Jumbo slapped his forehead. "Man, use your head. The program does all of the mundane killing. The one-hundred-and-sixty thousand plus deaths are taken care of. All you really need is someone who's going to put an end to all the undead, practitioners of illegal magic and other freak shows. You don't need a good guy. You need a *bad* guy."

Death tapped his bony foot on the linoleum floor. "How is a thief or politician going to help me stop the Unmentionables? Also, they'll need to get my dry cleaning."

"Come on, man." Jumbo sorted through the names. "Use your imagination. I'm not talking about the petty thieves. I'm talking about *real* villains. You know, the Big Bad Wolf."

Death looked over Jumbo's shoulder. He nearly put his clammy hand on Jumbo's arm but paused just before it landed. "Alright, I'm picking up what you're putting down. Good job."

"Thank you."

"What are you thinking?" asked Death as he picked up his mug and sipped out of it. Some Jack the Ripper serial killer or more of a Thulsa Doom cult-leader guy?"

Jumbo swiped at his computer screen a few times before stopping halfway down the list. He narrowed his eyes at a specific name, pointing on the screen toward a person's description.

"I had something different in mind." Jumbo smiled. "What would you say to a guy who grew up in Chicago?"

Death hummed.

Jumbo continued to read. "According to this, he was good in school, which is important, but had a tough upbringing that forced him into a life of violence. He's proficient in several fighting styles, has knowledge of both street and military tactics, and loves table-top roleplaying games?"

Death scratched at the top of his hood. "Jeez, what's this guy's profession? Commando?"

Jumbo squinted his eyes as he moved to the next column. "Actually," he laughed, "hitman."

1

Today was going to be busy. I didn't know how I'd fit a murder into my schedule.

For starters, I was out of coffee. I don't think anyone can really start the day unless they have a cup of joe. Not me at least. Since I live in a more *affordable* part of Chicago, there were no corner coffee shops charging mortgages for a fix within walking distance. Which means I had to drive deeper into the city to feed the shaky caffeine monkey beating on my back. I joined a local horde of zombies in a hipster neighborhood called Bucktown as they waited in a Disneyland-worthy line for a chance to be a real boy or girl again. This gave me time to think about my to-do list.

I needed to return my library books. I was finally catching up on my Bukowski novels after years of recommendations from friends. *Why is good advice so hard to swallow?* Since I paid for everything in singles and change, I couldn't just buy a book online. I had to check them out whenever a reading itch needed a scratch. Afterwards, I'd need to replace the squeaky brakes on the van, shower, and then pick up a new hammer strut pin from Denny's Pawn Shop. Denny and I had built a relationship based on trading illegal firearm parts, which was great for a guy that doesn't like proof of sale when it came to his career tools. Finally, my role-playing group had a six o'clock table reserved for our D&D campaign at the neighborhood gaming store. We were nearing level ten, and as the party's wizard, they'd need me to survive our latest adventure. Hmm, when could I possibly squeeze in work?

"That'll be twelve-fifty," declared the barista with black framed glasses.

"For a cup of plain coffee?" I stared at the register's cost display. "I mean, seriously?"

The acne covered art history major working the register didn't flinch. He must have been seasoned.

"Do I get a veteran discount?"

He shook his head. I used my sparse wallet insulation to pay for the mud, but only after my debit card declined. Now I was really running late.

After careful deliberation, I had decided to assassinate my mark just before D&D started. I started my day by returning *Pulp* to the library just hours before it was due. Once the scary Baba Yaga-looking librarian gave me the okay to take out another book, I fished for a lighter subject amongst the rows of brain candy. Andrew Smith would do. Nothing taps into a shattered childhood like kidnapped boys, melting men, and broken hearts. I hurried home with my new literature, ate the last Lunchable in my refrigerator, and then started on the van's brakes.

I'd cut my palm in the process and had to waste

precious time super gluing the gash across what a fortune teller once told me was my lifeline. I'd picked up the trick in the military. Super glue and tampons were a medics best friend overseas, but that's another story. The adhesive quickly stopped the bleeding.

I showered, dressed in my favorite suit, and hurried into my work car. The indistinct sedan was great for keeping a low profile. I drove the sedan across the hot summer town to Denny's pawn shop. Denny, who was on the most wanted list for diabetics, ate his deep-dish pizza dripping with grease with one hand while navigating his SmartPad with the other. He was reading the latest article from a local conspiracy theory blog known as the *Hex Files*. The title read, *"Missing Nursing Home Patients Part of President's Mass Alien Abduction Plan."* His store once was an 80's rug business, and the shag carpet on the floor hadn't been changed since. He did me the service of picking up his mullet-crowned head as I ambled into his outdated storefront.

"Buck," Denny croaked through oily lips. "Is today the day?"

"Today is the day," I lamented while bringing the briefcase I'd lugged in onto his dirty glass counter. The neon light above flickered as I clicked the brass hasps and opened the case up. Angels cried as the 1987 Second Series Punisher Issue One comic book waited for Denny inside. *I really needed this job to work out.* Denny's eyes lit up as he stared at the illustrated sex before him.

"You sure about this?"

"No, but I need that hammer strut pin. Unless you want to give me the pin for free?"

Denny used his pinkies, which had far less grease on them than the rest of his digits, to lift the plastic covered comic and bring it behind the counter. "Nope. Don't worry though. I'll take great care of it."

"Just give me the pin."

Denny wiped his hands on his standard fat guy t-shirt complete with besmirched mustard stains and stretched neckline. He handed me a Ziplock bag with the tungsten pistol part. "Hey, remember, if it doesn't sell, you can always come and buy it for market value."

"That's double what you're trading it for."

"Yeah."

"You're a monster."

I left Denny's cruddy shop and shuffled back into the safety of the sedan. After disassembling, repairing, and reassembling the forty-five-caliber I'd dubbed *Thing One* from the concealment of my tinted windows, I headed to the job site. I was running about ten minutes late, but my employer informed me that I'd have an hour window to locate and eliminate my target from the given vantage point. I finished one last cigarette in the car before getting to work.

I followed my employer's directions and entered the burnt brick building across the street from my mark. Instructions are different from job to job. Most first-timers let the artist apply their craft as they see fit. Repeat clients, control freaks, and sick-in-the-head types are a little different. They'd frequently give step-by-step instructions, and are willing to pay more for you to follow them to the T. I guess it's the whole *going to prison for life if we're caught* thing that stirs concern. My current employer was, without a doubt, the latter.

I headed up to the recommended stairwell that led to the advised abandoned office given to me by my employer. The door was open. I made myself comfortable at the dusty window directly across the street from my target's apartment. After locating my target's unit, I pulled up a leftover office chair and assembled the M40A3 long range rifle I'd smuggled through my satchel.

I fantasized about what spells my wizard would prepare in today's D&D session while spinning the sound suppressor to the rifle's muzzle brake.

Our party of zany adventurers were in the Mere of Dead Men, a place filled with black dragons, lizard-folk, and undead. You couldn't just go in using everyday swords and shields.

Come on, son, that's basic High Road bandit equipment. Your mindset needed to accommodate the situation at hand. We'd need special potions, magical rings, and holy items to survive this quest. Adapt or die, baby.

It was about thirty minutes into my daydream that I realized my mark was nowhere to be found. I placed my eye to the scope and took a look into his place. It was getting dark, and I could barely see into the poorly lit apartment supposedly owned by my mark. It struck me as odd that there were no signs of life. There were no bowls in the sink or phone charger plugged into the wall. In fact, as I used the scope to zoom in further, I noticed that the place didn't seem lived in at all. There was no furniture, wall paintings, or keys on the counter. It was spartan, as if it hadn't been rented out in months. *Something wasn't right.*

The unexpected clack of the lock snapped behind me. The creak of worn door hinges confirmed my earlier suspicion. I stood stock still. There was shuffling followed by soft shoe steps and then the distinct sound of a cocking handle being drawn from a machine gun. I lowered my rifle, raised my hands in surrender, and spun around. That's when the gunshots rang. *Well, this wasn't on the schedule.*

2

H ere's a question for you.

Have you ever had a bullet drilled into your skull? I just did, and it could best be described as *uncomfortable*. It wasn't the first time I'd been shot, but it was definitely the first one to the old noggin.

My body went numb, and a ringing drowned out the buzz of fluorescent lights, distant car horns, and anything else audible within the north side of Chicago. I could taste copper as if I'd been sucking pennies and my vision blurred. Meanwhile, that tiny little voice that I'd been ignoring my entire life, the same one that told me not to touch myself as a teenager and *definitely* not to take this job, took center stage.

At the moment that voice was telling me that I was an idiot. As my body kicked backwards and crashed onto the ground, that voice grew louder, replaying the many choices I could have made throughout my life to keep me out of this predicament. Blood began to seep from my forehead and into my eyes. Before long, I was looking up at the

commercial ceiling tiles through a veil of red. I wondered
how many people on the business end of my barrel felt
this way. Before I could consider, the tiny little voice cut in.
Not yet, it seemed to say. *Let's take this from the beginning.* I
could feel my guts and bladder let go of anything I'd been
holding back. I wasn't going to be buried in these pants.
So, with nothing left to do but die, I began to recollect life's
little mistakes. *Where did it all go wrong?*

It's a dime store novel, really. My name Buchanan
Palasinski, but people call me Buck. I'm a local hitman, or
at least I was, from Chicago. I grew up poor and busted on
the Southside and this is the result. My Old Man was a
second-generation Polish alcoholic who ditched the family
once burning us with cigarettes lost its charm. My Ma was
a Mexican immigrant who must have been high when she
tied the knot with Pops. Regardless, she tried her best to
raise my older brother and I while maintaining a fifty-hour
job at a fried chicken joint.

She was uneducated and spoke very little English, so it
was up to my brother and I to take care of ourselves. By
sixteen, my brother was in jail for a crime he's still serving,
and I'd already seen juvie several times myself. Shortly
after my brother's sentence, Ma made me swear that I'd
pay attention in school. Although I kept my grades up, I
hadn't seen the point. With no money for college, and no
idea how to apply for scholarships, I really only had a few
options. I could spend the rest of my life at my job in the
mall's cellphone kiosk or try my luck in the *stick-em'-up*
market. Neither had been very appealing.

Everything truly came to a head during my senior year
of high school. The stress of being a poor kid had snow-
balled for years, but one particular incident set the ball a

rolling. A few of the teachers had pressured me into joining an after-school program, and fortunately for me, it was a role-playing club. Every weekday after school at 3:15pm, I met several other kids in the library to play Dungeons and Dragons. The thought by faculty was that I'd let out pent aggression healthily by fighting pretend dragons instead of real street thugs. I met several good kids, and one terrible one. His name was Nick Griffin. He was in the club for the same reason as me. He was so bad in fact, that they had also forced him to join the school newspaper, botanical team, and anything else that would keep him out of trouble. Nick and I became close, getting high together on school nights and stealing from the mall on weekends.

Anyhow, one day some teachers requested that the chief of the newspaper put a special title under my yearbook photo. They wanted it to say *Most Likely to Work a High-End Job*. It was a pity title for a poor kid, but I appreciated the sentiment. Unfortunately, Nick caught wind of it, and thought it would be hilarious to shoot down any ambitions I might have. Come yearbook distribution day, I walked into a school filled with kids pointing and laughing at Buchanan Palasinski, *Most Likely to Work a Dead-End Job*. The jokes wouldn't quit, and before long, the fragile kid from the Southside hood gave up. I figured I was a failure by design.

Discouraged, I joined the Army. *Cue the American Eagle and fireworks*. I was assigned to the 10th Mountain Division based out of Fort Drum, New York. The army life wasn't fun by any means, but I was damn good at it. Unlike a lot of the guys, I had half a brain and nothing to lose, so the infantry was ideal. We were stationed in Afghanistan shortly after my second year, where according to my peers, I excelled. In my opinion, I'd survived a violent nine months of warfare by killing the bad guy before he killed me. Because of it, I not only became a scout, but was recommended for what fans of Tom Barringer movies know as *Sniper School*. After studying firearms physics, I reenlisted and became *Buck-Sergeant Buchanan Palasinski*, hence my nickname. It wasn't long before shrapnel from a landmine cost me a partner, two fingers, and vision in one eye. I was honorably discharged and returned to Chicago. I lived off checks from the government for God knows how long, drinking in my discount apartment while watching bad day television. Then I met Denise.

My experience in the military had taken a toll. I was still in my thirties, but my hair greyed to near white fifteen years too early. My right eye appeared milky, and I was missing the pinky and ring finger on my right hand. *Luckily, I was a lefty.* I hadn't thought that any woman could ever really be attracted to me.

Denise was a server at one of the many bars I'd frequented, and she was a drop of water in the Sahara. She'd come over to my table when the place was dead to flirt with me. I always thought that it was just for a better tip, but then one day she asked me out. It had been a while since I'd taken a woman on a date, so I invited her to a higher end joint along Michigan Avenue. *That night is frozen in amber for me.*

I was two baskets of bread and three Scotches into my wait. Denise was twenty minutes late, and I thought I'd been stood up. That wasn't Denise's style, though. It was her laugh I heard first. My eyes went from my watch to the restaurant entrance. The middle-aged maître d' flirted with her while he held open the door. Her beauty and curves parted the sea of other waiting patrons while she smile-walked to my table.

Denise was forged by gods. Her mom was a beauty pageant contender from Ghana who studied at Northwestern University. That's where she met Denise's father, a professor who looked more like a lineman for the Bears. The end result was a tall, dark beauty with the confidence and grace of freaking Cleopatra. I was so used to her wearing a t-shirt and jeans that I'd been taken aback by the sapphire dress that clung to her flawless body. The two of us picked up where we left off at the bar. We talked over dinner, joked over sorbet, and walked along Lake Michigan until our feet hurt. By the end, it was clear that we were a thing. We went that way for a good year before it all hit the fan in chunks.

If there's one person you can trust when they say that United States has a gun problem, it's an ex-soldier gone hitman. Due to the collective inability to recognize a growing problem, my relationship with Denise ended before it should have. All Denise wanted was a coffee. Unfortunately, so did some QAnon lunatic. When this gun nut spotted who he thought was a politician getting a latte, the lunatic tried to make a statement with his new high powered assault rifle. Three were killed, including Denise.

The news hit me hard. I think I stood by my window, smashed cellphone in hand and spilled Cheerios on the floor, from breakfast to midnight. I gave up hope and decided that if the world wanted to live like killers, I'd show them how scary it could be. Before long I was soliciting myself to betrayed housewives and bad business partners. I killed a dozen people before I ended up in this mess. Although I may have left one or two things out for our viewers at home, I'd probably have time to ponder them in the fiery pits of Hell. Okay, fun story. I think I'll die now.

My body felt empty, and my hands began to twitch. A darkness suffocated my vision, and just before I faded out of existence, I imagined someone's silhouette hovering over me. It was a man with slicked back hair. He was wearing a form fitting business suit; his crooked half smirk made me want to reach out my arms, if only I could move them, and strangle him. He shook his head before jolting around to look behind him. Something must have startled him because he darted away at blinding speeds.

Slowly everything went dark, then I died.

3

"Hey, man, get up," a nasally voice called out. The ringing between my ears went away; my vision returned, blurred but restored. There was a tapping on my foot. "Come on, we don't have all day." The tapping thumped harder. My heart began to beat again. Surges of blood palpitated through my arms, legs, toes, and fingers. I tried to move my hand and was surprised to see it wiggle. I wiped a smear of red from my eyes and took a deep breath. It was more of a gasp, and it filled my lungs with fire. I jolted up into a sitting position.

"He shot me," was all I could muster before my breaths were stolen from me. A strange steam leaked from my mouth. *I must be seeing things.* I inspected the room. It was a plain office with peeling wood paneling and floor tile that once could have been described as green, but now fell into the category of "bodily fluid." The oak desk and swivel chair were riddled with bullet holes. In front of me was a thin guy with a head of dreadlocks piled into a knot sitting in an electric wheelchair.

His thick, black-framed glasses complimented the blotches of acne on his dark cheeks. He swam in his long-sleeved shirt buttoned to the collar and tucked into skinny jeans. Resting on his combat boots was the instrument of my awakening—an extension arm with a plastic claw tip. It was the figure behind him that really drew my attention.

A towering frame, at least seven-feet tall, loomed over the man in the wheelchair. He wore a drab weathered robe stained with salt along its hem. His shadow stretched over the room and rippled like disturbed water. A skeletal hand protruded from his sleeve. *This has to be a joke.*

"Let me guess," I said while removing my leather gloves and feeling around my head for a bullet hole. "I'm either dead or you two are part of an anti-smoking campaign."

"Close, dude," said the guy in the wheelchair. "We're the guys that stopped you from dying."

I dabbed at my forehead. The bullet hole was gone. I grunted. "Why?"

"Because we need you, man," said the guy in the wheelchair.

I was confused. "You—need me?"

"Oh boy," the giant man in the robe sighed, "this guy is stupider than I thought. I don't think he's going to cut it."

"He's not stupid," the guy in the wheelchair protested. "He just has bad luck when it comes to thinking."

"I'm right here," I snapped. I tried to squeeze my hands back into my leather gloves. As I did, the pinky and ring finger I'd lost in the war jammed into their cotton stuffed sleeves. I marveled at my refunded digits. The guy in the wheelchair cut off that thought as he carted his vehicle closer. He extended his claw-stick to me. "Come on. Get to your feet."

"Thanks." I pushed myself off the ground. "But I'm good." I made note that there wasn't any of my blood pooled on the floor like there should've been. Nor were my pants soiled any longer. *Strange.*

"Let's start with introductions," said the guy in the wheelchair. "I'm Jumbo—"

"Cute," I bit. Ridicule was my defense mechanism when I was nervous.

Jumbo glared at me before continuing. "Once again, dude," he said louder, "I'm Jumbo and this here is Death." I looked to the guy in the robes. He gave a quick wave with his skeleton hand. I needed a smoke. I dug in my front pocket and pulled out my pack of *Lucky Aces*. I held the pack up to my mouth and culled out a cigarette with my lips. My hand, which had been trained like Pavlov's dog, intuitively dug in my coat pocket for my lighter. I flipped open the top of the metal fire maker and lit the tip of my smoke. The soothing taste of tobacco sent a wave of calm through my shoulders and spine.

"Tastes good?" Jumbo asked.

I took the cigarette out of my mouth and savored the flavor. "Yeah." I nodded as I exhaled. "Yeah, it does."

"Glad to hear, man," Jumbo crowed as he pointed with his extendable claw hand, "because you can smoke them all you want. You can't die any longer."

"Because you stopped it," I reiterated, my voice dripping with sarcasm. I took another drag. "I thought Death was supposed to *kill* people, not let them live."

"Aww." Death pressed his skeleton hands on his heart. "It's so cute when you try to talk about things you don't understand." I couldn't help but notice that Death sounded a little like Bill Murray.

Jumbo held his hand up to Death. "Hold on. Let me handle this." Death shook his head. "Buchanan, is it?"

"Buck," I corrected.

"Buck," Jumbo said with a smile. I noticed that Jumbo still had braces. "We've been watching you for a while."

"How long?" I asked.

"Long enough," Jumbo answered. "We've seen everything."

I blew smoke up into the air like a locomotive. A cigarette never tasted so good. "Even on the toilet?"

"Even on the toilet," Jumbo repeated.

"Sorry," I apologized.

"Everybody poops," Jumbo responded, "but we're not here to talk about your need for Number Two." Jumbo shifted his weight, making himself more comfortable on his chair. "Buck, it's safe to say you haven't lived a very peaceful life."

I shrugged. "You could say that."

"I just did." Jumbo's lips drew a hard line. "Your trip to the afterlife isn't going to be good."

"Well." I put the butt of my cigarette out on the floor, "I ain't no saint."

"No, you're not," Jumbo confirmed. "It's going to suck."

Death shook his head slowly. It was kind of strange seeing the guy on horror novels and bad movie covers in the flesh...or bones.

"Well." I rubbed the stubble on my chin. "What're my options?"

"See," Jumbo cheered as he looked back at Death. "I

told you he's not dumb. He knows exactly where this is going."

"Thanks," I sang dryly. Death hadn't moved.

"Buck." Jumbo brought his attention back to me. "You're in a position that hasn't been offered to anyone for a few hundred years. Now you have a one-way ticket to Hell, but we can change that. We want to know if you'd like to work an internship for Death instead?"

"Like." I looked at Death. "Getting him lunch?"

"Mmm," Jumbo hummed, "kind of. You see, Death has been working hard, and he deserves a break." Jumbo cupped his mouth and whispered. "Between you and me, man, the guy's is kind of a workaholic."

"Here we go again," Death bellowed.

Jumbo smiled. "Anyhow, we need you to learn his trade and then take care of some special work while he's out."

"You want me to kill people?" I asked.

"No," Jumbo objected. "Well, kind of. We don't want you to kill the everyday people. That would be messed up. We just need you to take care of the ones that refuse to die."

"LIKE MADONNA?" I asked, managing a straight face.

Jumbo snorted. "I like you." He looked back to Death. Death waved his hand in a spiraling motion as if to say *get on with it.* Jumbo turned back to me. "More like the people who go out of their way to cheat death."

I tried to guess where this was going. It was all a bit overwhelming. Not mere minutes ago, I was some scumbag contracting executions for cash before getting gunned down. Now, here I was face-to-face with Death and his handicapped buddy. Unless this was some Stanley Kubrick plot, I was in a one-in-a-million kind of scenario. Most people might poop their pants in a circumstance like this, but I'd been conditioned to adapt to weirdness since I was a kid.

Evictions, my brother's arrest, Afghani ambushes—the trick is to deal with the situation first, and then panic later. *Simple damage control.*

"Define people who cheat death for me, please?" I asked feeling my shoulder for kinks. I'd knocked it out of its socket several times, and the pain was something I dealt with daily. For some reason it was gone. Jumbo squeezed the mechanism on his extendable claw hand, causing it to pinch open and closed. I don't think he was aware that he was doing it. He hummed while staring at the floor.

"I could tell you," he said as he maneuvered his chair so that he could see both Death and I, "but I'm not sure that will *tell* you." Jumbo turned his attention to Death. "Maybe it's time for a field trip?"

"What the heck." Death pulled up his sleeve to reveal a fitness watch. "I could use the exercise."

I tried to hold back a laugh, disguising it as a cough. You don't want to tick off the guy keeping you away from eternal damnation. Death walked toward the office entrance. Jumbo followed. Death grabbed the shabby bronze handle of the outdated wood door. I was told that this was an abandon lawyer's office that I could use to set up my shooter's position, but looking at the lettering peeling on the glass, I should have known better. The sticker letters on the office entrance were so far removed that you couldn't make out any title. Had I done a little research, I would have probably learned that this entire building was owned by my employer. Previously-alive me had definitely been set up. Death used his delicate skeleton knuckles and knocked on the entrance to the tune of *Shave and a Haircut*. He pulled the door open and to my astonishment, a wall of rainstorm-grey water blocked the hallway. Before I could ask any questions, Death plunged through the wall of liquid and disappeared. Jumbo studied my face. I bounced my eyes back-and-forth between him and the doorway.

"You'll get use to it," he insisted. I looked around the office and spotted my oversized computer satchel and rifle. I went to collect the items, but Jumbo spoke up. "You won't be needing those things anymore. Trust me." Jumbo moved toward the door and drove through the waters. He might be right about the rifle, but old habits die hard. It was a Hitman 101 no-no to leave evidence. I grabbed the rifle and disassembled it as quickly as I could before shoving it in my leather satchel. I slung the strap over my shoulder before hurrying toward the door. I took one deep breath before slipping through the shimmering surface. *Here goes nothing.*

A stream of cold smothered my skin. My sight left me, replaced by undulating grey fog.

Pressure pushed down on my body like I'd been trapped at the bottom of an ocean. A hollow despair as deep and dark as the day Denise died filled inside me. It was an emptiness so raw that I began to struggle, thrashing about in a futile attempt to escape it. Quickly as soon as it started, it had ended; my head came up from the water. I was wading in an onyx stream thick as tar that flowed into an endless cave. Not far from me was a rickety, long boat made of tattered wicker. Death and

Jumbo were inside it. They were dry. Death held a single wood oar.

"Come on, man," Jumbo called out. I swam to the boat. The water didn't give me any resistance nor did it splash up. Death extended a paddle and waited for me to climb aboard. I slopped my computer bag onto the planks of soft wood padding the boat floor.

Jumbo pursed his lips. "Man, I thought I told you that you wouldn't need those things anymore."

I used Death's oar like a monkey bar to pull myself inside. Once I had gained my balance, I shook off the boggy water from my coat and pant legs. It ran off me as if it were snow. "I'm not comfortable with leaving evidence," I stressed as I took a seat. Jumbo looked to Death with a silver braces smile.

"Smart," he complimented, turning his attention back to me. Death shook his head and steered us forward.

The river's path was filled with rocky passages. There was a soft glimmer of green mushrooms and fungi that lit up the otherwise murky caverns. The air was crisp and the atmosphere cool. We pushed on, and while Death navigated, I watched as the water I'd shaken from me crawled away from my feet, climbed up the boat walls, and leapt back into the river. *Not creepy at all.* After a short while, Death moaned. Jumbo and I looked ahead and saw a boat similar to the one we'd been riding, only it was in pieces. There was a splash near the broken boat, and I could see the top of a large serpent swimming through the debris. It was something straight out of the Jurassic Park, chewing on the whicker of the starboard planks with its crocodile like mouth.

"What the hell is that?" I asked as I reached for one of the two .45's concealed under my coat.

"That's Miss Hissy Face," Jumbo said in a low voice. "The real question is, who was in the boat?"

Death grumbled. "It was probably that damn mummy again. If I ever figure out where she's hiding, it's going to be epic." Jumbo frowned. The massive serpent swam over to the boat. Death reached out and petted her scales with the oar before she submerged. "Good girl," Death praised. "Kill the infidels." I kept my mouth shut.

The boat waded through the river long enough for me to untie my dress shoes and empty out the creepy, not-wet water. As I tied my laces back up, the raft came to a sudden jolt. I looked up and noticed that we'd pulled up onto a rocky shore. Death stretched his long skeletal leg and stepped out of the boat. He then reached back in and dragged the entire boat onto shore. I fought to get Jumbo's heavy wheelchair off the brim of the canoe.

"Would you just add a handicap ramp to this thing already?" Jumbo pressed his hands in prayer.

I stepped out first and pulled at the front wheels, eventually half-dumping Jumbo onto the shore. I stumbled backwards and felt a strange crunch. I looked down expecting to find shells, and instead I made out thousands of little rodent skulls. I squeezed my eyes closed and took a breath, mentally erasing the dead mice and squirrels. I opened my eyes again and saw that Death and Jumbo were headed in the direction of a decayed steel door. There was an electronic keypad next to the tarnished lock stile and after Death dialed several numbers, the door drew open with a moan from the hinges. A drape of beaded curtains hung from the threshold, blocking any chance of seeing what was inside.

"Hurry now," said Jumbo as the two split through the beads.

"Is this a trust exercise?" I paused, left alone. No one answered.

I crunched through skulls and entered the beaded fortress. As I pushed through the curtains, I found that I'd leapt into a hall stuck in the disco era. There were peeling eggshell walls and a wicker mail table with envelopes scattered on top. Potted bamboo trees and macramé planters decorated corners. Glow in the dark paintings of psychedelic tigers and girls on roller skates were "tastefully" arranged on the wood paneling. Clearly, Death had a different perspective of time.

Death and Jumbo made it to the end of the corridor and turned right. Curiosity drew me to the mail table covered in FedEx boxes and promotional offers. I *so* wanted to know who else lived here but stifled my interest. I tried to catch up and found that they'd made their way to another hall filled with a dozen marked apartment entrances. Death and Jumbo were parked in front of a door marked double zeros. I watched as Death dug into his sleeve and removed a key with a *Hello Kitty* face on top. He stabbed it in the keyhole and turned it several times before finally twisting the doorknob. Death pushed inside, then stopped to block the entrance.

"Dang it." Death slapped himself on the side of his hooded head. "You two stay here. I totally forgot something." Death hurried into his apartment. I could hear death metal and moans from neighboring units.

"Creeped out yet, man?" Jumbo asked. I was. After all, I

was about to go into Death's house. Who knows what I'd find? The tough guy in me wasn't about to admit an ounce of fear to my future employers. If I failed to convince them I was the guy for the job, I'd probably get sent to a fiery abyss, where I'd be tortured with endless Enya music.

I cleared my throat. "Are you kidding me? I'm having a great time."

The apartment door swung open, and Death hurried out with white badges and a sharpie in his hand. On his chest was an ivory sticker with a label that read "*Hello, my name is.*" Written in underneath was '*The Big Cheese*' in handwritten letters. Death peeled another label off its backing and carefully handed it to Jumbo. It read "*Hello, my name is: Jumbo the I.T. Guy.*"

"You're joking." Jumbo patted the label on his shirt.

"This is new hire orientation." Death handed me a sticker that spelled out *Hello, my name is: Buchanan Palasinski.* Underneath in all caps it said, *I'm an applicant*, which was underlined three times and topped with a frowny face. Death took a step back and inspected us. "Perfect. Okay, you can come in now." Death whirled around and hurried back into his apartment.

"Well, man." Jumbo grinned. "If you thought the boat ride was strange, just wait until you see Death's apartment." Jumbo pushed the joystick on his controls forward and the chair wheeled through the door. I took one last look down the endless apartment hall, half expecting *The Shining* twins to appear. I needed another smoke, but I didn't think that Death would approve. Instead, I looked up at the ceiling and took a few deep breaths. Whatever I saw in here, I'd need to be ready. I took two brisk steps forward and entered Death's apartment.

To my astonishment, there wasn't a tower of skulls or a stream of tortured souls. Oddly enough, the walls were sky blue, bad IKEA furniture, and a bookshelf collection of 80's Classics DVD's. I could smell fresh coffee brewing. Death and Jumbo went passed a closed door marked *Server Room* in pencil and into a living room. I looked at John Cusack, who was staring at me with doubt from a pair of tilted sunglasses along the cover of "Better Off Dead." *No, the irony wasn't lost on me.* I tried to center his go with the flow sense of humor before moving along.

The front room was open and neighbored by a small octagon kitchen. While the front room was plain with its leather couch, mid-sized television, and empty fish tank, the kitchen was booming with activity. The Spanish wall tiles were covered with picture frames of happy people at parks and in front of fireplaces. I studied the photos and made out lettering that read "*8 x 10 frame*," along with the brand of the frame company. On the kitchen table was an array of blinking lights from a laptop computer, a *Maximus 5.0* coffee machine, and high-definition printer. There were notebooks and newspapers scattered along the floor, and an opened cardboard box with Styrofoam peanuts filled to the brim. I looked inside. An Optimus Prime action figure still wrapped in its package lay at the top.

"This is my home." Death motioned to the kitchen. "Would you like a cup of coffee?" Death's voice was inviting for the first time. "I have tea too if you'd like?"

"Thanks," I grunted. "But I don't think I need any more caffeine today."

"Alright," Jumbo spoke up. "Thank you for coming. We brought you here to show you what your internship will entail. Death, mind booting up the files?"

Death was all legs and arms balanced on a too-small steel chair. I wondered how uncomfortable his brittle looking bones felt sitting there, his dark robe pooling around him and onto the floor. He clicked the keys of his laptop several times to light up the screen. A *Thundercats* screensaver greeted him. Death moved the mouse over a dark blue icon folder with an orange cartoon skull. He double-clicked it, opening a list of files labeled by titles and names. Death scrolled down through the records.

"Hmm," he hummed. "Which one. Oh," he exclaimed as his mouse stopped on a specific file. "This will be perfect."

Death clicked the file open, and a neatly written profile popped up. It read like a Dungeons and Dragons character sheet, complete with the person's name, nationality, and history. A picture also hung in the top right corner. I scanned the document. The name read, Peter Crane, a.k.a. "Zombie Pete." I wasn't sure what I was seeing. A pale, purple-skinned man with yellow eyes and half a nose eyed the camera. He had bad rocker's hair with crimped bangs and a jean-vest studded with shoulder spikes. His hand, which was wearing a fingerless biker glove, was balled into a fist near his rotted chin.

"Is there a new Evil Dead remake coming soon?" I asked.

"No," answered Jumbo. "Though we do need you to summon your inner Ash. This here is Peter Crane. I chose him because he's from your hometown of Chicago. That should make things easier. He's known as Zombie Pete on the streets and is a real pain in Death's ass."

Death nodded as he poured himself a cup of coffee. "I hate that guy."

"You see," said Jumbo. "Zombie Pete uses a guitar bought from the crossroads to steal the life out of his audience. Though he should have been dead in 1991, Zombie Pete survives because of his Fender Telecaster. While his body decays, he continues to cheat death."

Death brought his mug of coffee up to the area where his mouth should be. Though there was a void where his entire face should be, I could hear slurping. "He's not even a decent a musician."

This was getting hard to comprehend, and that's saying a lot for me. Compared to most people, I had lived a pretty wild life, unethical, but wild. Yet in all of my time, never did I think the Grim Reaper, water serpents, or undead rockers ever existed. Had I not felt the bullet, I honestly would guess that I was having a relapse of that acid I tried in '01.

"I didn't go to college, Jumbo." I looked over Death's shoulder at the screen, "but I'm going to guess that you don't need me to write a review for his next Double Door concert."

"I think he's catching on," Jumbo said to Death. Death stayed lurched over his laptop but gave a thumbs up from over his shoulder.

"You need me to off him." I read more of Zombie Pete's information.

"Frag." Jumbo shrugged. "Assassinate, execute, whatever you want to call it, man." My eyes continued to scan the profile. I reached for a note that was marked *Undead Talents*. Along with the ability to steal life from his victims through music, the description noted that Zombie Pete couldn't be killed through conventional means.

"Question," I asked. "How am I supposed to eliminate

the target if I can't kill him?" Jumbo cleared his throat. "Death, Charlie has the golden ticket. I think it's time."

Death stood up from his chair and paced to a skinny closet door near the pantry. He opened it and plucked out a six foot long, wood handled scythe. Its stem was a dull brown with hundreds of small marks and dimples. The curved steel blade had been oiled, but the metal itself bore scars along the bridge. I was now looking at what millions conjured up when they imagined their untimely demise. Death and his scythe. He walked it over to us and gently placed it on the kitchen table as if it were made of glass.

"Old Lilith," Death introduced. "She's been with me since my first time on Earth."

I whistled. Never would I assume that this simple farmer's tool had taken the lives of kings and peasants alike. It was so ordinary looking. Yet here it was, likely the most powerful weapon in existence, inches from me.

"So back to your question," Jumbo spoke up. "How do you kill something that can't die? Well, here you are. The scythe was given to Death by the Big Man when times were simpler. It can end anything, including immortals. Death has been using it for millennium to stop demons, undead, and anything else that tries to bypass the system."

I grunted. "God gave it to you, huh?"

"The one and only," Death answered in a plain voice. "Though he has a thousand names in a thousand cultures."

"I still have questions," I cautioned. "There're already some serious flaws in this plan. I'm a hitman, not a ninja-farmer. I can't sneak up on this zombie guy with a six-foot scythe and make a clean kill. It's impractical."

"No, it's not." Jumbo wagged his plastic claw. He was

clearly leading me on through this conversation piece by piece. "It's adaptable to the user. Death, who grew up in a time of farmers and pharaohs, loves the scythe."

"I'm a big fan of the metaphor," Death defended.

"But," Jumbo continued, "it's been other things before too. You see, Buck, you're not the first intern ever taken on. Death had a few other assistants, but unfortunately, he's a bit of a control freak."

"Thanks," Death mumbled.

"For Longus, it was a spear," Jumbo went on. "For this colonial guy, it was a flintlock pistol. It is what you need it to be."

"This is some Harry Potter Sorting-Hat shit," I baited. Jumbo's forehead creased.

"Don't diss the Potter series man," Jumbo hissed.

"Yeah, sorry." I pumped my fist. "Go Harry,"

"Well, there's not much more to say." Jumbo pushed the bridge of his glasses. "Death needs a vacation, but first he needs a reliable intern. We did some research and found you. So now as a test, you're going to take the scythe, turn it into something that suits you, and go kill Zombie Pete. If you can finish that guy, we'll accept you into the internship program and delay your time in the pits of Hell for all the atrocities you've committed."

"Damn it, Jumbo," I grumbled. "Do you have to put it like that?" Death pointed at me. "Poor life choices."

He had a point. I took a deep breath and jonesed for a cigarette. "Well." I approached the scythe. "I didn't see this happening when I woke up today."

"Go ahead," Jumbo insisted. I reached for the scythe. The thing was heavy and unwieldy.

I raised it to my chest and in a blink of an eye, the

ancient tool changed. I was now holding a M24 Remington similar to the one I'd trained with in sniper school. The 7.62 caliber bolt-action rifle had a grimy silver barrel with a dull wood stock just like the scythe. The killing machine was complete with an advanced optic scope, deployable bipod, carrying strap, and sound suppressor. It was a gorgeous death machine, and that was always my problem. While one part of me tried to be a good guy, I tended to side with my lizard brain when it came to things like guns and destruction. Maybe I wanted to punish everyone for my rough upbringing, P.T.S.D., and losing Denise. Whatever the reason, I was just so damn good at being violent.

Death bobbed his head. "Cool gun."

I held my tongue. After all, the guy controlled my fate. I needed to treat him like my superiors once upon a time. You endured the bad jokes and broken egos. Old Lilith felt good in my hands. I was surprised that Death was so willing to let me use it, but then again, I'd assumed he'd thought it through. You don't give someone the keys to your Porsche unless it's insured.

"Gentlemen." I looked through the scope. The vision magnifier had several different modifications, including lowlight lenses and something marked G.S. on the display optics. Jumbo crossed his arms while Death hovered over the rifle. I looked up and smiled. "I think this might be the beginning of a beautiful relationship."

4

D eath and Jumbo took me back to Chicago through the John Carpenter-themed water park. We oared to another island of bones with a single iron door built into the cave wall and went ashore. Death used the *Hello Kitty* key and when he opened the door, my favorite grey wall of water awaited. Jumbo sat with me near the boat. I must have given him a clue that I didn't want to go through the gloom door again.

"Sorry, man," Jumbo apologized. "But it's the only way to get through the underworld. It's supposed to suck. It keeps people out."

"They say that travel," I said as I stared at the freaky supernatural doorway, "broadens the mind."

"Ha." Jumbo snapped his plastic claw. "That's true, dude. Alright, so remember, we'll be evaluating you. Knock this out of the park and the job is yours. I'm rooting for you."

"Copy that." I stepped toward the wall of bog water. Death held the door open for me like a hotel bellman. I took one last deep breath. "Ah, this is going to hurt." I stepped toward the gloom water. Sure enough, I was engulfed in an ocean of despair, sending warped images of the worst moments of my life spinning in and out of focus. The buddies I had lost in Afghanistan appeared one by one, lingering on my sniper partner who blew up in front of me. Then, the memory of Denise in her final moments, terrified one second and spluttering blood the next.

Luckily, just as I'd thought I couldn't take anymore, it stopped.

I'd come through a janitor's closet along the subway. I inspected a nearby *L-Rail* map posted over the baby blue tile walls. It told me I was at one of the Green Line stations. *Perfect.* I stared at the framed glass map and caught a glimpse of myself. My peppered hair had bleached bone white. *Yeesh, this is getting weird.* I broke away from my reflected Anderson Cooper look- alike and slipped my hand into my coat pocket to retrieve my train pass. The weight of my satchel was twice as heavy now that it kept both my old rifle and God's instrument of destruction inside. I fumbled to get my wallet freed from my pack of cigarettes, which were calling my name. I didn't dare. Jumbo said I couldn't die, but he had no idea how merciless Chicagoans were to people with tobacco addictions.

It didn't take long for the Green Line to arrive. I checked my watch and found that hours had gone by. It was now late morning, and the train was mostly empty. I sat down in one of the corner chairs inside and listened to the robotic voice of the automated douche bag over the speakers.

"This is Randolph," the CTA Robot announced. "Standing passengers, please do not lean on the doors."

"Jim Morrison made his music for people to lean on," I said as I rested in my chair, satchel on my lap. The laugh track never started.

Obviously, it had already been the strangest day since the doctor made me cough, and it wasn't even noon yet. I started to count on my fingers everything that had happened. I died in an ambush, came back like Jesus, met Death and his I.T. guy. There was a River of Styx thingy, a leviathan, and a supernatural internship. After mulling it over, I put down my fingers and decided I needed that smoke before any more math could be done.

I didn't have a middleman to get my jobs like some of those fancy hitmen, so I relied on word of mouth. Every one of my contracts was a reference except this last one. I should have known better, but the price was right. Some lady with a birthmark the shape of Idaho on her face had approached me in a coffee shop during my morning breakfast. She insisted on protecting the source but claimed to know who I was. She complimented me about the Tucker and Polanco jobs, so I figured she couldn't be a cop. She offered me triple the going rate, half in advance, to take out some bad business partner of hers. I was back on the rent due to some recent liquid therapy binges, so I jumped at the chance.

Idaho-Face was generous enough to offer me a burn-file with information on my target, which included a place across the street from his apartment where I could spy. It was a high-rise building filled with mostly empty office rentals that gave me a clear line of site, and also later the place of my death...and resurrection. The burn file also had a photo of the slick haired smirking guy and times when he frequented his place. I'd only scoped out the apartment once, from my vantage point and found that the guy, whether coincidence or not, made his home pretty kill-proof. He draped his windows with red velvet curtains until dusk. The problem was after he pulled the curtains, he left the house shortly after. When I returned the next day just before sundown, I decided to jump at any chance my target gave me. But as I sat in that window spying on his home, little did I know that the hunter had become the hunted.

The door busted down, but by the time I had whirled around a storm of bullets were buzzing in my direction. The guy went old school, filling the room with lead from a damn Thompson submachine gun. One kissed me on my forehead and that's all she wrote. A stupid rookie mistake. Had I just turned down the job, I wouldn't be here. Had I just secured the door better, I wouldn't be interning for the Angel of Death. Then it hit me.

Holy shit, I'd been brought back to life by a mythical being and was now working for him.

I'd put the thought off while rubbing elbows with Death to keep a cool head. But now the gravity of it all was all catching up. I was literally taking a job from the man in charge of everyone's demise. My brain began to boil with *what ifs*. What if this is a downward spiral? What if I become some distant supernatural monster? What if he makes me wear one of those gross cloaks? But before my head exploded from horror, I was interrupted. The smell hit me first.

"Excuse me, sir," said a vagrant who kind of sounded like he was trying to impersonate Arnold Schwarzenegger. He stood a few feet away by the exit, but the odor of rotten eggs and sewage hit my nose like a punching bag. He had a puffy beard, raggedy beige long coat, White Sox baseball hat and sunglasses. "But I'm on a mission from da 'future. Could you spare some change so that I may stop John and Sarah Connor?"

I dug in my pants pocket for change and pulled out a few dimes and pennies leftover from when I bought cigarettes.

"Here you go." I offered it to him. The man took it with his grimy fingers.

"Thank you, sir." he palmed the change. "I missed the last dimensional door near Buckingham Fountain, so this will help."

"Well, be careful, Terminator." I stood up for my stop.

"T-1000," the vagrant corrected.

"Sorry, T-1000." I apologized as the robotic announcer called out my station's name. The doors opened. "Those dimensional doors aren't what they look like on television."

I stepped off the Green Line to get one last look at the cyborg assassin. He stared at his palm, counting the change. I did a double take as the Green Line passed by. Not but a few seats behind him was a bizarre stranger whose eyes followed me with a lunatic's gaze. I couldn't tell if my voyeur was a guy or girl due to their sharp elven-like features, and I wondered how I had missed them before. The stranger had toxic green hair molded like a torch, yellow feline eyes and bright red lips wrapped around an enormous toothy grin. They wore a candy cane striped suit coat with matching tie and had silver chord around their neck clasped to a flickering light bulb. They wore a pencil skirt with fishnet stockings. The two of us exchanged stares before the train drove out of sight.

"Chicago's getting weird," I said to myself as I dug for my cigarettes.

The late summer sun beat down on me as I smoked cigarettes all the way to my apartment. I was taking the internship for Death thing very seriously, mostly because I didn't want to burn in Hell for the rest of eternity. My head went into military mode. I processed the objectives, putting aside all the mental side banter. Zombie Pete was an undead jerk off who needed to play concerts to drain the souls out of people to survive. I'd need to do some research on where he might be playing next. I didn't think there were many dudes like him, so it narrowed my search. As I used the key-fob to enter the main gates of my apartment complex, it dawned on me that the guy was nothing without the guitar. So, if all else failed, I could try to Karate Kid that Fender Telecaster in half.

I reached my apartment door and noticed there was a *late rent* notice taped under my peephole. I grabbed it with my teeth while pulling the handle and twisting the key in the lock, pushing my way in. The air conditioner in my unit had been left on. A wave of cold ran over me. It reminded me of the gloom waters in the underworld— holy hell the *underworld!* I spit the notice onto my coffee table, and after lighting up another smoke, I opened my laptop in the crowded area that was meant to be a dining room for hobbits. I pushed aside the Dungeons and Dragon books and gun magazines to give myself some space to take notes. I used a promotional bank pen to write on the back of an old character sheet, and I began my internet search for Zombie Pete. Sure enough, my first search pulled up a dozen or so references.

I clicked on the official "Zombie Pete" website and

began to build a profile. Zombie Pete was what hitmen called an easy target, and what survivalists call an idiot. He was using his rotten visage as a gimmick to attract Goth kids. He had several smaller venues listed on his tour index. I put two and two together that this guy didn't outright murder his crowd when he played, as that would have gathered police attention. He must be more of a bottom feeder, taking bits and pieces of people's souls as he performed. It reminded me of the Grave Bard my gaming group had fought at level six. My wizard, Sarsicus, wiped him up with a single fireball. The only difference is that the Grave Bard was siphoning the souls of Princess Mary and Prince Jonathan for power while this bad boy fed on people who frequented Hot Topic.

Zombie Pete's next show was tonight. I found that far too coincidental. Clearly Death and Jumbo wanted me to hit the ground running. *Damn.* Zombie Pete was playing at a hundred-year- old bar on the West side just past the expressway. With a usual job, I'd scope out the area in search of obstacles, places I could perch, and a clean getaway. Now I'd have to rely on internet pictures. I jumped on the venue's Facebook page and studied several photos of the place. It was your typical storefront concert hall with a basement like theater with a two hundred-person fire capacity. Since the concert was being played on a weekday, I assumed that the crowd would be light.

Good, fewer witnesses.

Scrolling, I mapped out a bar near the entrance, an opening with stools and cocktail tables. Past that was an area for the crowd that reached to the makeshift stage. I scrutinized every picture in an attempt to spot a bathroom or back office that I could fire from. There were a few okay places that I could take advantage of if desperate. I found the picture that showed an area of the venue that screamed "*kill people from up here.*" Over the bar was a balcony reserved for V.I.P. customers that could watch the show from the comfort of movie theater seating. Every picture of the reserved area showed that it hadn't been used in ages and was now storing extra tables and chairs. Better yet, there was a single window taped by cardboard that led right to it.

I drew up a strategy that would knock the socks off Death and Jumbo. I scribbled it down on paper and began to probe it for flaws. Nothing ever went as drawn out, but the more backup plans you had at your disposal, the better. Offing someone was one-part planning, one-part adaptability, and one-part good aim.

I had less than eight hours. Time was of the essence.

If there's one thing I learned in the trenches, it's 'know your tools.' I retrieved Old Lilith's scope and toyed with its optics. The lowlight feature was handy, but nothing I hadn't seen before. It was the G.S. lens complete with flashing ghost icon that piqued my interest. Pressing my eye to the scope, a flush of blue colored the apartment just like last time. I decided to try it out along different angles and light sources throughout the flat. I bumbled from the long dim hallway to the cramped pitch-black bathroom. There were no optic or thermal adjustments. However, as I neared the light of my front room window, something remarkable happened.

First the icon caught my attention. The ghost token locked solid with red X's over its cartoon eyeballs. As I glided the sights along the street side, a tall cerulean form strode along the sidewalk. It was a pellucid man in a Zoot suit. He spun a chained pocket watch as he strolled down the path. A gold glowing bead flickered over his chest, then a second figure ten feet away adorned in a dated postal uniform drew me to him. A semi-opaque mailman with a gold bead heart went from building to building, slipping clarion letters into nonexistent mail slots. It wasn't until my optics passed over the building directly across my apartment complex that I truly understood the G.S. lens.

Along the third floor, Miss Lopez played a piano from her French window as she'd done for the last decade. The local celebrity had toured with several jazz bands in her heyday but resigned herself to personal children's lessons after retirement. I watched Miss Lopez passionately dance her fingers along the keys of her baby grand. The sight gave me chills, especially since Miss Lopez died six months ago at that very same spot. I pulled away from the scope. I couldn't see any of the blue figures with my naked eye. When I returned my eye to the G.S. optics, there they were, swaggering down sidewalks, delivering mail, and playing piano as if nothing was amiss.

Shocked, I returned the scope to the satchel without looking, fixed my eyes on the sparse bookshelf across the room, and stumbled over to my couch before sitting down in a stiff upright position. My back tightened as I stared at the stained spine of a George R.R. Martin novel, distraught. It took time to process the information into my new mental X-Files folder, but after a rigid and uncomfortable minute, I settled down. If there was an afterlife, which I'd confirmed by dying and returning, then it was only natural that there were ghosts. I just hoped I wouldn't have to eliminate any of them at this point in my paranormal career.

Now anyone who tells you that hitmen are supposed to wear plain black suits with straight colored ties is only *mostly* wrong. The key is to blend in with your surroundings so that you're forgettable. Since most hits are zeroed in on business CEO's and stock exchange folks, it only makes sense to wear sheep's clothing. But a *good* contract killer is just as likely to dress up as the Xfinity employee, boring sweater guy, or construction worker. Any identity that helps you blend in.

And that's only if we're talking about the bang-bang, shoot em' up contract killers.

There's a whole slew of poisoning seductresses and freak accident conductors who could blow me out of the water. I had a box of more elaborate disguises in my van, but tonight I was planning on climbing on the roof of a bar and slipping in unnoticed through a side window. It was best to wear dark clothes that didn't look street strange.

The sun was just going down when I put on my disguise. I checked myself out in the mirror. I was wearing a tight fit leather jacket with a high square collar, raven colored t-shirt, jeans, and boots. I'd covered my conspicuous white hair with a White Sox hat and hid my milky right eye with sunglasses. I'm not a fan of Corey Hart, but people tended to focus on my creepy glossed pupil, which drew in more attention than shades.

Just like the last one, the realization hit me.

I could see out of my creepy pupil.

I lifted my sunglasses. Though my eye was still milky, I could see clearly through it. It was a Christmas miracle. I followed my index finger several times, verifying that I had twenty-twenty vision again. After playing ophthalmologist for another half hour, I decided to count my blessings and head to work.

I checked both pistols I kept in shoulder holsters under my coat to ensure they weren't peeking out. Afterwards, I collected Old Lilith, who was still sitting cozily in my computer satchel, and headed to the van. I had bought the VIN-less primer grey beast from a junkyard and filled the back with crates full of DVD's I'd bought from a second-hand store. The idea was that if I were caught during my casual escape by cops in search of a killer, they could run my background and I'd simply come up as Buchanan Palasinski, a jobless lowlife selling movies out of the back of his van. I'd have to leave town afterwards, but at least I'd escape.

I hid the beast down the street in an abandoned lot. She stunk of stale carpet that the former owner laid down in the back. I lifted the loose layer of rug and hid the computer case, as well as my notes in a small compartment I'd hollowed out in the floor. Subsequently, I started the van and drove to the spot I'd decided to park via a search engine's map application. Technology, making murder easy since 1990. This wasn't one of my most thorough plans, but it wasn't the worst either. I'd never killed a zombie before, so I was going to have to remember to stay on my toes. I needed to remind myself that Death and Jumbo were somehow watching too. It was like I was a guest star on one of those career reality shows. *Welcome to another episode of Dirty Jobs. Today we follow Buck Palasinski as he completes a high-profile contract killing.* This job was either going to show them how serious I was about the internship or it'd be a drop-dead hilarious flop.

Well, here goes nothing.

5

*Z*ombie Pete's venue wasn't busy, yet it still showed signs of life. A custodian emptied a trash bin into a dumpster and, luckily for me, left the backdoor open behind him. I walked through the garbage-lined alley and lit up a smoke. I could see staff inside setting up cocktail tables. Casually, I picked up a Styrofoam coffee cup littered near the doorway. I peeled the top lip from it, crumbled it in a ball, and once the coast was cleared, pushed the bead into the lock's latch hole. The door would serve as my backup plan should I not be able to escape from the roof. The custodian returned with a pilsner box filled with bottles. He didn't take notice of me, and after dumping the cardboard carton, he hurried back inside.

Now, ever since the Chicago Fire, public officials have been proactive about fire safety. It's why you'll never see a wooden building downtown. It's illegal. There's also an ordinance that forces all buildings to have a fire escape of some sort. Older buildings on the West side have classic fire escapes. You know, the hanging iron ones with ladders that paint the backdrop of any gritty crime drama. I made like a gorilla and hopped up to one of the hanging ladders, using its pulley system to drag the metallic ladder down. It took a great deal of strength, and by the time I'd brought it to my level, I was half sure someone heard the moan of rusty hinges. I checked over my shoulder. No one was around.

I scaled the extendable ladder to the roof. Once on top, I towed it back up. The top of the building was bare, with an electric generator, exhaust pipes, and outdated satellite dish. A swirl of fog from the neighboring complex misted a portion of the roof with a fresh laundry aroma. It reminded me of the mist coming from my mouth during my resurrection. I used it as cover, taking in the smell of fabric softener. They'd need a lot of Tide Pods to clean up the stains I was about to make. I ducked under the lacteal laundry clouds to the window I'd mapped out along the theater's shoulder. It was still covered in cardboard, like in the internet pictures.

Buildings in Chicago were tightly packed onto each block, usually only an arm's reach apart, so I climbed over the edge and pressed my back to the neighboring condo while using my limbs to crawl down to the windowpane. My gloved hands had a hard time finding any loose seams from the duct taped beer box, but once they did, I gingerly pried it off. Beneath the beer box was mostly intact glass with a single hole from a baseball or rock. It was quickly growing dark out, so I doubted anyone inside noticed the dull shine from nearby streetlights leaking into the building. Now I'm no cat burglar, nor do I care about the property value of the bar, so I used an old technique to get through. It's called the "Breaking Shit" approach. I made sure I was firmly pressed against the walls before leaning my shoulder onto the exposed hole in the glass. I carefully added a little more weight every second until I heard a crack. The trick was to not apply too much pressure as to shatter the pane.

By the time I was done, there was a spider web of cracks along the hole. I used my leather-shielded fingers to pop a few of the large shards out quietly. This gave me a big enough gap to fit my arm in and unlock the window from inside. I pulled the window open. My legs were now burning, so I entered in a hurry. I plopped onto the indoor balcony floor and crawled my way to the theater seating. The rat droppings and dust layer confirmed that no one had been up here for a while. I peeked over the seats and watched employees set up the stage. They conducted microphone checks while I assembled Old Lilith. Once she was ready, I leaned the gun barrel's bipod onto one of the arm rests and began to toy with the sights.

I'd inspected the weapon before, but still had a few questions about reloading, recoil, and scope adjustments. Regardless, the rest of the rifle seemed to work just fine. Once I verified a clear line of sight between myself and the stage, all that was left was to wait. After an hour or so, the lights dimmed, and a manager called out that she'd open the doors in five minutes.

I used that time to visually review my escape route. I'd left the side window open on purpose. Once I'd confirmed Zombie Pete's death, I'd climb back onto the roof and hurry to the escape ladder. After I clambered down, I'd walk casually through the alley to the van. Those were the most dangerous moments. In most cases, bystanders panicked and ran over one another, but occasionally you'd get the ex-cop or war veteran that worked the door. Their eyes were trained to spot the bad guy and would give chase. It never had come to that yet, luckily, but if it did, I'd use Thing One and Thing Two, who slept under my jacket.

I heard the doors open, and a clamber of stomping feet and voices echoed throughout the concert hall. Dozens of misunderstood college students and self-dubbed music bloggers poured in. I searched through my sights, using the lowlight modification to brighten up the room. *What the hell.* Most of these kids didn't look old enough to drink. Their smooth little faces were painted in dark eyeliner and studded with piercings. They slurped beers in their black leather pants and underground band shirts. One by one they nested around cocktail tables and gathered along the shores of the stage. I wondered how kids who pretended to be obsessed with death would react to watching their favorite musician's brains explode.

Purple stage lights and a cheap fog machine suffocated the stage. I could have cared less, but then I noticed that the cheap Halloween trick drowned out my clear shot. The entire stage was smothered by an accumulation of smoke. And *this* is why I never go see shows anymore. I played with the scope a bit, but it was no use. The crowd began chanting. At first it was a just a few clearly alcohol-driven slurred war cries, but before long, the entire crowd cheered.

"*Zombie Pete,*" they shouted in unison. "*Zombie Pete.*"

"Attention," called a loud grimy voice from the speakers. "Attention you little shits." The crowd roared in approval.

"Are you ready for some fun, you pathetic fools?" The horde of fans whooped.

"Are you ready for some real music?" The throaty voice asked. The horde cried louder.

"Then get on your feet and make some noise because you're ready for Zombie Pete!"

A ballad of the electric guitar serenaded from the amplifiers. I winced from the pressure of the bewitching melody filling the hall. Whoever was jamming strummed the bad boy at an alarmingly rate. The electric sex was soon joined by drums and a bass guitar. It sounded like Black Sabbath and Garage-Rock had a baby. I peered through my scope but could barely make out the hazy silhouettes of several band members on stage. Their definition was too indistinct to tell who was who. Not only would shooting them all be a dick move, but I didn't know if I had enough bullets to cover it.

"*I want to buy booze for kids,*" the smutty voice sang. "*Like the law forbids.*" There was a quick guitar rift. "*I want to teach Grandma to draw...with my chainsaw.*" The crowd shouted in unison. "*I want to party with Mom—*" the guitar sped up "*—with no clothes on.*" The drums banged with the words. "*Cuz' I'm Zombie Pete. I'm Zombie Pete. Give me your soul cuz' I'm Zombie Pete.*"

I kept flipping through the different optic settings while the music went on. When I passed the ghost-view, my eyes went out of focus. Dozens of small gold glowing beads ascended from the kids in the crowd. They hovered above the assembly like a swarm of fireflies. As the lead guitar went into a short solo, the orbs of light flew onto stage where they were swallowed up by the amethyst lit fog. Zombie Pete was collecting his immortality. I peeked up over my own head but didn't see any little glowing lightbulbs.

There's irony in that, I'm sure.

"Now ladies and gentlemen," Zombie Pete's voice called out while he continued to play the Telecaster. "Before we continue our show, I want to introduce a special guest. You see, not everyone is a Zombie Pete fan." The gathering booed. "I know, I know. But that's okay because we have a special surprise for our music critic. You see ladies and gentlemen; I've been tipped off that a certain assassin in our stands has come to wipe me out. So, Mr. Hitman hiding on the balcony." Zombie Pete finally stepped out from the fog onto the center stage. He was shirtless. A network of ebony veins pulsated from his bare mauve chest. His eyes shined a gold that matched the souls he'd just swallowed, and his serrated teeth and Gene Simmons tongue hung out of his mouth. "Say hello to my groupies."

I jumped back behind my scope to see if I could take a shot, but just as I centered my aim on Zombie Pete's forehead, an extra from *The Walking Dead* shambled out from the backstage and stepped in front of him. The grey-skinned corpse wore a denim vest and red bandana. One of its eyes hung from its sockets and its gnarled teeth gnashed from a lipless mouth. I squeezed the trigger and a luminescent bullet fired from Old Lilith's barrel straight through the creature's brow. Green slime sprayed over Zombie Pete, but his undead meat shield blocked me from finishing the job. A pack of twenty other zombies shuffled out from backstage and through the crowd. They were headed straight to the roped off stairs that led up to me.

Zombie Pete laughed into his microphone. "Looks like you won't get to hear my encore, Mr. Hitman," he mocked as he strummed his guitar.

I had two choices. I could either take out the horde of zombies headed my way or risk having my guts ripped out to focus on Zombie Pete.

Remember the mission.

I strained through the scope and targeted the Fender Telecaster. Zombie Pete continued his rift, collecting souls from the now hushed crowd. I fired, and the fluorescent bullet shattered the guitar, sending shards of wood into Zombie Pete's guts and ribs. A spray of tiny stars poured from the instrument's fretboard and showered back into the audience. As pieces of soul reentered Goth kids, their bodies fell over unconscious. *Strange.* Though Zombie Pete's Fender stopped its beat, his band continued to play. Zombie Pete looked up to the balcony, eyes wide. I didn't wait. I pulled the barrel up, zeroed in, and fired again. The blazing bullet kissed him between the eyes, causing his head to explode like a pumpkin loaded with fireworks. Zombie Pete's body dropped to the ground.

"Insert catch phrase here," I said to myself in celebration. *Thump, slap, thunk.* The sound of sloppy footsteps clamored up the nearby stairwell. "Time to freaking go," I muttered as I slung Old Lilith from her strap over my shoulder.

THE LEAD ZOMBIE wailed as she reached the top step. An emaciated girl with blonde pigtails and a trail of chunky drool oozing onto her Radiohead t-shirt led the pack. Her eyes were white and her cheek wore to the bone. The zombies behind her, including an aproned cook with a fork in his shoulder and a nose-less lady that looked like Angela Lansbury, shoved Pigtails forward with their clumsy shuffle. There was no way I could make it to the window and scramble up to the roof without these things taking a chunk out of me. I needed to put some space between us. I dug in my jacket and drew out the two silver .45's. Pigtails reached out to grab me, but I gave her a stiff kick before opening fire. Two bullets pierced her clavicle before the third cleanly went through the top of her skull.

"Sorry," I unleashed more rounds into the horde. "No last meals."

The front row of walking corpses collapsed from the gunfire, creating a pile for the others to clamber over. I hoped that it bought enough time and sheathed the hot guns back in their holsters. I scrambled to the window. Moans grieved behind me. I leapt out onto the ledge and pulled my way up. I dangled from the roof, using every ounce of strength to pry myself up out of harm's way. As I did, a rotten hand grabbed my boot. The creature went to take a taste of my ankle, but I hurriedly practiced the removing-dog-mess-off-your-heel system to peel the thing's fingers off. I then used the zombie's head as a stool to boost myself up as quickly as humanly possible. Once on top of the building, I rolled onto my back.

Holy shit. I'd almost been zombie dinner.

"No time to rest, soldier-boy," I whispered as I stood. I hurried to the fire escape and scrambled down until I was a safe jumping distance to the ground. I took a leap of faith, which for some reason didn't cause my bad knees to cry for help. I fast-walked down the alley, my rifle clutched at my breast like a baby in a poor attempt to conceal it. I glanced over my shoulder. No one ran out of the bar. There were no screams or police sirens. *Highly unusual.* I kept up my brisk pace until I made it to the van.

I slid into the back of the cab and locked all the doors. After disassembling Old Lilith, I hid her in the hollowed space and then made for driver's seat. The primer grey dragon roared with life as I turned the key. I put the van in drive and rolled out of the crumbled street. As I did, I noticed that my rearview mirror was crooked. I adjusted it, and when I did, there was a massive shadowy figure huddled behind me.

"What the hell?" I shouted. My eyes did a double take. Death was reading the back of a bad kung fu DVD.

"Sorry, man," a voice from the passenger seat apologized. My free hand went for a pistol while my eyes narrowed toward to the passenger seat. Jumbo sat slack in the carpeted chair, his seatbelt holding him upward. "Easy, it's just us."

My heart stampeded and my nerves surged with life. "How did you even get in here?"

Jumbo pointed his nose downward and looked over his glasses. "Seriously? Are you really asking that?"

My hand crawled away from Thing One and instead pinched the cigarettes in my coat pocket. I pulled out the pack with my free hand, and then pressed down the car lighter. After plucking a smoke out from the package with my lips, I grabbed the charged burner and lit my guilty pleasure.

"In the army," I said between puffs. "We call people like you *Hide-and-Go-Seek Champions*. You get a special prize and everything."

"Okay, dude, I'll bite." Jumbo smiled. "Why?"

"Because every few years," I explained. "A soldier who thinks he's funnier than he is hides in the bush to scare friends from his squad. When he leaps out to say *boo*, he gets shot. Whether he survived or not, his platoon always refers to him as the Hide-and-Go-Seek Champion."

"You army guys are sick," Jumbo laughed.

"Yes." I agreed, rolling down the window to blow out fumes.

"Anyhow," Jumbo kicked in. "You can tell war stories later. We're here for your evaluation."

"This should be rich," I sighed. I could already feel pitchforks poking me. "I'm assuming I didn't do well."

"On the contrary," Jumbo objected. "You scored very well."

"How?" I turned onto the expressway. "He was ready for me. It was a freaking ambush."

"Yeah." Jumbo licked his braces, "I know. We tipped him off."

"You did what?" I hit the brakes.

"*WE*," Death said slowly. "*TIPPED*," he annunciated louder. "*THEM OFF.*"

"Thanks, you clown dicks," I hissed, cigarette clenched between my teeth. "May I ask why you did that?"

"Buck," Jumbo said in a low steady voice. "Think about it. Anyone can kill someone. It doesn't take much. What we needed to see was how you did with adversity. You know, when the deck is stacked against you."

"That's weak." I hit the gas again. "Have you ever heard the phrase '*clean kill*'? Hitmen take it very seriously."

"Man." Jumbo unrolled his window and breathed fresh air. "Do you think that the Unmentionables–"

I gave him a cross look.

"You know, things that cheat death?" I nodded.

"Do you think they are easy to kill? They're not, man.

They have all sorts of backup plans and ways to protect the only thing that they have left, their stupid existence."

"This was all a setup?" I questioned.

"Not a setup," Jumbo explained. "A test. Death could have wiped up Zombie Pete, but we wanted to see what you could do before we made you an intern." I took a moment to digest it all. I had two options. I could have a hissy fit about it all, or just deal with the fact that Death and his sidekick could have made me the next meal for a bunch of literal zombies.

Real clever. Ha,ha, you got me. Besides, it sounded like they enjoyed the show.

"So I'm in then?" I smashed my cigarette butt in the van's ashtray.

"You have some things to learn, dude." Jumbo put up a finger. "But we like your style. The rooftop thing was pretty pedestrian, but the fact that you took out the guitar before finishing the job was beautiful. Everyone was returned their soul."

"About that." I flicked on my blinker. "What happened back there?"

Jumbo looked back at Death before returning his stare to me. "It's complicated." He shrugged. "Getting your soul back is kind of a big deal. The audience pretty much went into shock."

"Are those zombies going to eat the crowd?" I asked.

"Nah," Jumbo asserted. "Those things were the byproduct of being at too many of Zombie Pete's shows. You know—*groupies.* They only had a shelf life of a few minutes after the guitar was destroyed."

"Alright." I slowed along the expressway exit ramp. "What now?"

I watched from the rearview mirror. Death dug in his cloak and pulled out a sticker pad and sharpie. I heard the squeaks of the marker tip as he wrote. He extended his skeletal hand between Jumbo and me. A new name badge stuck to his finger.

Hello, My name is Buck. I'm the new intern. Ask me for coffee.

"Death and I will video-chat you in the morning." Jumbo removed his seatbelt. "Make sure to have your computer on."

"My flight leaves early," Death warned in his usual morose tone. "Set your alarm."

"You'll get your first official target," Jumbo instructed. "Until then, go home."

"Copy." I stopped at an intersection a block from my apartment.

"Be ready for an early video-chat," Jumbo grinned.

"Out of curiosity, how long is this internship going to be?" I inquired as I turned to face them. Both Jumbo and Death were gone. "Again. Seriously?" I grumbled as I checked the back of the van. It was empty. I turned back to face the road. The light went from red to green. I pressed the petal and drove. There was nowhere to go but forward. Whether I liked it or not, I was now Death's intern.

6

Every few nights during Operation Enduring Freedom, enemies programmed crude timers on rocket launchers aimed at our mountain camp. Around 0300 hours, the screech of rocket propelled grenades screamed toward base. Ninety-nine percent of these attacks were off target, and the enemy was always long gone. As time went on my internal alarm clock trained itself to jolt me to life just before the attacks and I'd stir from my cot to listen. Only the rocket alarm clock never went away. Sixteen years later and I'm still waking up, waiting to hear the explosions.

The V.A. had prescribed Zoloft and said it would go away.

I jostled upright. The clock on my nightstand glared 3:03AM in its bright glowing numerals. After shuffling for that first cup of coffee, I started my routine. I went down to the cruddy gym in my building. The outdated treadmill and corroded weights still did the trick in getting my blood pumping, even after my resurrection. It was a

hard pill to swallow, dying and then returning. I stared at
the tired walls and lumpy punching bag hanging under
buzzing shop lights. They'd always been constants. They
were strangers to me now. Too much changed.

I'd finished my routine but didn't feel winded in the
slightest. Curious, I did an entire extra set of weights and
another ten minutes on the stair master. Still nothing. I
wrote it off as a busy mind evading a body's scorn and
moved on. I returned to my apartment and started breakfast. After a second coffee, two stale donuts, and six cigarettes, all I could do was buy time until Jumbo called. So, I
did a little online research on the Grim Reaper.

According to an occult blogger, *Well_Hung_in_Tomb-
stone*, the Grim Reaper frequented a diverse stretch of
global cultures from East Asia to Latin America. There
were a few widely accepted similarities in his myth.

First, he was a holy agent created by the top being, be it
God or Gaia, to do a dirty job. He could take different
forms but tended to don the all famous black death robe.
His embrace could slay any mortal, but it was his scythe
that could unmake even the devil. While the world feared
him, scholars understood that he protected the afterlife
from unbalance. Should his realm ever become unstable,
it could halt existence.

Well, that slightly explained the stick up his ass.

Finally, at 5, just as the sun was starting to rise, my
laptop chimed. I activated the video-chat. The digital
screen painted a picture of Jumbo and Death huddled over
Death's kitchen table. Bags hung under Jumbo's
unshielded eyes. He massaged his eyelids before placing
on his glasses. Death stood behind him with a Hawaiian
shirt buttoned over his cloak.

"Good morning," greeted Jumbo as he straightened out the camera on his computer.

"Glad to see you didn't fail your first task, rookie. Punctuality is everything."

"I'm an overachiever," I said with a straight face.

"So after careful consideration." Jumbo shuffled through some papers. "We've decided to give you a very distinguished target. Buck, you'll be hunting a wily Unmentionable that may have been tampering with our Death-Program."

"Death program?" I leaned into the computer's glow.

"Yeah, dude." Jumbo clicked on his keyboard. "It's a special integrated system we created to manage the everyday deaths around the world. It handles the six-hundred-thousand or so casualties a day. Now, part of the reason you won the fate-lottery is because you're a Chicago native. There's been an abundance of unscripted deaths in that area, and we think your target might be up to no good."

"Wait," I interjected. "You're telling me that a Chicagoan has figured out how to corrupt the system? I'm shocked."

"Sarcasm?" Jumbo asked.

"It's one of the services I offer," I lit up another cigarette to help me concentrate. "Alright, tell me about the target."

"Already on it." Jumbo clicked a button. "Check your e-mail."

"Yahoo or G-mail?" I asked.

"Come on," Jumbo laughed. "Who am I, your ninety-year-old auntie? No one uses Yahoo."

"Right." I opened a new window and checked my e-mails. There was one new message with an attachment from the user, *ICanSeeYourPixels*. I downloaded the attachment. The file opened and a profile came up. My eyes grew as I saw the name.

"His name is John Dillinger," Jumbo said through my laptop speaker. "Heard of him?"

"You have got to be kidding me." I took a puff of my smoke. "Like, *the* John Dillinger?"

"Born in Indianapolis in 1903," Jumbo recited the profile in front of me. "And supposedly died in Chicago in 1934." I took a moment to scroll through the rest of his profile while Jumbo continued. "In life he was charged with bank robbery, murder, assault, assault of an officer, and grand theft auto. But it's his afterlife that's really juicy."

"Wait," I sputtered in confusion. "It says here that he was shot down in the alley of the Biograph Theatre."

"He was," Jumbo confirmed. I looked up at the screen. Jumbo nodded. "Dillinger knew that the FBI was on his trail, so he set out to find an ancient Romanian vampire who could change him. No one knows the deal Dillinger cut, but eventually he became undead. He then arranged for it to look like he was being betrayed by some lady friends. Women from Romania to be precise." Jumbo raised his brows up and down. "He lured three agents into the theater's alley and tricked them into opening fire. After the coroner pronounced him dead, of which he technically was, he was taken back to Indiana where he was buried. But being a vampire has its perks, Dillinger dug himself out and had a clean slate from there."

I scrolled down and stared at the black and white mug shot of John Dillinger. He had slicked back hair, shortened near his big ears, a devil-thin mustache and a strong cleft chin. However, it was his stare and smirk that hit a chord. I had the strangest feeling that I'd met him before, but that was impossible, *wasn't it*? That's when it dawned on me. There was a modern security camera photo of Dillinger in a casino. His hair was shorter and his mustache even thinner. He wore a snug navy business suit with a skinny red tie. Most importantly, his skin had grown ten shades more pallid, and his bright green eyes turned gold. *This was the man that Idaho-Face hired me to kill. This was the guy that murdered me.*

"Son of a piss wizard," I blurted.

"What's wrong?" asked Jumbo.

Death stopped humming Jimmy Buffet over Jumbo's shoulder.

That's when my street smarts kicked in. I didn't want to lie to my new employer, who was the only reason I wasn't burning in Hell's furnace. Then again, Dillinger being my last target seemed to be an awful big coincidence. Jumbo and Death had lied to me before. How could I be sure this wasn't a similar setup? Maybe I'd confess a little later when I had my bearings, but for now, I decided to hold my cards close to my chest.

"I'll tell you what's wrong," I rebounded. "There's nothing on this list that tells me how to kill a vampire. I mean, are they allergic to sunlight like in the movies? Should I just have Giordano's deliver him a deep dish with extra garlic?" I cross my fingers that they didn't see through my bullshit. Jumbo stared at the computer monitor for a moment. He turned back to Death before shaking his head. *Uh oh.*

"Man, rookie, who ties your shoelaces for you?" Jumbo rubbed his forehead. "I've already told you that Old Lilith can kill anything. And yes." Jumbo's voice calmed.

"Dillinger is allergic to sunlight. But the rest of the lore and superstition depends on what type of vampire they are. You're a smart guy. You'll figure it out."

"Great." I feigned a sigh while I finished scanning the attachment. "Alright, anything else I should know? Any rocks that can be unturned?"

"If we had any leads," Jumbo answered. "Death would have taken care of this guy long ago."

"Alright," I said, picking roof soot from the bar out of my fingernails. "I'll figure something out. I always do."

"Good boy," Death stopped humming Margaritaville to jeer as if talking to a puppy.

I scrunched my face but bit my tongue. My life currently felt like a test I didn't study for.

"Now, don't mess this up. I'll be gone one week."

"I hope," I said dryly. "That things aren't too painful for us while you're away."

"Life is pain, Highness," Death declared in a dramatic voice. "Anyone who says differently is selling something."

"Sure, Westley," I snorted, recognizing *The Princess Bride* reference.

"As for you," Death said as he patted Jumbo on the head. "There're pizza puffs in the freezer." Jumbo looked to the computer with a frown.

"Alright man, well I'm going to let you go." Jumbo clicked his mouse. "E-mail or text me if you need anything." And with that, the screen went black.

Deja Poo, I feel like I heard this shit before.

I stared at my laptop and wondered who the bad guy was here.

Was it Idaho-Face?

I mean, she had been the first to hire me to kill

Dillinger. Plus, her offer was way too good to be true. On the other hand, Death and Jumbo were definitely leaving a suspicious number of breadcrumbs.

First, how was it that the guy that killed me just so happened to be the man they brought me back to destroy? Second, we were on a *need-to-know basis*, which typically means that some heinous bull was going down. Then that wicked little voice in my head reminded me that technically, I was the bad guy here. After all, I was the guy going around killing people for others, be they evil geniuses or otherwise. I filed the unanswerable questions in my head as *things to look into* and then began planning the hit.

7

John Herbert Dillinger, head of the Dillinger Terror Gang, had robbed twenty-four documented banks in the early 1930s. He was known as Jackrabbit John for his guile in eluding capture. He'd escaped prison twice and could have likely stayed free had he not been addicted to the lifestyle he'd carved for himself. Some admired the bank robber as a Robin Hood figure due to his defiant bravado documented in the media. That is until he was accused of murdering a police officer in East Chicago, which quickly launched him up the ranks to Public Enemy Number One. Dillinger went into hiding, staying with girl-friends and fellow criminals in hopes that the nationwide manhunt for him would eventually come to a halt. He even went so far as to have two warts, a scar, and his dimples removed with plastic surgery. Dillinger continued to hide, but according to history, his lust for Cubs games, pretty ladies, and movie theaters ultimately caused for him to be gunned down in an alley at the Biograph Theater in 1934.

It's rumored that only a few days after Dillinger had been buried, his grave was dug up in Crown Hill Cemetery.

I thought about Idaho-Face's job again. All the details she'd given to me had to be a damn lie, but she had provided one crucial piece of information that Jumbo and Death didn't: *Dillinger's apartment*. The place was in Old Town's merchant area on Wells Street, snuggly hidden between a few small businesses over a four-story nail salon. I decided to have another visit. This time I'd be ready for that scab sucker. I dressed in a casual business suit with no tie, packing Thing One and Thing Two under my grey jacket. I'd have to disassemble Old Lilith again, but she was definitely coming with. In fact, I think I'd wear her as closely as whitey tighties from this point forward. After I took her apart, I packed the supernatural rifle in my computer satchel that I slung over my shoulder.

I'd left my black sedan reserved at the murder scene in front of Dillinger's place. It wasn't even lunch time, so I had hours of sunlight on my side if Johnnie Jackrabbit happened to be stupid enough to return. I took the green line, then transferred to the blue to get to Dillinger's place. The sedan waited for me in front with several tickets on the windshield. I'd have to transfer fake license plates when I returned home. After scrapping the tickets, I kept up with my investigation. Dillinger's apartment had an open-door policy, with no doorman or security, so getting through the main entrance was a piece of cake.

As I entered the building, I took a look at the offices across the street where I'd been shot down. The perfectly angled shooter's nest, conveniently abandoned office, and close proximity alone should have been an obvious sign that this was a set up. *If only I hadn't taken that stupid job.*

John's mailbox was marked Frank Sullivan. I went up the stairs and to his door as quietly as possible. Once I saw the coast was clear, I dug my gloved hands out of my pockets and into my computer satchel. The building was old, so I assumed the warder's keys I'd purchased at my local hardware store would pick the lock just fine. *$19.99 at O Malley's Home Improvements.* I tried each key until finally one pick did the job. Once the lock clicked, I tapped the door open with my shoe and crept inside.

Dillinger's place was quiet and dark. The drapes had been drawn, so I left the door behind me a crack open to shine some light in from the hallway. His home had glossy white walls and very little decor. I crept further to find that the place appeared to be a studio. It had a wide living area with a miniature kitchen that hadn't been touched in some time, and an open door that led to a closet size bathroom. The only furniture was an outdated record player with Ella Fitzgerald on the wheel and a six-foot long Christmas green rubber storage container. I pulled open the drapes in the place so that the studio was bathed in sunlight. Cautiously, I pried open the container. There was a pillow and blanket inside, but no Gentleman John.

"Damn it," I swore. I dug through the blankets and pillow for any clues. I found one. There was a sheet of crumbled magazine paper with rentable storage facility listings. A cheap converted factory building on the far westside near Midway Airport had been circled in red marker. It looked like Dillinger either hopped around a lot or he was going into the storage business. I continued to check his apartment for more leads or clues of any sort, but came up empty. I closed up Dillinger's place and headed back to my car, which already had a new ticket on it. I removed the city's love letter, punched the storage address into my phone's GPS, and headed west.

The building was close to the Metra tracks in an area once known as an industrial zone. Time had worn the bustling neighborhood down to near extinction. The streets were eroded, the sidewalks exchanged for gravel and the only traffic was semi-trucks that delivered inventory.

Midway Airport's traffic whooshed from above. After finding Dillinger's building, I parked across the gravel road near another decayed storage facility and observed.

The four-floor storage facility was made of dull bargain metal. It had a large pebble lot with a single silver Audi A6 parked near the main entrance. I planted myself at an empty neighboring property and continued to canvas Dillinger's complex. It was only a football field away. I nearly face palmed when I noticed two out of place gargoyles perched on its front corners. It didn't get more vampirish than that. Besides the stoner twins, there was nothing out of the ordinary. For nearly two hours I waited, marking possible places to force entry, positions with a clear line of sight, and escape routes. After noticing a lack of activity in the area, I hopped out of my car and walked over to the building.

I thought I could be dressed well enough to play the part of a prospecting construction manager should anyone catch me, but when I tried the doors, I realized that there was no one around. Everything was silent inside. I attempted to get a view from the windows, but they were covered in soot. So, the *Curious George* in me decided to have a closer look. The door locks were a bit too advanced for my warder's keys, so I went to one of the side windows and applied a similar method to the glass at Zombie Pete's bar. The wide pane took more patience due to its industrial strength, but persistence rewards. After a few minutes, I'd cracked enough of a hole to fit my hand through to unlatch the window fixture. I crawled inside and dusted myself off.

The interior was dark and even after removing my sunglasses I found that it wasn't enough. I dug into my computer satchel and removed Old Lilith's scope. After flipping on its power, I used the lowlight mode to navigate my way around. The center storage area sprawled out like a grocery store and was polluted with stacked wood crates that resembled a game of Tetris. The open ceiling reached up four floors to the top of the building. There was a thin wrought iron staircase that led to overlooking mezzanines crowning the second and third levels.

On those upper levels were small glass offices. If anyone were upstairs, they could easily lean over the side to shoot me up like fish in a barrel. That only further inspired me to tread lightly. I tiptoed toward the stairs with one hand glued to the scope over my eye and the other hand clung to Thing One. The plan was to search office to office in search of Dillinger. I took my first step up the stairwell, and the cast iron reverberated. It was only moments later when I heard the rumble of the large engine outside. The mechanical thunder bellowed like only a tractor or big-rig would.

There was a groan of tires, then the muffled creek of a vehicle door. Heavy feet hit gravel and then shuffled toward the building's loading dock doors.

Damn, I thought to myself. *I rolled a 1 on my sneak check.* I hurried to an amassment of crates and hid between them. Someone outside fumbled with a lock. Soon after, the door rose a foot open before a figure rolled underneath. The muscular silhouette stood up and reached for a chain that dangled from the top of the loading dock door.

They pulled the iron links several times, forcibly raising the door higher and higher. Finally, the barrier reached the top and sunlight poured inside. The back of an orange semi-truck faced the entrance. The Herculean figure walked back to the driver's seat. I could hear the drag of a few gears as the vehicle beeped and backed up until the bed of the truck plugged the entrance, making everything dark again.

The tail of the trailer bed drew open. I wondered if my hunch was a bust. Maybe Dillinger circled this place on the advertisement because he was interested, but never actually committed to rent it. Perhaps I'd broken into *Bob Nobody's* legitimate establishment, and was now forced to hold the big guy up if he discovered me. I watched from my hiding spot as four disheveled workers with chevron mustaches poured out of the back. Along with the strapping driver, they unloaded cargo into a neat pyramid just outside the trailer. I focused on the driver with my scope. The wrestler sized figure wore his coal hoodie over a snug Blackhawks baseball cap that shaded his eyes. His worn workman's gloves competed with his raggedy jeans and tatty construction boots for *Scruffiest Clothing of the Year*. While his men worked in teams to get the heavy boxes off the truck, the big man worked alone.

An imaginary light bulb flickered above my head and I had an idea. I flipped the scope's optics to G.S. vision. It was just as I thought. An overlay of electrical tendrils crackled along the truck driver as if he were a storm cloud.

I unplugged my eye from the site and compared. There was nothing sparkling over the truck driver. Maybe my instincts were right after all.

I decided to get all creepy ex-boyfriend and watch them from my dark corner. The process took at least an hour, but by the time they unloaded the last container, I'd made a few strange observations.

All four of the laborers looked exactly the same. Each scowled face had feathered pepper hair, narrowed eyes, and a broad mustache. Their skin had heavy creases and their jaws stayed tightly shut. They wore flannels, denim jeans, and dirty sneakers. I subconsciously began to sort them out as Charles Bronson A through D. They worked together like ants, silently understanding the others' intentions.

As for the beefy driver, he seemed to be the ringleader. I noticed a slight German accent when he'd give orders like, "Put dat' over there," and "put dat' box next to dat' box." The Charles Bronson Foursome obeyed. As for the driver's physical appearance, I'd say he was due for a visit to his dermatologist. What little skin he had showing was scarred and littered with heavy stitching. I didn't know if he'd been in a road wreck before this but if he had, maybe truck driving wasn't his true calling. In the end, I was convinced that I definitely was where I needed to be. It was all far too weird to be natural.

"*Folge mir,*" he said in a throaty form of German. "Our host should be awake soon." The Charles Bronson Quartet followed behind the driver as he stomped his way up the wrought iron stairs. He passed the second level to the third floor. Together with his minions, they entered an office that was out of my line of sight. *Damn.* Everything was now a high-risk guessing game like *Battleship,* only I had a chance of winning. I settled down and continued to observe. If this was a waiting game, they'd find that I could be as patient as Prince Charles standing by for the throne. By the time the sun went down, I'd memorized every exit, put together Old Lilith, and mentally balanced my checkbook. My back should have ached and my knees should have given me hell, but they didn't. I wrote it off as the benefits of my new high fiber diet. Finally, I heard activity upstairs. At first there were footsteps, followed by muffled conversation.

"*Guten Morgen,*" said the truck driver.

"*Guten Tag,*" responded an American man's voice that I didn't recognize.

"*Es ist Zeit für...*" the truck driver continued in German, which I didn't understand in the slightest. "*German, German, German.*" He carried on about something that sounded like a buffet involving Sigmund Freud. *I thought German was a dying language?* The two went back and forth. Since I didn't understand any of it, I decided to make a move while they were distracted. I put weight on the balls of my feet and crept toward' the pyramid of freshly unloaded boxes.

There were several heavy-duty Rubbermaid chests with snap latches and three tall wood crates hugged in chains. A pungent ammonia smell stung my nostrils. I flipped the latches of one of the plastic chests and peeked inside. There were cheap steel bars lined in rows. Well, that was a letdown. I slipped toward the chain, my eyes locked on the balconies above. I leaned on one of the tall wood crates. There was the distinct sound of heavy breathing from inside. Slowly and cautiously, I turned around and peered through a small crack along the corner of the crate, catching a large yellow eye blink. I backed up, but the creature had already begun to growl and shake its prison. Chains rattled and wood moaned.

"What was that?" the American voice from above asked.

"*Die Hunde,*" the truck driver exclaimed.

I didn't think that the snarls were coming from an affordable South Korean scooter, so I put some distance between the box and myself. I slipped behind the truck trailer and watched as the chained crate continued to rock. There were scratches clawing from inside the box. Like a chemical reaction, the second chained box wobbled and barked, and then the third. Soon there was a chorus of howls and snarls.

"Go have a look."

I strained to hear the truck driver's order over the grunts and growls. A weak flood light from above flipped on. Not to be outdone, the Charles Bronson Band looked over the railing and studied the boxes. They exchanged glances briefly before making their way downstairs.

This was getting hairy.

I kept Old Lilith slung over my shoulder and removed Thing One and Thing Two from their holsters. I wasn't looking for a fight, but I'd be ready if the jig was up. I crouched close to the massive driver side tire and watched from under the front bumper as the Charles Bronson squad made it downstairs.

Three of their heads were cut off from my view, but I watched as the fourth Charles Bronson in a red flannel beat on one of the crates with his fists. Whatever was inside stopped, causing its neighbors to do the same. All went still. Seconds later, as if the chained box was filled beyond capacity, the crack of cedar cried out and the crate erupted. I watched as a blurred figure pounced from the broken remnants onto red flannel Charles Bronson.

The beast was blanketed in black fur and as large as a grizzly bear. It clawed at a now prone red flannel Charles Bronson. Charles Bronson in blue plaid came into view. He leapt on the creature's back while orange flannel Charles Bronson picked up a nearby pry bar and started hitting the creature's wolfish head. Green houndstooth patterned Charles Bronson readied to leap into action when a second chained crate's seams burst open.

Shouldn't have cut down on shipping expenses.

A colossal brown furred creature with a head like a German Shepherd dove at houndstooth green Charles Bronson, sweeping the retro action star's legs with a front paw.

"Well, no time like the present," I whispered under my breath. I scurried past the cargo.

The third chained box rattled once I reached the bottom of the wrought iron stairs. I was going to get my target damn it. As I reached the second step, a set of fingers grabbed my ankle. I looked down to find that red flannel Charles Bronson had crawled his way to me and was trying to keep me from advancing. I narrowed my eyes and studied the wounds on his face. He had gaping lesions across his eyes and nose, but where gore should be, there was an interweaving of wriggling maggots. My jaw dropped, and as Charles pulled me forward, I blurted out my surface thoughts.

"What the shit am I looking at here?" I asked him. His bushy brows furrowed as larva poured from his face.

"*Mensch!*" shouted the German truck driver from above me. I glanced up. The truck driver and John *freaking* Dillinger were leaning over the third-floor balcony. The truck driver's eyes bounced between the commotion and myself, but Dillinger's glare was directed straight at me.

"Who are you?"

"That's a funny story," I answered over the cacophony of madness on my floor. "Just stay right there and I'll come up to tell you."

John Dillinger's sleek eyebrow lifted. "Hey boob, you're armed." I looked to Thing One and Thing Two readied in my hands.

"Huh?" I said as I looked the pistols over. "How about that? Well." I pointed the pistols up at Dillinger. "Use it or lose it."

I fired three shots from each gun. Now most people bold enough to sport a pair of pistols do so because they watched way too many John Woo movies. For me, it was because before a day ago, I was mostly blind in one eye, and needed to take as many shots as possible. My batting average didn't get any better this time around, as four of my six bullets ricocheted off of walls and railings. One entered the bulky truck driver's beefy arm. A spark of electric glinted outward from the bullet hole. *Strange.* The second should've hit Dillinger in his neck, but somehow, in the blink of an eye, John sprang sideways.

Dillinger dusted his shoulders off and shook his head. "Hey, Abercrombie." He gave a smug smirk. "I thought Mr. Rodgers taught you better." Humor during high-stress circumstances; I might like this guy. Too bad I had to kill him.

The truck driver's mouth bent into a clenched half-moon. He looked around the hall and grabbed a corroded barrel from a collection nearby. I didn't like the idea of my head getting crushed in, so I targeted Charles Bronson's wrist along my ankle and unloaded my pistols. The bullets didn't quite saw through as I'd hoped, but they did enough damage so that I could tug hard with my leg. A sound similar to tearing paper split in my ears. Maggots poured onto the stairs from Bronson's wrist. I leapt up the steps with a hand gripped on my ankle just in time to dodge a whirled barrel. The drum rolled down and over Charles Bronson. I kept climbing up, but as I glanced at the balcony, I noticed that Dillinger was gone. The disappearing act didn't stop the truck driver from pretending he was Donkey-Kong. He hurled another barrel that I narrowly escaped.

I'm getting jealous of people that never met this guy.

I holstered my pistols and unslung Old Lilith from my shoulder. The rifle was unwieldy and took all of my concentration to control. I put my good eye into the scope and aimed at the truck driver's heart as he lifted another drum but just as I squeezed the trigger, red flannel Charles Bronson leapt in front of me. The luminous bullet drove through Charles's shoulder. All at once, the maggots began to explode like popcorn. Charles Bronson's skin flapped in a pile at my feet along with his clothes. The truck driver's eyes flared.

"*Angry German words,*" he shouted as tendrils of electric covered his skin. At once, he leapt helter-skelter over the rails. Like a grasshopper, the truck driver covered a far greater distance than anyone his size should. He landed feet first on the cement, fracturing it into a web pattern. He stood unharmed and darted toward the semi's cab.

I flipped my head and saw that Mr. Electrodes was now behind the wheel of the truck. The engines grumbled with life. Near the back of the trailer, blue plaid Charles Bronson was being ripped to ribbons by the black dog monster. Green houndstooth Charles Bronson, who had been torn in half, dragged himself toward the fray. I had no idea where orange flannel Charles Bronson or the brown beast was. I unfastened Old Lilith's bipod and leaned the supports along the stairs 'guardrail. I peered through the scope again and aimed at the dog monster's head. I pulled the trigger. The creature lurched forward from the impact of Old Lilith's radiant bullet before collapsing upon the leftovers of blue plaid Charles Bronson. In an instant, the creature shifted into a nude woman.

Suddenly, from the back of the stacked cargo, a howl cried out. I peeked over my scope and saw the creature with a German's Shepherd head coming out from the stack. It strode to the nude woman and sniffed. It must not have liked what it smelled because it roared before setting its sights on me, its teeth pulled into a vicious grin. I drew back the rifle's bolt-action to put another bullet in the chamber and then plugged my eye in the scope. The monster rushed forward. I did what you're taught *not* to do and took panicked shots. My first bullet missed wide. I pulled back the bolt-action again and fired into a box as the creature hurried past. I reloaded another time and fired. The bullet drilled into the first step of the stairwell that the monster climbed. If my count was right, I had one shot left, but I doubted I'd cock it in the barrel before the beast reached me. I was about to find out what being in a blender felt like.

As the creature reached within striking distance, it

winced in pain. My hands hurried to put the last bullet in the chamber as orange flannel Charles Bronson, who only had one hand now, bashed the German Shepherd with his pry bar. The wolf palmed orange flannel Charles Bronson's skull and crushed it like a tomato. Maggots rained down. I put the scope to my eye and aimed. The beast turned to me and lunged. I pulled the trigger. There was a scream from the creature as we collided. The impact was too much. Together with the monster, I flipped over the railing and down to the bottom headfirst. It was about the time when my head met the cement that I lost consciousness.

WHEN I WOKE UP, the sun was out in the warehouse. There was an overweight woman on top of me with a bullet wound in her neck. Together we wallowed in a pool of her stale blood. I pushed her off and stood up. The truck had left, and the building was quiet. Though the bodies of the two nude women were still around, the Charles Bronson quartet was gone. I should have felt like a bag of dicks, but miraculously, I was fine. I checked the upstairs for any signs of life, but there weren't any. I made my way to the pyramid of cargo in hopes to find something I could work with. As I made it back downstairs, the third chained crate rattled.

"I just can't catch a break," I mumbled aloud as I checked Old Lilith. There were no bullets left, nor was I given any spare ammo. I dug in my jacket and removed Thing One, reloading it with one of the spare clips I kept on me. Afterwards, I used the pry bar leftover from orange flannel Charles Bronson and bent a small opening between two pieces of wood. My plan was to give myself just enough of an opening to unload the pistols should I need to. To my astonishment, there was no demon wolf-bear inside. Instead, a sobbing child lay curled in a ball. She was a little girl, no older than six, with beaded black hair tied into a single braid. She had ripped pink pajamas and the shredded leg of a doll. She looked up at me with her tear-stained eyes and frowned.

"Well." I pulled the boards out so she could squeeze through. "This just got a whole lot more complicated."

8

Once upon a time there was a hitman. A sad contract killer, who was terrified to face the consequence of his heinous deeds in life, took a job as Death's intern in order to put off his eternal fate. Death and his sidekick Jumbo gave the hitman all sorts of bullshit jobs, from killing zombies to slaying a vampire. One day, just after the hitman finished a fight with multiple Charles Bronson's and werewolves, he found a little girl in a box.

That's it.

The freaking end.

I was never really good at fairytales. Anyhow, I was in quite the predicament. I couldn't just leave this poor girl to fend for herself on the mean streets of West Chicago, but I also wasn't up to turning her into the police. If she was anything like her wicked stepmothers, she'd tear the precinct to pieces. Maybe, though admittedly unlikely, this girl had a mom or dad who knew just what to do with her. I crouched down and tried to hide my freak eye by putting my sunglasses back on. It didn't work. The girl scooted farther into the corner of her box. I cleared my throat.

"Hi." I gave a tiny wave. The girl curled into a tighter ball. "I'm not going to hurt you." I paused. "Then again, I'm sure you've heard that before." The girl eyed Old Lilith. "I know," I demurred, my hands palm down on my lap. "But it's empty. It can't hurt you either." The girl blinked at me. "Do you have a ma or dad?" The girl shook her head no. "Brothers or sisters?" The girl shook her head no again. "Okay, no family. You've probably been kidnapped." The girl just stared at me. "Listen, I'm *honestly* not going to harm you. I promise. Did you want to come out of that box?" There was a prolonged period of quiet trepidation. The girl moved to her hands and knees before crawling out.

She took in the building around her. She'd probably never seen more than what she could make out from her crate. She was a little under four feet tall. Her knees were scabbed, and her fingernails were dirty. She tucked her lip over her large buckteeth, but they were far too long and bulky to completely cover. Her gaze wandered from the boxes to the railings, to the two dead bodies on the floor. The woman who'd dragged me off the stairs was blonde with blue eyes and the one nearest was grey haired with olive skin. I didn't think they were related, but then again, it didn't make things much better. The girl blinked several times, eyes locked on the corpses.

"Yeah." I rubbed the back of my neck. "Sorry about that. But they were going to kill me." I cringed at my own words. "Were they related to you?" The little girl shook her head. "Were they your friends?" She furrowed her brow and frowned before shaking her head again. Then she stepped toward the woman with grey hair and dipped her fingers in the old woman's wound.

She rubbed the blood on her face and spat at the old bag.

Holy shit, this kid was too legit to quit.

I watched how the girl stared at the crone. Her mouth stiffened, her forehead creased, and her hands balled into fists. Grandma over here must have done something real bad to this kid. I walked behind her. She was barely to my waist, but she still made me nervous.

"Did she hurt you?" I asked. The kid nodded. I took a shot in the dark. "Did she touch you?" The girl looked at me as if I were wearing polka dots and a clown nose. She wiped her nostrils with her hand before shaking her head 'no' again. "Did she try to get you to do bad things?" The girl looked up to me and nodded briskly. "Ah," I said while smacking my lips. "I see. They were using you as a weapon." The girl didn't say anything. She just stared down at the body. "Well, hey, I can take you somewhere if you want. Do you know anyone that will take you in?"

There was a pause before she lifted her head and shrugged.

"Okay. You clearly don't have anyone. How about we just get out of here for now and come up with a plan as we go. We're kind of hanging out at a crime scene." The girl remained hush, but as I started to test the waters by heading toward the exit, she followed. I kept track of her as I walked to the car near the neighboring warehouse. She pursued, putting safe distance between us while observing the empty road, warehouses, and the summer sun. I wondered how long she'd been cooped up, but my concentration changed beats once I noticed that the Audi once parked outside was gone. Dillinger had escaped, and he was now aware of my presence. He was a professional criminal and would likely go into hiding.

The summer heat baked the inside of my vehicle to volcanic temperatures. I turned on the car and air conditioner before retreating back outside to wait for everything to cool off. I hid in the shade of the perched gargoyle and advertised for the cigarette companies. I puffed the cancerstick and blew out. The girl fixed her sights on the cloud plume. I took another waft and blew out a few smoke rings. The girl watched them rise and disintegrate. Her face went from a frown to blank.

"Okay kid," I annunciated slowly as if she spoke another language. "Lesson one." I pointed to the cigarette. "This is dumb." I then tapped on my head. "I am dumb. Please, don't be dumb." The girl titled her head at me. The slightest tickle of a smile spasmed along her lips. "Dumb," I repeated while lifting the cigarette and throwing it. "Now that we've established my intelligence level, it's time to go. You can come with if you'd like, or you can stay." I hoped she wouldn't want to be left here alone. Ditching her was a bluff. I couldn't abandon her. I opened up the driver side door and slipped in. The cooler temperatures were a relief. The girl moved to the passenger side door but didn't come in. I fanned myself and mouthed the word *cold*. She blinked several times. I could see sweat coming from her forehead. She slowly opened the passenger door, inspected the interior, then slipped in.

"See." I put my hand by the air vent. "Cold." She held her hand up and put it along the airway. Her eyes shut as her little fingers wiggled. She opened them back up, looked at me once, and then buckled her seatbelt. "Well, alright," I said as I put the car in drive. "Destination unknown."

We cruised out of the Westside and onto the northbound highway. I didn't really know what to do with the girl or what the hell Dillinger wanted with her. So I did what I usually did when I hit these little snags. I headed to my favorite gaming store. *Gamer's Pair-a-Dice* was a hobby and role-playing shop where local gamers met to escape the world. The little money that the place made on role-playing books and miniature monster sales barely paid the rent, but what it did for the outcasts of Chicagoland was priceless. The weird neighborhood mail delivery guy or nerdy tech support girl at the office didn't have to worry about being judged here. They were accepted without question. Though most patrons were as socially awkward as the Dalai Lama getting a lap dance, they made up for it in brains. The place had more MENSA members than NASA. I visited whenever I needed some perspective, as intelligent people who pretended to be elves were surprisingly insightful.

I parked the car along the side lot and shut off the engine. The once-growling girl I now dubbed Little Wolf stared at the poorly painted logo on the exterior's side wall. The tropical tree's coconuts were replaced with Icosahedron shaped dice known to nerds everywhere as "twenty-siders." I patted my chest, and for reasons unknown, spoke to her in caveman.

"I go in building," I announced way too loud. I pointed to her. "You go with?"

Little Wolf pursed her lips over her rabbit teeth while furrowing her brow. I was fluent in the subtle art of dirty looks and this one said, *I'm not stupid or deaf.* She watched as a squat fat kid and acne covered boy with thick glasses emerged from the store. They were as geeky as they were harmless. Little Wolf didn't say anything.

"Okay, it's fine," I said as I opened my door. "You can stay inside. I'll be right back. By the way, there's napkins in the glove compartment if you want to wash the blood off your face."

I left the car and started to walk toward the entrance when I heard a second door slam shut. I turned to see that Little Wolf left the sedan to follow me as she rubbed a McDonald's napkin on her cheek. I gave a half smirk and waved her over. "Come on then. Let me show you what a room of virgins smells like." She followed with a raised brow.

A gale of chilled, musty air hit Little Wolf and me as we entered the gaming store. Darren, the middle-aged man who worked the register, sported his frequently worn Hawaiian shirt. If you looked close enough, you'd notice that the hula girls were replaced by roaring orcs. He was talking to a pudgy man with an outfit that screamed *lower-office management*. Darren spent most of his work day patrolling the seven tight isles for gamers sadistic enough to take pieces out of boxes or read books without purchasing them. When his great patrol was over, he tormented visitors with conversation.

"Mark my words," Darren warned as he tied his balding ponytail into a man bun. "China will beat everyone else to Mars and then they can hold the entire world hostage with their planet- to-planet laser. They have the technology you know?" The pudgy man with no neck opened his mouth to comment, but Darren quickly cut him off. "I mean, if you like communism that's fine, but if

not, I'd be ready to build the second Great Wall by 2030."
Darren's eyes grew to saucers when he saw me. "Buck,
what a pleasant—"

"No," I objected.

"Wait." Darren's eyes followed me. "What are you—"

"Shush," I interrupted again, standing in front of Little
Wolf in order to shield her from the shameful display of a
man. I could feel her little fingers tug at the hem of my
pant leg. "I'm busy now. Can I ignore you some other
time?"

Darren frowned. The two of us had a rare dislike for
one another similar to a buzzard and a crocodile. Darren
loved to squawk about his vast knowledge until it was
downright demeaning. Then I would remind him that I
had killed people in the Army. It tended to scare him into
leaving me alone for the remainder of my visit. Today
wasn't the day to play our little game though. I had proper
nerds to consult. I pushed Little Wolf, who now clung to
my leg, ever so gently by the shoulder, guiding her to the
gaming room entrance decorated in a chain of Hawaiian-
themed leis.

Little Wolf and I entered the back room, which was as
large as a typical old basement, and just as dingy. It had
several makeshift tables that were strewn with tiny castles,
forests, and other battle maps. My group, who we'd
dubbed "Sword's Edge," was scheduled for this afternoon
at Table Five. It was strange, but just seeing them made a
unicorn tap dance in my heart. I had no real family or
friends of my own, so these guys and gals were the closest
thing I had to a healthy relationship.

"Dhat's' when the pregnant ogre comes chargin' at you,"
Nolan exclaimed in his thick Chicago accent that comes

complimentary with any working-class family. "Her club in the air. You see, she had been protecting her young and now yous' guys are trespassing on her home." Nolan was our Game Master, and he was a damn good one. He stood at the head of the table like the one-hundred-and-thirty-pound king that he was, describing his imaginary scene.

"Damn it, Nolan," Nikolai, who joined us three years ago as an exchange student from Russia and had never returned home, complained. "Why must you make every scene some, how you say, existential crisis? I don't want to question my character's morality. I just want to kill some monsters." Nolan gave a grin that matched the evil smirk from Lo-Pan on his t-shirt.

"Perhaps you'd like to join Table Three," Karen, an overweight Native American accountant with a preciously dark sense of humor, jabbed. "I'm sure they have a spot for you." Nikolai grunted.

"I have an idea," Beth, the career band nerd, cut in. "I cast *Sleep* on the ogre. That way we don't slay her but win the encounter."

Atari, yes, that was his real name as far as we knew, cleared his throat.

"That's true," Atari declared with a crack in his voice, pushing the bridge of his glasses upward. "According to Dragon Wiki, you do not need to slay the monsters to gain the experience." Nicolai's shoulders dropped.

"Why did I even make a blood thirsty barbarian?" Nicolai slurped his Red Bull. "I should have made a damn Red Cross volunteer." The group laughed.

I waved Little Wolf to follow me as I loomed over Table Five. Nolan smiled when he saw me.

"Ladies and gentlemen," Nolan announced. "Our resident wizard, Sarsicus, is here." Nolan's brows raised when he saw Little Wolf. "And he's brawt a friend."

"Greetings, homies." I saluted. "Unfortunately, I won't be able to play today."

Nicolai, whose cheeks were covered in craters from old zits, leaned down to Little Wolf.

When Nicolai wasn't gaming, he was abusing basement-brewed steroids or using his discount hair clippers to buzz bizarre designs into his temples. It made him look like Ivan Drago's ugly stunt double.

"Hello, Little Girl," he greeted with his thick accent. Little Wolf hurried behind my leg.

Beth swatted Nicolai's arm.

"You're scaring her," Beth chastised in her helium pitch voice. She offered Little Wolf an unwrapped Snickers bar. "Here you go." Little Wolf grabbed the candy bar and scarfed it down in two eager bites.

"Gosh," Karen cried out. "Buck, when is the last time this girl has eaten?"

"Great question," I said. "That's actually why I'm here. Um, Nolan, can we put the game on pause for a quick second. I need a little smart people advice." The group shared in a collective set of blank stares.

"Hey team." Nolan clapped his hands together. "Why don't we take a 'tirty minute break."

"Great idea." Atari held onto his stomach. "I'm starving. Anyone want some Wendy's?"

"No," Nicolai objected. "I will solve Buck's problem," he declared with the confidence of
a bull charging a red cape.

"Oh gosh." Beth slapped her forehead. "I'll stay to counter any advice Nicolai gives."

Karen sighed. "I'll go with you, Atari. We can take my car." She tossed her keys up in the air before catching them.

"Pick me up a pop, please," Nolan requested. The pair walked out, leaving Little Wolf and me with Nolan, Nicolai, and Beth.

"So, buddy," Nolan said while waving at Little Wolf. "What exactly is going on?"

"I found a kid." I looked down at Little Wolf. "And I don't know what to do with her."

"Well," Beth hummed. "Isn't it obvious. You need to take her to the police."

"No can do," I objected.

"Uh, Buck," Nolan stepped in. "Why not?"

"Isn't it obvious?" Nicolai spoke up. "He kidnapped her."

I cocked my head back. "What? No. Damn it. I did *not* kidnap her." Nicolai shrugged.

Nolan twisted his lips, tapping on his chin.

"'Den Buck." He tilted his head. "It still begs the question. Why not?"

My little gaming group didn't know that I was a hitman. There was never a time to just open up about how I killed people for money. Instead, I masqueraded as a wounded veteran who lived on government checks. Little Wolf was my only link to Dillinger, and I was pretty damn sure she was a damn werewolf, so I couldn't just give her away. I needed to dream up a reason why a war vet wouldn't want to give a little girl up to authorities. Then it hit me.

"She's Denise's niece," I lied. Everyone knew about Denise and her murder and walked gingerly around the subject. "Yeah, you see, Denise's sister is addicted to well, *everything*, and her daughter here ran away. I barely recognized the kid on the side of the street and decided to pick her up. If I turn her in, she'll go to the State, which we all know isn't any better. So, I'm kind of in a funk. Suggestions?"

"No father?" Beth asked in a calm, inquisitive tone.

"Afraid not." I shrugged.

"No udder family?" Nolan jumped in.

"None that are responsible." I patted Little Wolf's shoulder.

"No clothes?" Nicolai asked while inspecting Little Wolf's raggedy shirt and pants.

"I'm working on it." I frowned. "This all just happened."

"Well, buddy." Nolan took a deep breath, "I can only tell you what I'd do."

"Yeah." I smiled. "It's kind of why I'm here."

"I'd hold on to the girl for a few days," Nolan continued, unaffected by my response. "I'd let her Ma know she's safe of course, 'den check in with her periodically to see if she's cleaned up."

"What?" Beth argued. "He can't do that."

"Beth," Nolan called out, turning to her. "I was adopted. I remember how bad the orphanage sucked before my parents picked me. It's cruddy food, wounded children, and underpaid care. You can't hand her over to the cops. I don't see anything wrong with Buck being the girl's guardian angel until Ma is better as long as he lets her know that her girl is safe." Beth bit at her lip. Nicolai crossed his arms.

"Suppose you're right." Beth blew her blonde bang from her face. "How will Buck know when he should give her up?" Nolan looked me in the eyes.

"I trust Buck." Nolan nodded. "He'll know. Won't you, buddy?"

"Okay." Beth bit her lip. "She'll need some clothes for starters. Buck, my sister's fifty daughters are outgrowing clothes like spring plants. If you want, I have a wine date with her after our game tonight. Come here tomorrow morning and I promise I'll have loads of extra clothes for..." Beth paused and stared at Little Wolf. "What's your name, Sweetie?" Little Wolf gave a blank stare.

"Uh." I swallowed a lump in my throat. "Funny story. I only met her once. I don't know and she won't speak. She must be really spooked about her last few days."

"Oh." Beth frowned. She bent down, hands on her knees, and smiled to Little Wolf. "You don't want to speak?" Little Wolf shook her head. "What would you like to be called, Sweetie?" Little Wolf pointed to Beth. Beth looked to the three of us. Nolan smiled.

"Look behind you, Beth," Nolan laughed. The four of us took a glimpse behind Beth. Displayed in a clear plastic display shelf was a miniature of the fantasy goddess with midnight skin, white hair and pointed ears. She held a moon shaped sword in her hand. It was Luna, Queen of the Night Elves. *Oh, sweet irony.*

"That's Luna." Beth smiled. "Goddess of the Night Elves." Little Wolf grinned, and I swear to you, I'd never seen anything sweeter.

"Luna it is then," Beth laughed. Nicolai put his fist to his chest.

"This little girl," he said with a furrowed brow. "Is what we call in my country, a *badass*."

"No, uh," Nolan said matter-of-factly. "'Dat 's pretty universal." Nicolai leaned down and patted Little Wolf on the head.

"Luna." Nicolai saluted her. "You may join my army someday."

"On that twist of fate," I cut in. "I had one piece of business I wanted to discuss. Who would I talk to in order to ask about vampires and werewolves?"

"Quite the subject jump." Beth smirked.

"I'm a wild card," I said in my best James Dean, cool guy voice. Beth laughed.

"I'm gonna guess that you've recently started dabbling in Chronicles of Darkness," Nolan guessed. I nodded.

"Please don't feel cheated on," I apologized. "It's online. You'll always be my boo, Nolan."

"Well 'den, buddy." Nolan tried to hide a smile. "You'll need to talk to Freddy. I'm useless when it comes to modern day monster. It's dragons and wizards for me."

"Freddy," I groaned. "Uh, never mind."

Fredrick L. Waters was a resident gamer. He dressed like Brandon Lee from *The Crow* and rode on the fact that ten years ago, his screenplay for a vampire movie was made into a pilot that crashed and burned within its first year on cable television. Nerds of little confidence felt it an honor to know someone like Freddy. He was smart no doubt, but so odd that it was taxing. I looked over to Table Nine, where the Goth dorks hung out, and spotted him. Freddy was in a cheap oversized trench coat that had been washed so many times that it was grey. He was plump with long greasy hair. He wore eyeliner and plum lipstick.

"Well, ders' your guy, Buck." Nolan shrugged. "Take it or leave it."

"Alright," I said through gritted teeth. "Here goes nothing."

"Meanwhile," Beth spoke up. "I'm going to take Luna here to peruse the gaming shirts to see if anything will fit her." Beth held out her hand to Luna. "Would you like to go with me, Luna?" Luna gave a single bob of her head. "Great. Come on."

I casually strolled over to Freddy, who appeared to be in the early stages of setting up Table Nine's combat map. He didn't look up as I approached but tilted his head ever so slightly.

"Speak, mortal," Freddy pressed in a low voice while lining up a Frankenstein miniature along a graveyard map. Oh God, this was going to suck.

"Hey, Freddy." I did a little karate bow. "I needed your expertise on some creature questions."

"Do you now?" Freddy added undead revenants to the map. "So, the darkness calls to you then?"

"Uh." I paused. "Yes. It definitely calls to me. Say, Freddy, if I were a modern-day werewolf, when would I be able to transform into a savage hunter?"

"Ha," Freddy said without feeling. "While it's true that lycanthropes must transform on certain moon phases, that's not the only way they change. A real lycanthrope transforms during certain triggers as well."

"Triggers?"

"Yes. Some morph in the presence of silver while

others change when their loved ones are being threatened. Each pertains to the lycanthropes' spirit."

"Oh. Makes sense."

"Does it?" he challenged. His eyes never left the table.

"Uh, I think. Say, one other question. Modern day vampires, what's their story, right? I mean, I'm old as hell, yet need to drink blood. What am I doing all night? Am I waiting in a castle like a spider, hoping my next victim will come to me?"

"No, not even kind of."

"Oh?"

"Vampires need mortals. Without their blood, vampires are nothing. They must disguise themselves. Wear sheep's clothing. Only then can vampires insure they will have immortal life and energy."

"So, vampires surround themselves with their food?"

"You wouldn't understand, but yes."

"So, I should go to places where people are?"

Freddy stomped his fat fists on the table and finally looked up at me. "You wouldn't just *go* to places where people are. You need to hunt where your victims are impressionable, susceptible to your advances. Yet, you're decades, if not centuries old. You have style and a need for decadence that no one can understand. You want to surround yourself with beauty, though you're confused as to what that still is. So, you'd cast yourself amongst the most alluring mortals in the finest establishments, trying to remember what grace was before you confined yourself to a kingdom of opulence. You are a blood god after all, if you're to have a prison, a child of the night should have the best."

I must have had one of those faces that says, "*Are you*

nuts?" because Freddy flung his hair in his face and continued setting up the vampire lord onto the game board.

"Well." I smacked my lips. "Thanks."

"Buck."

"Yes?"

"There's more to the night. When you're ready to truly understand." He paused and extended what appeared to be a fridge magnet. I glanced the black and red advertisement, which read Fredrick L. Waters, Occult Expert. Below the title was a poorly drawn cartoon of himself with a sword next to his phone number and address. "Return to me."

"Lovely. Will do."

I hurried away from Table Nine as quickly as I could. Nolan and Nikolai had returned to Table Five and were measuring out the distance between an ogre miniature and Tonak the Barbarian. Nolan dignified me with a smirk.

"So," Nolan laughed. "How'd it go?"

"As well as the Hindenburg's last flight." I shook my head. Nicolai and Nolan laughed. As I digested what just happened, I felt a tug on my pant leg. I looked down to see Luna with an oversized ruby shirt that said, *Dear Mr. Dungeon Master, Please don't kill my character.* I grinned.

"It was the smallest shirt they had." Beth hung her hands on her hips. "It's a little bit of an upgrade from the ripped grey top, which I will burn once you leave." I put my hand on Beth's shoulder.

"Thanks, Beth," I said, appreciative. "I owe you one." Beth waved me off. "On that note, Luna and I must be off. I should get her a proper meal, after all."

"See you next week?" Nolan inquired.

"If you peasants can get past the ogre," I said in my best impersonation of an old crabby wizard. "Then Sarsicus will be there."

Shortly after, Luna and I were loading back into the car. There was a long checklist of things to do. I needed to get her fed, settled, and feeling safe. That was going to be tough, seeing that I lived in an apartment that was one murder short of feeling like a haunted hotel. I'd start by using the emergency fifty-dollar bill in my glove compartment to raid a fast-food menu. I also had research to do if I wanted to find Dillinger. The wily vampire probably had something against vampire hunters trying to kill him. I'd need to act fast.

As we picked up McDonalds, I thought about what Freddy had to say. If Dillinger really was like the vampires of role player's lore, then I had an idea of where he might be. If my suspicions were correct, then I had a lot of work to do. So, along with a werewolf chewing a mouthful of French fries in the passenger seat, I put the car in drive so that I could kill a vampire for the Grim Reaper.

Yeah, you heard it right.

9

I expected judgment from Luna when we returned to the flat but living in a crate must have made her far more forgiving than most. Upon entering, Luna sniffed the air, scanned my crooked bookshelf, and then walked over and picked up a ceramic Wolverine book end, ignoring the roach on the linoleum. I showed her the bathroom, and then brought out some old sheets from my closet, making her a makeshift bed on my secondhand couch. Luna sat on the plaid blanket chewing the last of a fried apple pie. I had work to do but I didn't want to be rude, so I flipped on the television, searching for the best basic cable had to offer.

"I need to do a little work on the computer," I explained while pointing to a *Chips* episode. Erik Estrada was chasing a bad guy through the streets of Los Angeles. "You can use this—" I handed her the remote control. "—to watch anything you want." Luna took the remote, curled up under the blanket, and watched wind blow through

Erik Estrada's beautiful angel hair. By the time I pulled out my laptop and powered it up, Luna was sleeping.

I started to research the many trendy, highbrow attractions Chicago had to offer. I sorted through private boat tours, fine dining establishments, and nightclubs that might be a chic vampire fit. If Freddy was right, then John Dillinger would be looking for someplace that spoke to his old style, but still had plenty of young pretty necks to suck on. It wasn't long until I found it.

The Violet Hour was a swank cocktail lounge in Wicker Park that posed as a luxurious speakeasy of old. It had only just recently opened back up from the pandemic. The front door was disguised as the boarded-up entrance of a condemned building with a single light bulb dangling from its front. If you knew what you were looking for, you could enter the dim interior decorated in high-backed sapphire chairs clustered around marble bars. The lounge sold cocktails that cost more than most meals and played early twentieth century jazz. A reviewer even posted that they spotted Al Capone drinking bourbon there. It was right up Dillinger's alley.

The plan would be to scout the place out, and if I somehow was right, track Dillinger to his home. Once I knew where he lived, I'd go all *Abraham Van Helsing* on him. If I was wrong, I'd investigate the list of other possibilities I found like the vintage Drake Hotel or classical Chicago Cut Steakhouse. This was a game of cat and mouse. It could take days.

I put down the laptop after an hour of note taking. Luna was snoring and snarling in her sleep. I wondered what the hell Dillinger wanted with her. A wise person once said that it's easier to build strong children than it is to repair broken men. I rarely looked back on my child-hood. There was no good reason. Psychoanalyzing every time my old man decorated my face with a black eye or every night I went without dinner because Ma had to choose heat over groceries didn't change the fact that it happened. I never wanted to admit that my upbringing had any power over me.

Now, as I glimpsed at Luna, my past scared me more than ever. I couldn't imagine what Luna, or whatever her real name was, might have been through in her short time on Earth. I was pretty sure the girl was a legitimate were-wolf. I didn't know how you inherited the condition, but her first change alone had to have been a shock. All the movies I'd ever watched made the transformation look like a front row seat to a *House of Pain* concert. What that had to do to a child's psyche was dizzying to think about.

Then there was the fact that she had been a prisoner, locked away in a crate. Luna, without saying anything at all, suggested that the other crated were-women harmed her somehow. I had to imagine that they weren't the only transgressors. She had been transported like feral cattle. Chances were that her emotional wellbeing wasn't her captors' priority.

What did the future hold for a little girl forged in flame and branded by pain? If I couldn't upend my life after a laughably easy childhood compared to Luna's, then what chance did she stand? Maybe I was projecting my own contrite guilt on the girl. Maybe she could right the wrongs she'd witnessed. I hoped for her sake and my own that she was stronger than I was.

That dark thought led to another. It dawned on me that typically, once I started honing on my next target, I'd fantasize about how to spend my contracted money. There were overdue bills on my coffee table. I'd often pay in advance as it could be months before my next hit. This job was different, though. There was no money involved. Payment was a possible extension of my eternal soul on Earth instead of the fiery pits of Hell. While that was far more important than cash, it still begged the question as to how I was going to pay rent. Not only was I behind, but I now had Luna to look after for a while. I was a shit role model already.

It was getting late. The poor kid was exhausted and wouldn't likely wake up until morning. I debated whether or not I should start scouting this evening, but it didn't feel right to leave Luna alone without an explanation. She could rise in a panic, murdering all my neighbors. Besides, I still needed to restock my inventory, clean out Old Lilith, and figure out how to reload her. I wasn't given any extra ammunition, nor did I think I could purchase *Magic-Death Bullets* at Denny's pawn shop.

After a round of pushups and the last of my prescribed Zoloft, I decided to call it a night. I left a single kitchen light on for Luna, then locked all the doors, including the one to my bedroom. I dragged my clothes cabinet in front of the door in case Luna decided she felt a little wolfish and placed a pistol under my pillow. I imagined that regular parenting wasn't as hazardous, but then again, I'd seen those little monsters at the park. They were vicious.

10

When my eyes opened back up, The Grim Reaper was standing above me. He had a colorful Hawaiian Lei around his neck. Gripped in his bony hand was Old Lilith, now back in scythe form. He lifted the wood handle as if to strike. I withdrew the pistol under my pillow. The Grim Reaper snickered. I pulled the trigger and a joke flag sparked out with the word "Bang!" imprinted across its red surface. The Grim Reaper shook his head.

"You, sir, are an oxygen thief," The Grim Reaper sighed. "Jumbo was wrong." He struck down at my head with inexplicable speed.

I leapt from my bed in a cold sweat. The room was empty. A labored hum from a cranky air conditioner was the only sound in the room. I looked at the clock. It read 3:02AM. I put an ear to my blockaded bedroom door. I could hear Luna lightly and ever so sweetly snoring the way that only kids can. I wondered at what developmental age snoring turned into lawn mower sounds. I fell back into bed and stared at the ceiling. It took some time to

persuade my body to return to sleep, but eventually I went
down.

I WOKE up again around dawn. It was no use trying to force
myself down again, so I dragged the dresser from my door
and started breakfast: instant oatmeal and a mushy
banana I'd stolen from a hotel lobby. Luna was still asleep
on the couch. I tried my hardest to be quiet, but the
microwave beeps and coffee in the air was likely too much.
Luna shuffled into the kitchen. I smiled and handed her
the browned banana. I half expected her to throw it at my
head, but once again, Luna was merciful. She gulped down
the banana in two bites. I pushed the steaming bowl of
Insta-Oaties across the kitchen table. She sniffed it before
taking a test bite. After squishing it around her cheeks, she
added sugar and finished the bowl. I waited for her to
clean up with a fast-food napkin before trying my hand at
some diplomacy.

"So," I lit a cigarette. "You can understand me, right?"
Luna winced as secondhand smoke hit her face. I waved it
away, then in an act of divinity, crushed the death stick into
an ashtray before it hit the filter. I took a sip of coffee and
tried again. "Sorry, but you can understand me?" Luna
nodded. "Well, that's the most important part. If you
understand me, then I'm going to assume then that you
can talk, but just choose not to." Luna gave me a blank
stare. "Regardless, let's get this out of the way. I apologize.
I'm a terrible example of an adult. I smoke, drink, and live
in an apartment that a frat boy would scoff at." Luna's eyes
shifted back and forth between the crushed cigarette and

my stained ceiling. I don't know why, but for the first time in a while, I felt uncomfortable. I was exposed for who I really was, a dried up, repressed murderer living in a rat's nest. I took a breath and braved on.

"With that being said." I took another sip of black mud. "I thought it over and it would be best if you went with me today. We have a lot to do, so if you feel like you've eaten enough, I can find you a towel to shower, and then we can hit the streets. Is that okay with you?" Luna put her finger to her lips and puffed them. She tottered back and forth for a moment before nodding. "Great. Shall we get started then?"

After finding a mostly clean towel, waiting on Luna to shower and then dress, we were on our way in the sedan. The sun was still raw and colored Chicago in an early orange. We stopped at a ruddy gas station, and as we filled up, I raided the station's basic overpriced grocery aisle. After buying cereal, milk, donuts, and laundry detergent, we were back in the car and headed to *Gamer's Pair-of-Dice*. Derek was unlocking the door while chewing on a breakfast sandwich when I arrived.

Finally, he was quiet.

I tried to be as quick as I could, collecting the clothes that Beth had promised to bring over. True to her word, Beth had left two garbage bags of children's clothes along with some kid's books and toys with Derek. I waited for Luna to use the store's bathroom to choose some new clothes, avoiding Derek by pretending to read the back of new role-playing book, until she emerged. She was wearing a pastel blue shirt with matching flower printed shorts.

"Look at you." I smiled. "You're a real kid now." Luna

covered her buck teeth, but the ends of a smile curled from
behind her fingers. Back in the car, we headed north
through the dismal Chicago rush hour. I wanted to scout
out The Violet Hour and compare it to the notes that I'd
found online. Traffic aside, the morning was an ideal time
to visit, as there'd likely only be a skeleton crew in the
building in charge of cleaning and taking deliveries. I
parked across the street along the corner of North Damen
Avenue and Wicker Park Avenue near a playground. I
pushed Luna on the swing a few times before letting her
take over. She eyed the city, her gaze darting at cars and
people from the safety of the park gates. Once I saw that
she was content, I slunk past the park fence to the sidewalk
to case the place. The building was old with boarded up
windows and doors. I though it seemed like an ideal place
for a vampire to live.

Like clockwork, the stock trucks came in one-by-one. I
watched as a blond employee, who looked like a Ken Doll
with his plastered hair and perfect complexion, pushed
open a steel trap door from the sidewalk to let the beer guy
in. Ken Doll watched like a smiling hawk as the beer man
wheeled in several kegs down to the basement. When the
beer guy returned to the surface with an empty dolly, Ken
waved goodbye and watched the delivery man and his ten-
footer drive away. Ken then secured the trap door and
double tested the handle to ensure it was locked. Talk
about employee of the year.

Not much else happened after that. I continued to take
in little details. The front wall of the building was spray
painted with vibrant cartoon skateboarders and a depiction of a radio pouring out musical notes. It was quality
urban art that I suspected was commissioned given its

detail. In the background of one illustrated scene was a depiction of a smirking Prohibition-style gangster with a thin mustache. My instincts told me that the image was just a little too coincidental. I was on the right track.

I hardly noticed Luna returning to the car and starting to read some of the books from Beth's nieces when I remarked on the time. I'd been in the car for hours. It was lunch time. I looked in the rearview mirror and made eye contact with Luna through the reflection. She stared up with her deep brown eyes but didn't say a word.

"You hungry, kid?" I asked. She nodded. "Great, I know a place around the corner."

If Luna wasn't here, I'd have staked the place out for at least a few hours more, but I was okay with leaving. Having Luna to look after didn't feel like a burden. I enjoyed making someone else happy for once, especially since I was inept at doing it for myself. We headed to a cheap diner down the street where I used all but ten dollars of my emergency money. We sucked down the lunch special: greasy steak sandwiches and fries with ice-cold pop. Once we were done, I thought it would be best to hurry back to the flat before traffic stiffened. I wanted to go over my checklist, inspect my equipment, and clean up before returning to The Violet Hour. I'd take the van for tonight's expedition as returning with the sedan could raise suspicion for anyone who saw us earlier. That meant that I'd need to tune it up as well. It was strange, but I had a strong hunch that Dillinger would be at the lounge tonight. It was dangerous to go off of impulses. You needed to have ice water in your veins. Regardless, I wanted to be ready, so we headed home. There was plenty to do and not a lot of time to do it.

11

A choir of angels sang from the heavens. Wind chimes jingled. Gregorian monks chanted to the tune of a pan flute. Then suddenly, a woman's voice, gentle as snow, spoke up.

"Welcome to the Karma Repair Shop," the speaker greeted. "Where we'll shock your chakra with kindness. I'm your hostess for this meditation session, Clarity Moonchild. Now, before we begin, let's start by finding a comfortable place to sit."

Death, who'd been fidgeting his bony legs along the stiff plastic airport chair, inspected the seats beside him. An old man snored like an opened mouth hog to his left and to his right, a young lady held a pair of Pomeranians, who yapped incessantly at him. Death shrugged and squeezed the earpieces tighter into the spot where fleshy people would have ears.

"Good," Clarity complimented. "Now, take a deep breath that goes all the way into your belly. Let the breath remind you that you're alive."

Death slowly shook his head.

"The key to relaxing," Clarity announced. "Is releasing your inner conflict and struggle. Feel your body let go of its worries. There are no schedules."

Death pulled up his airplane ticket, which showed a boarding time for his connecting stop from Kansas City International Airport at 12:30PM to San Diego. It was now 3:17PM.

"There is no work."

Death felt his phone vibrate. He peeked at the touch screen leaning on his arm rest and saw six texts from Jumbo. One was titled, *911. This is Jumbo, but not Jumbo. Call me ASAP.*

"There is no pressure," Clarity proclaimed. "Because you are a simple, humble and loving human being. The Universe does not need you to continue. Nothing, in this moment, is a matter of life and death."

Death ripped the earbuds out from his hood and let them fall on his lap. He sat in his airport chair as the Pomeranians continued to bark. His gaze explored the dirty white tiles and advertisement pasted walls of Kansas City International Airport. Death watched a nearby woman shush a screaming toddler in one hand while rocking an infant with her other. He overheard a pair of middle-aged men arguing over what might make America great again. He followed a hurried man in a three-piece suit throw his Styrofoam fast food container on the floor near a garbage can, then watched as a poor little custodian with the name Jose on his uniform curse as he quietly picked it up.

"I don't get it," Death mumbled to himself. Or so he thought he did.

"Yeah," the old, once snoring, man answered while he rubbed his eyes. "I don't either." Death swiveled his neck and bore down at the old man.

"I'm pretty sure we're not talking about the same thing."

"Don't be so sure, *bubeleh*." The old man smiled, pressing a plaid trilby hat on his head. He was short with bushy grey brows and a stringy mustache. He had small, glinting eyes and a wide grin. "I've been around a long time."

"You don't say," Death praised with a dry tone.

"Oh, yeah. Saul, by the way." He extended his hand. Death eyed the man's liver-spotted palm. He wondered if Saul was on the list anytime soon. A few days early couldn't hurt. Death decided against it.

"I don't do handshakes."

"Suit it yourself," Saul shrugged. Just then the woman with her dogs stood up and shuffled to the restroom line. Saul stared at her backside as he dug in his pocket, removing a few shelled peanuts that he started to pick apart. "Like I was saying, I know what you don't get."

"Oh?"

"Yeah, you're talking about life. I mean, you're looking at your ticket there, fussing in your chair. There's dogs barking and babies screaming. It's enough to make anyone ask the same question."

"Huh."

"But can I tell you something, bubeleh? You're looking at it all wrong."

"I am?" Death questioned in his unflinchingly bromidic tone.

"Oh, of course." Saul patted Death on the arm. Death

ogled where Saul had unwarrantedly touched him. "Even weeds have flowers to smell."

"I'm losing you, buddy."

"Look around. What do you see, bubeleh?"

"Eh." Death sneered. "Existence."

"Bingo. Whether you like it or not, it's there. Now, there's only two real choices once you dignify that existence ain't going anywhere. You can either get *angry* about the barking dogs or you can *enjoy* their owner's nice ass."

"Oh, wow. Well." Death looked at the ticket in his hand and stood up. "Thank you, weird old man."

"Saul."

"Thank you, Saul, but I think it's time to get yelled at again by the ticket agent again." Saul tugged Death's cloak. "Think about what I said, bubeleh."

"Trying to forget it." Death tugged his cape and straggled to the ticket counter.

The employee working the computer chased another frustrated customer in front of Death away with a blend of disgust and politically correct script. Death watched the defeated customer return to a sea of other angry passengers. He took in the ticket agent's subtle deep breath and temple rub. She looked exhausted.

Death wondered if his complaint would really do anything besides add to the orchestra of whining. He thought about what Saul said. Death realized that things sometimes were just out of peoples' control. The plane would come when it did.

"Maybe Saul was right," Death muttered.

"Sir," the ticket agent called out through a mouthful of bubblegum. "It's Susan. Now, how can I help you...again?"

"Oh, uh, hey, Susan."

Susan blew a bubble and then bit down viciously, popping it.

"I," Death stammered. "I just wanted to say that it's okay. You're doing what you can and the airplane will come when it does. It's all about weeds and flowers, and stuff."

There was a pause. Susan fixed her eyes on Death. "Sir." Susan coiled her head like a cobra ready to strike. "I have a lot to do, and you are holding up the line. I will repeat one last time." She wagged her finger. "The plane is refueling. We will announce when it's ready. Please don't inquire anymore until then. Now, is there anything else?"

"Uh, I like your nice ass?"

Susan's eyes went big, but just before she could verbally unload on Death, the phone beside her rang. Susan's gaping mouth twisted into curled lips.

"Welcome to National Scarelines," she greeted. "Where our prices are so low, they're scary. This is Susan, how can I help you?" There was a moment of quiet. Death wondered if he should crawl away, but before he did, Susan spoke up. "Thank God." Susan lifted her other hand then dialed an extension; her glare set on Death. "Ladies and Gentlemen, on behalf of National Scarelines, I want to announce that bordering for connecting Flight A13 from O'Hare to Kansas City International Airport to its final destination of San Diego International will begin. All VIP and A category passengers may line up near the door with tickets ready."

Susan slammed down the phone.

"Well." Death looked down at his ticket, which he had checked in bright and early to ensure he was first to board. "That's me."

Death didn't wait for Susan's response. He filed in with

the other early passengers and readied his ticket. Seemed things did work out eventually. Maybe perspective was key. Death thought about everything else he was worrying about. Jumbo could handle whatever was brewing. Death believed in him. He powered off his phone and put it away. As for Buck, maybe Death was being too hard on him. After all, the guy was hand selected because of his professionalism. Death was sure that Buck had everything under control and it was going like clockwork.

12

Never underestimate a man running late. Traffic stretched miles longer than expected. By the time we returned to the flat, it was nearly time to leave again. I heated up an oven pizza for Luna while prepping for the evening. I readied a black tailored black suit, checked over Thing One and Thing Two then examined Old Lilith. Miraculously, the rifle's clip had a new set of bullets in it. Strange happenings like reappearing ammunition were becoming the norm. One worry to check off the list. After burning my hand on the stove to feed Luna, I hurried down to check the oil levels on the van and fill it with diesel. Then it was a quick shower and shave before I was ready to take on Count Dillinger and his ghoul gang.

I was all about bringing Luna with me for the scouting mission, but a deadly soiree with a vampire was different. The plan was to keep her locked in the apartment for the night while I hunted the hunter. She'd be safer here, especially because several websites confirmed that it definitely wasn't a full moon. I slipped the satchel where Old Lilith slept over my shoulder before cracking my neck. It was time to give Luna my *Lock the door* speech.

"Okay, kid." I kneeled down next to Luna. "Time for me to go. I'll double lock the door behind me." Luna was nested on the couch, finishing off the last slice of pepperoni. "Don't leave the house. Don't let anyone in. I'll be back by midnight." Luna shook her head no. "Uh," I crooned. "Okay, eleven-thirty?" Luna's forehead creased as she stood and walked toward me. "Kid, it will be very quick. Just watch some television and enjoy not being crammed in a box." Luna's face was frozen in a scowl. I tried to ignore the death stare by smiling before heading toward the door. Luna let out a strange squeal and grabbed at my leg.

"Whoa." I waddled to the front door with Luna on my leg. "Kid, come on. Stop." Luna tightened her grip. I tried to pry her off. "Kid, I have to go to work. If I don't, we won't have this flat." I pointed to the dirty walls with a frown. "And all of its majesty." Luna clutched my leg harder with one arm, pointing outside with the other. I didn't speak mime. "Kid, are you trying to say that you want to go outside?" Luna waved her hand before directing her index finger at me. "No, you can't go with me. You could get hurt." Luna gave a little kid growl, but I wasn't about to budge. I was diving into the danger zone, a place of no return. Hopefully there wouldn't be any violence, but there was a chance that outright bloodshed could occur. I wasn't about to bend. Luna could *not* go.

WE DROVE down North Avenue in the rumbling van, Luna reading her children's books in the cab. If I parked the van far enough away, Luna should be safe, and I'd still have an escape vehicle to run to if things got hairy. We pulled up near the club around 10:30PM. I'd had a long stern talk with Luna during the trip, and I was about fifty percent sure that she understood that she could not leave the van no matter what. I found a suitably well-lit, but not *too* well-lit spot two blocks away and parked. I left the keys in the ignition so the air could stay on and locked up. Luna gave me a half smile from behind her book as I tested each door. Once I'd determined she was safely locked in, I walked toward The Violet Hour.

A single light bulb hung on a chain glowed near the boarded-up entrance. I tested the seam of the door and found a notch along the side where I could squeeze my fingers in. I pried at the door and was surprised to find that it opened with ease. Before me was a shed-sized room draped in cerulean curtains. An attractive woman with dark features and bright red lipstick smiled behind an oak podium. Next to her was the blond, pretty Ken Doll from earlier. Both wore black.

"Good evening," the woman greeted with a wide smile. "Welcome."

"Yes, good evening," the Ken Doll jumped in. "I second that. How are you today?" I took a moment to examine the odd couple, looking them over for radios or headpieces. There were none.

"As good as I look," I answered. "You?" I looked for a way into the lounge.

"As good as it gets." The woman gave me a pair of finger guns.

"And I'm even better," the Ken Doll added in the same happy tone. I narrowed my eyes at them.

"Is this a bit?" I asked.

"I'm sorry?" The woman with an enormous smile bit her lip.

"Do you two have some sort of act that you do?" I challenged. The woman and Ken Doll looked at each other with raised brows. "Never mind. I just need a seat at the bar."

"Oh, great," the woman rejoiced. "Let me see if we have an available seat." She separated a split in the curtains that I hadn't noticed and then pushed open a door, poking her head through the threshold. I could hear the fog of dozens of people talking. The Ken Doll stared at me with his perfect blue eyes and horrifically white smile. The dark-haired woman returned to her podium. "Yes, sir, you're all set." She grabbed a small paper menu pressed on a clipboard and waved me over. "I have just the seat for you. Follow me, please." I shadowed the woman. Ken Doll followed me with his stare.

"Have a good day." Ken Doll grinned. "Or better." I gave him a quick frown of disgust before following the hostess through the curtain. As I did, I was hit with a visual and audio torrent.

The heather ceilings were adorned with crystal chandeliers that lit up the teal walls and hardwood floors. Sectioned off by more curtains was a sea of cocktail tables littered with guests in business suits, slit dresses, and trendy outfits. At each table was a flickering candle that created a canopy of marigold stars. The aroma of expensive perfumes and fresh leather flavored the air. Clanking glasses, muffled conversations, and soft laughs sang in my ears. I followed the hostess through the main hall toward a filled bar. There was a single stool at the end where the hostess stopped.

"Here you are, sir." She placed my menu down on the bar top. "Enjoy your night."

I sat down while the hostess returned to her station. Judging by expensive watches, lavish jewelry, and tailored suits, I was shoulder-to-shoulder with Chicago's finest. Affluent men and women meant two things, lots of money and lots of secrets. I wondered if I'd worked for any of these people in the past. The man behind the bar saw me sit and made his way over. He appeared to be in his late twenties with a handlebar mustache, forearm tattoos, and a pair of plug earrings. He wore a classic barman's outfit from the early nineteenth century that included a white button up shirt with its sleeves drawn up, a pinstriped red vest, bicep garters, and a waste apron. I assumed it was part of the uniform.

"Good evening." He placed a cocktail napkin in front of me. "What can I get you?" I studied the tiny menu I'd been given and noticed that it was all unrecognizable. Gourmet drinks like the *Gold Dust Illusion* and *Delinquent Daydream* required you to read the description to understand what went in it. I studied the little list as if it were written in math equations. The barkeep tried to suffocate a grin as he watched me struggle.

"What's the most popular drink?" I asked while studying the ingredients for an *O'Leary Scrambler*, which included whole milk and hot whiskey. "Because whatever it is, that's what I'll take." The bartender, who seemed to be as equally uninterested in me as I was in this whole scene, gave a nod.

"Coming right up." He collected my menu.

I wasted no time scoping out the crowd. There was a blend of middle-aged desperate souls and young beauties bunched together, all dressed like peacocks. The guests were all so striking in one way or another that they weren't distinctive at all. The bartender delivered my drink. It was slime green with seltzer bubbles, a carrot stick for a stirrer, and steam coming from the top.

"What's this?" I asked.

"You asked for the most popular cocktail on the menu," the bartender replied plainly.

"I asked for a drink. This looks like you shoved the Easter bunny in an acid vat." The bartender blinked several times. I handed him my last ten-dollar bill so he could leave and continued to inspect the congregation from behind my cocktail.

I watched for nearly an hour before doubt polluted my thoughts. Either my timing was off, or John Dillinger didn't come here for Bloody Mary's. I decided to visit the washroom to better probe the lounge. I still didn't see anything out of the ordinary as I checked staff doors and tested corners, doing a fake pee-pee dance. That is, until I reached the back of the lounge where the dining hall met the kitchen. There, near the restrooms, was a concealed section tucked in the corner and covered in wall-to-wall curtains. Its only opening was the seam gripped open by a waitress taking orders. Inside was a circular table with several posh women and men chatting over cocktails. A man whose back was to me kept his crooked ears partially hidden with immaculately slicked hair. He wore a tailored, silver pinstripe suit and had one sharp nailed hand that dangled from a chair with a large, gold, signet ring. Maybe

John "Jackrabbit" Dillinger was here after all, socializing with his dinner.

I made my way to the bathroom. I was hoping for a single room with a toilet and lock, but that wasn't the case. The washroom was a long with a chess-patterned floor, housing two stalls and a set of urinals. There was a musky air freshener scent and a pair of ivory sinks with automated faucets. From the entrance, I could see a set of feet wearing raggedy gym shoes in the front stall. I heard Jumbo's voice reminding me that *everybody poops*. I passed by the stall likely being used by kitchen staff and went into the neighboring lavatory. I sat on the lid of the throne and took a moment to consider my options.

First, I needed to confirm that it was in fact Dillinger sitting with the crowd of beautiful people. Freddy told me that a "blood god" would surround himself with the prettiest people and things, but I had to be sure. However, I couldn't just trot over to the table and introduce myself. That would be really bad for my cover, especially since John Dillinger had seen my face before he freaking murdered me. I also couldn't sit at the bar all evening waiting for Dillinger to leave as Luna was sitting ever so patiently in the van. *Being a single parent is hard*. There were only really two options. I could either assemble Old Lilith, burst into the sectioned area, and finish off Dillinger, likely getting killed in the process, or go check on Luna and wait outside with the van until I saw Dillinger leave.

It was about that time when my musings were interrupted by the main door of the bathroom opening again. A set of heavy footsteps constructed from iron stomped inside. I didn't pay much mind until the Decepticon plodded directly in front of my stall.

"*Ocupado*," I declared. No answer.

I studied the shoes, a pair of workman's boots specially made for Sasquatch parked at my flimsy door. From the corner of my eye, I caught my neighbor's raggedy gym shoes shift slowly from a sitting position to being pointed at the partisan between us.

Zoinks.

I walked my hand to Thing One, unclasping its cover band and removing it from the holster. Both sets of feet remained still. Without hesitation, I used the other hand to reach into my coat pocket and remove the silencer before screwing it on. Still nothing from the foot patrol. I pushed off the safety and pointed the gun toward the door.

Crash! The door broke from its hinges and smashed into me. Luckily, my face eagerly blocked it. I was stunned. My eyes watered. I could see the outline of a large man dragging the broken door out from my stall. The throbbing in my nose and lips was uncanny, stopping me from even the simplest of actions, like lifting my arm and pulling the trigger. I was doomed. Strangely, a cold substance snaked up my throat. My jaw forced itself open and a milky fog bloated upward, steaming into my eyes. The strange substance was doing something. Like the flip of a switch, my vision refocused, and the pain went away. I didn't hesitate, locking onto my future murderer. The scarred German truck driver from the storage facility was staring me down—*Yes*, the same douchebag that had kept Luna as a prisoner.

Instinctually, my finger squeezed the trigger of Thing One, delivering three popping noises through the silenced barrel. The German truck driver's chest spurt black blood, but the giant man didn't budge. He stared down with a grimace before lifting his head and shaking it. I didn't let him finish his scare tactics and fired four more times into his face. While one bullet went astray into the tile wall, the others struck true, hitting the truck driver in the cheek and nose. It was the final bullet however, the one that drove into the truck driver's forehead that crossed his eyes and forced him to fall backwards.

I filed what had just happened under *Time to Get the Hell Out of Here* and jumped over the truck driver's thick garbage can-sized leg. Shockingly, he was still waving his hands around, but struggled to put thoughts into action. I made my way to the door and was intercepted. I recognized the dirty shoes of my toilet neighbor as he tackled me, hurling me into the wall. It was orange flannel Charles Bronson. Now prone with Charles Bronson on top of me, I jabbed Thing One into his gut and unloaded my clip. Maggots poured onto my tailored suit, guaranteeing a dry-cleaning bill I couldn't afford. Charles Bronson tried to grab at my throat with his open hands but was unable to reach due to my knee pressed in his chest. I kicked him off and leapt to my feet. Charles Bronson used one hand to scoop up the heaps of maggots into his gaping mouth while flailing his free arm at me.

My hand hovered over the bathroom door, but just as I was about to pull the handle, the door kicked back at me like a speeding car. The wood edge smashed into my hand, numbing it. I looked up and could see a handsome man with dark hair and pasty complexion looking me over with a glower. His silver pant leg didn't quite lift as much as it flashed forward into my stomach. I doubled over, my guts churning with fire before John Dillinger himself pushed me onto my backside with the strength of ten men.

Dillinger stepped into the bathroom so that the door shut behind him. He straightened his tie before bending down so his copper eyes met mine.

"You don't give up easily do you, Abercrombie?" John Dillinger licked his bottom lip.

His eyes blazed red drawing my attention. As I studied them uncontrollably, my mind went slack.

"You can relax now though, Mr. Hitman," he commanded. My spine loosened and my muscles slackened, rendering my body limp. "It will all be over soon."

13

In 1931's *Dracula* movie, Bela Lugosi waves his fingers in dramatic fashion at the camera before a gaffer dims the set lamps and a production assistant beams a flashlight over the actor's eyes. Only then can Dracula deliver his hypnotic gaze to his victim. That's what I'd been expecting from Dillinger should he try to hypnotize me.

Unfortunately, for yours truly that wasn't the case at all. In a split second, the slick monkey's flashing red pupils pulled me under his spell. It felt as if I were falling asleep with my eyes open. The stress in my neck released and my muscles relaxed. My conscience quieted to a squeak, able to think but not act. Dillinger commanded me to return my weapon to its holster. I watched from my hazy state as my body obeyed. Subsequently, Dillinger instructed me to follow him out of the bathroom. As if sleepwalking, my rubbery legs passed through the restroom exit, through the back hall down a staff stairwell, and into a creepy basement.

Basements in Chicago are nearly ubiquitous. I was told

once that it was because frozen soil below a structure in wintertime can crack a structure's surface. They come in two varieties. The first version is the suburban remodeled den that comes with a bar, couch, and half bath. It's where most parents hide to wrap Christmas presents or have sex while kids play video games upstairs. The second type is your classic haunted murder cellar. It's where pools of excess rain ferment along the dirty cement floor and spiders grow to be as big as house cats. I was in the latter.

My lazy conscience tried to catalogue everything in the basement while Dillinger tied me to a lounge chair with an extension cord. There was an octopus-style furnace with arms that stretched over the ceiling, a rusty washer-and-dryer set, and fifty or more kegs with tubes leading upward into the first-floor bar. The kegs hissed and puffed as the compressor pushed the gold ale through clear tubes via compacted air tanks. Perhaps most fascinating, though, was a black turn of the century safe sitting behind Dillinger. It was waist high with reinforced steel, a worn turn dial and the gold words *Trumbull Safe & Vault Co.* inscribed across the surface.

I must have been in the basement I'd seen the beer man delivering kegs to this morning. When I'd scouted earlier in the day, I had noticed a trap door that led to the front sidewalk off of North Damen Avenue. I searched for the exit, and sure enough, spotted a hydraulic lift with a simple control mechanism hovering below a set of metal doors that withdrew to my salvation. If only I could shake myself from Dillinger's grip.

I heard the cry of the worn basement stairs as several more visitors stopped by to say hello. In addition, an anodic buzz followed by thumps told me something with electric wheels struggled to climb down each step. Maybe it was a power dolly hauling a refrigerator that they were going to store me in. Dillinger continued to stare at me as our guests ambled behind him. Charles Bronson came into sight first, a patch of duct tape along his belly. He was followed by the German truck driver, who still had several bullet holes leaking oil. The ogre-man walked over to Dillinger and handed over a tome wrapped halfway in silk cloth. Finally, the dark-haired hostess and Ken Doll came into view. They still had their creepy game show host smiles on as they studied me, but as I inspected them in the light, I noticed pale complexions and Rosie the Riveter Band-Aids along their wrists.

"Oh wow," the hostess blurted. "You have him all tied up. Nicely done, sir."

"Very nicely done, sir," Ken Doll repeated.

"Is this him?" Dillinger asked as he tucked the mystery book under his arm, his swirling red eyes still on me.

"Absolutely, sir." Ken Doll nodded. "He was watching the building all morning."

"No doubt," added the hostess. "That's him."

The German truck driver dug into his breast pocket with his cigar-sized fingers. He plucked out a pair of D batteries, removed them from the packaging, and swallowed them like jagged pills. He pressed his bunched fist to his heart and winced before sparks flared from his bullet holes. I watched as the wounds sealed up and disappeared, leaving only singed holes in his clothing.

The Duracell Rabbit finally has competition.

Meanwhile Dillinger picked up my satchel. The warm burn of panic set into my chest.

"Now, Abercrombie." Dillinger stared at me. "I'm going

to release you from my gaze so I can concentrate on the little conversation we're about to have. Let it be known no one can hear you down here. Screaming or doing anything stupid will likely end in you being my next meal."

Dillinger snapped his fingers; his eyes went from neon, almost firetruck red to pale copper. I could feel my body wake up from its stupor, but I didn't yell or try to wiggle myself free. Dillinger turned his back to me and approached the safe. Several clicks rang before he twisted the handle open. He placed the book inside next to a large stack of cash and a small pistol. He was about to shut the safe door when he suddenly paused.

"Let's see if I should put anything else into here," Dillinger declared as he opened the satchel. "Oh, Mr. Hitman, I'm disappointed." Dillinger picked up Old Lilith's scope. "I thought you knew already. Guns can't kill me." He continued this search, digging through my fake I.D.'s. "You did know that—didn't you." He narrowed his eyes as he read my fake license. "Mr... *Shaw*?"

"I know," I said dryly, "but a stake through the heart just doesn't sing the same beautiful song as a long-distance rifle."

"Well, you have a point there." Dillinger continued to despoil the contents in my bag, tossing out the fake laptop cover that hid several clips for Thing One and Thing Two. "So," he sighed while tossing my mag light on the ground. "I have a problem. You see, you've tried to kill me twice now, which means that I'm bringing a lot of heat."

"Let me pretend I care," I shrugged. The German truck driver raised his massive hand to slap me, but John waved him down.

"No, Adam," Dillinger commanded. "That would be

foolish. Mr. Shaw here needs all of his teeth to tell me who hired him."

"Funny story," I said dryly. "Because I was actually hired by two separate people to kill you." Dillinger cocked his head back.

"Really?" he inquired with fake enthusiasm in his voice. "Please explain."

"Buddy," I sighed. "I don't have the time or the crayons to explain it to you." Adam growled.

"It's okay." Dillinger's eyes stayed on me as he waved off Adam. "He's just yapping his gums. Everyone does it at first," John continued, this time through a toothy grin. It was the first time I'd noticed that John was sporting a pair of sharp, polished canine teeth. "Besides," John put all of my equipment back into the satchel, "I kind of like him."

"Aw. John," I cooed. "I'm starting to like you too. Unfortunately, I still have to kill you." Now I know what I was doing seems foolish, but it was all part of the plan. I was fishing for violence. I wanted someone to whack the hell out of me. I wanted to fall over in my chair, gasping several times as I wiggled around. That's because Dillinger used an extension cord to bind me. The wire had a polished waterproof plastic coating over it that could be loosened. All I needed was some sort of cover in order to start squirming myself free. Unfortunately, Dillinger didn't take the bait, *yet*.

"Mr. Shaw." Dillinger licked his incisor. "My car headlights are brighter than your future if you keep this up."

"Why don't you just flash your eyes again and compel the answers out of me?" I asked while wiggling my arms a bit to loosen my bindings.

"I wish it worked that way, Mr. Shaw." Dillinger

clucked his tongue. "I'd have the one percent's savings in my account by supper. Now, let's stop yappin' and talk business. There's a slight chance I could let you go." I laughed. "No, really. I may need you to send your employer a message, but first, I'm going to need some cooperation. So, let's try again. Who hired you?"

I thought about it. It totally felt like Idaho-Face had set me up. Why was I protecting her? Besides, this could be a golden opportunity to learn a little more about her. As for ratting Death out, well, to call myself an idiot for doing something like that would be an insult to stupid people everywhere. Let's hope one name would be enough.

"You know what." I gave Dillinger a once-over. "I like you, so I'm going to cooperate." Dillinger's expression hardened. Adam shook his head and sighed. I paused, waiting for everyone's initial doubt to clear. "If you're telling me I could live by squawking on the people that sent me after a damn vampire then you've captured my interest. Obviously, those people didn't want me to survive. Cross my heart and hope to not die."

"Okay, Mr. Shaw," Dillinger said plainly. "I'm all ears."

"I mostly work with repeat clients," I confessed. "It's safer that way. They can be trusted since you have dirt on them. However, the bills piling up on my coffee table aren't going to pay themselves. So, foolish me, I took a risk and met with a new client. Now, if you're going to ask her name, let me stop you right there because I don't know it. I never ask and they never tell."

"Naturally." Dillinger forced a smile.

"She did have something about her, though, that was very distinct," I added.

"Oh?" Dillinger's brow raised.

"Yeah." I slowly wiggled my arms. "The entire time that this woman was detailing your whereabouts, I just couldn't stop staring. It's not because she was a beauty, though I do love Latinas." I winked at the hostess. Her smile twisted into a frown. Adam, the stitched face giant, didn't budge. "No, the reason I was staring at her this entire time was because she had a birthmark on her face shaped like Idaho."

John tried to keep a poker face, but his lip quivered ever so slightly. He looked back to Adam, who was far less subtle. The muscles in his jaw tightened as he gnashed his teeth. His fists tightened, cracking bone. I could tell that I was starting to distract them.

"I'm guessing you know her?" I looked down from the bridge of my nose. "Maybe an old girlfriend of Adam's? Nah, maybe not." Adam stomped forward, ready to kill. "Nothing personal, Big Guy. I'm just saying that the last time I saw something like you, I flushed it down the toilet."

"That's it," he seethed in his ridiculously thick accent. "I'm going to break his neck." His hands opened up like a crab to squeeze my head off, but Dillinger's quick reflexes stopped him. In a flash, Dillinger was grasping Adam's wide wrists with both hands and pulling him backwards.

"Adam, stop," Dillinger ordered with the first real sound of fire in his voice. "This is my final warning. You can go upstairs if you're getting upset."

"He's mocking us." Adam punched his fist into his other palm.

"I know." Dillinger rubbed his temples. "It's intentional, and you're playing right into it." Dillinger was cleverer than I'd thought. I wasn't dealing with some ordinary ex-gangster-gone-undead. He had nearly a century of experience under his wing. I crossed my fingers that he didn't know exactly what I was up to, but my gut feeling told me he had an idea.

"*Was würdest du mich tun lassen?*" Adam spouted in a low throaty octave.

That's it. Should I survive this, I'm taking German.

Dillinger responded, matching the tongue. Adam nodded and then waved the group to follow him. Charles Bronson, the Hostess, and Ken Doll trailed after Adam up the stairs. I couldn't decide whether my escape plan had just improved or worsened. Once the basement door was shut and the muffled customers on the first floor could no longer be heard, Dillinger, who was as still as a coiled cobra, reacted. He grabbed another cocktail chair from a stored stack along the wall and placed it across from me. He sat down and smirked.

"Sorry about that." Dillinger shifted his weight on the chair. "Adam has seen a lot, and it has shortened his temper."

"It doesn't help that he's undead garbage." I bucked. "Like you."

"I'd argue that he's not undead at all," Dillinger said nonchalantly. "I'd contend that he's more human than you or I, Mr. Shaw." Dillinger crossed his legs and leaned back in his chair.

He was talking to me as if we were having coffee, which frightened me. When a dangerous individual with considerable secrets starts opening up to you like you're Ann Curry, chances are you're about to die. "You see, Adam was created by human hands long ago, the eighteenth century to be precise. His maker was a real piece of work, so Adam liberated himself. Since then, the poor guy has wandered

Bavaria, Geneva, and the Arctic exploring what it is that truly makes man who he is. When he decided it wasn't worth the trouble, he took that all popular boat ride to the Americas." I wasn't the sharpest spear on the rack, but I knew historical horror novels when I heard them. It was hard to believe that the scarred pro-wrestler I'd been poking fun at was who Dillinger said he was.

"Are you telling me," I laughed. "That's Frankenstein's Monster?" Dillinger's postmark half-smirk stretched wider, but he didn't answer.

"You're a hitman, Mr. Shaw," Dillinger pressed on, tapping his long fingernails together. "In my time, that was a well-respected profession. It was necessary for business. I still think it is. So, I don't blame you for taking work. Unfortunately for you, your employer doesn't rattle her tail before she bites. The dame used a middleman to tip me off about your attempts to take my life days before you tried. Shame on me, I should've asked Zombie Pete more questions. The guy isn't exactly trustworthy. Or at least, he wasn't."

"What rotten luck," I sighed. "Do me a favor though, John, and tell me who the hell this woman is?"

"The lady with Idaho branded on her face represents someone heinous. You see, there's a political uniform in the supernatural world. We have new rules and organizations that keep us away from the suspicions of man and his pitchfork and torch routine. Your first employer represents people trying to hostilely break down those walls."

"Good for them," I complimented. "Monsters like you need to be stopped."

"No, you've got it all wrong. Her kind isn't trying to kill monsters. They're using paranormal entities to..."

Dillinger paused, looking behind me as if there was someone else there. I could hear a creak over my shoulders as if someone was shuffling in a seat. For the first time, I realized that when the crowd of freaks had come down to watch my interrogation, they hadn't all shown themselves. "Well, they're using paranormal entities to reestablish the old way. Ways that would end up with mortals being slaves." I leaned forward, trying to stretch the chords around my chest and arms. I could feel them loosen slightly.

"Then I think I know who *they* are," I whispered while taking a deep breath to put stress on my bindings.

"Do you now?" Dillinger tapped his chin.

"Yes." I cleared my throat. "They're working on a machine of mass destruction that can destroy entire civilizations." Dillinger's eyebrows rose. "If we let them construct it, we're all doomed. There's hope, though. A young boy named Luke Skywalker lives on a planet called Tatooine." Dillinger closed his eyes and pressed his lips together. He remained that way for a moment. I must have finally chipped away at his patience. I continued to shift in my seat, masquerading my intentions of loosening the extension cord as an act of discomfort.

"Very funny, Mr. Shaw." Dillinger opened up his eyes again. "It's good to have a sense of humor, especially in your situation. Now, let's get serious again. You haven't told me anything about your second employer."

"If you thought my first employer was bad," I said while testing the bindings. They felt loose enough to make some sort of move. "Then the second is a real doozie." Dillinger leaned back in his chair again. "You see, after you gunned me down and I lay drowning in my own blood, someone interfered. I wouldn't exactly say they saved my life as much as they didn't let me die." I wriggled one arm up ever so gently. All it would take was an upward thrust to free it. "That's because my second employer was—" I paused dramatically. Dillinger tilted his head, eager. I braced my arms, ready to heave off the extension cords, and then coiled my legs to my chest.

"Karate Kid," I shouted while bucking my legs into Dillinger's chest. Dillinger wasn't ready. He fell back into his chair as I propelled my arms upward. Unfortunately, I hadn't loosened the cords as much as I'd thought, and I had to struggle for a few more essential seconds to release myself from their grip. By the time I'd hurled the extension cord to the ground, Dillinger was back up on his feet, dusting himself off. I grabbed my satchel and took several large footsteps toward the cluttered wall of kegs. Dillinger must not have been too concerned because I could hear his shoes slowly tap my way.

Bad move on his part.

I plucked the beer tubes from the compressors, causing a fountain of gold and amber to spray violently from the kegs. In addition, the air tanks feeding the kegs gas sprayed a sharp mist that created a thick gilt fog. Both of us were blinded by the storm, but I'd been busy memorizing my escape route. I crawled toward the lift, hopping on top of its hydraulic platform. I pounded on the up button and could feel the conveyer ascend. I made out a foggy set of red eyes struggle in the gold mist as several kegs fell from their stacks, rolling along the floor.

As I took in the beautiful sight, I made two very vital observations. First, the escape hatch above me had a padlock on it. If I didn't loosen it, I'd be crushed. Second, near the stairwell was the cloudy outline of a hunched figure sitting in an electronic scooter. I couldn't be sure, but I swear I'd seen that silhouette before. Maslow's Hierarchy of Needs reminded me that along with food and air, not being crushed like a bug was essential. So I withdrew Thing Two, unloaded on the lock several times, and then donkey kicked the trap door open, wiggling out the opening feet first.

The smells of freshly cooked steak, sweet grass, and truck exhaust told me that I was back on North Damen. Due to the late hour, there were very few people around to see me sprout like a booze god with my gas and beer fountain. I hurried my way to the van, looking behind my shoulder during the entire half block sprint. No one pursued me.

I reached the van and banged on the glass. I could see Luna peek her head out from the cab. I must have been soaked and bloodied upped because her eyes grew ten times wider. Her hand hovered over the lock before finally deciding to pull the latch up. I jumped in the seat and kicked the car into drive with one motion, my door still open. Luna ambled her way into the passenger seat. We leapt out from our parking spot like a rodeo bull released from its pen. I closed the door with one hand while steering with the other, my eyes scanning for Dillinger, Adam, or anyone else. I was screwing up by the numbers and needed to take shelter so I could put the pieces back together.

14

I have what's called a *genetics problem*. While some people nearly murdered by Count Chocula and his gang of miscreants might go hide in a hole, I was already trying to figure out a new way to take out Dillinger. I'm sure that if I dusted off a few old memories, my ability to rebound in stressful situations was related to a childhood stemmed denial mechanism. Nothing like the shame of being poor and abused to keep you going.

Isn't reflection fun?

I needed to dissect the moving truck's worth of information I'd just taken in. Fact: Dillinger's hunting grounds included The Violet Hour. Fact: he had minions including Frankenstein's monster, Charles Bronson, and his juice box hostesses to help him with his wicked deeds. Fact: Dillinger was part of a larger establishment of supernatural creatures that were trying to keep order within their horrific ranks. Fact: Dillinger was a bit of a badass, and I should be happy that I escaped with my life.

As for unanswered questions...those were piling up at

an alarming rate. For starters, it was obvious that Death wanted Dillinger dead because the vampire was cheating fate, but what about Idaho-Face? She had seemed pretty alive when we connected, plus it was morning, so she wasn't some neck biter. If she was part of some undead resistance, what would killing John Dillinger do for her? Why would she tip Dillinger off about me if she hated him? The questions kept pouring in. Why did they want Luna? Who else was part of this Monster Organization? Why did I puke up body smog? Who was in the scooter at The Violet Hour? What hair color did they put on bald people's driver's licenses?

As we drove the last part of our trek home, I made one last check for cars shadowing me. I'd taken the effort to lose any tail earlier in the trip. I weaved between vehicles on busy streets, took sudden turns, and cruised through a pay-to-park building. Now that we were in the rougher part of town where I lived, the cars were sparser and the streets lonelier. There wasn't anyone on the road besides my van. I reminded myself that although today was a disaster, I still had one distinct advantage. I knew where John Dillinger stalked his prey, while Dillinger was clueless as to where I called home.

Luna and I emptied the van. I collected my satchel while Luna grabbed her toys. We locked up then hurried to our building. Living in the tougher part of town has its advantages in my line of work. There was bad lighting and no one along the sidewalks. Hurried walking wasn't suspicious. It was common. The van was parked a half block away. Luna and I speed-walked to our apartment complex's front door. I shuffled with the keys while Luna drew swirls along the glass with her sweaty finger. I took a moment to watch as she entertained herself. She must have felt me staring because she shot a glance back up.

"You good, kid?" I asked with the best smile I could conjure. "Because I can take you somewhere else." Luna twisted her lips and raised an eyebrow. "I'm just saying," I twisted the key in the knob. "There're shelters out there where they can find you a family. I'm sure someone out there could give you a good home." Luna shook her head, growled, and then shoved the door open as the key clicked. "Okay, okay." Luna stomped inside. "Jeez, anger issues."

I went to the wall where all the mailboxes stood and checked my slot. There were four pieces of mail, all with *Final Notice* warnings along the cover. *Did they have to print them like that?* I could feel a sickness bubble in my stomach. Working for your soul didn't pay well. If I didn't do something soon, I'd be living in my van. That would work wonders for my reputation. "The Hobo Hitman, he's begging to kill for you." I was in the middle of taking deep breaths when a pounding came from the glass entrance. I jumped out of my skin, digging in my jacket for Thing One.

"Buck," hollered the muffled voice of Bethany as she fogged the glass. I exhaled, released my fingers from the pistol grip and then shuffled to the front door. I opened it to find Bethany with a department store shopping bag in her hands. She crinkled her nose and gave a crooked grin.

"Sorry." She shrugged her shoulders. "I tried to call, but I realized I didn't have your number. Also, did you get attacked by Cujo or something?"

"Uh, hey Bethany, I didn't know you had my address."

"I got it from your gamer registration card. Darren pulled your delivery store file."

"How DID you get him to do that?"

"I flirted with him?"

"Genius. Maybe that's what I'm doing wrong."

"Why? How do you get things from him?"

"Death threats, mostly."

"Yeah, you might want to change your approach."

"Come in." I waved as I moved from blocking the door. Bethany stepped in and her eyes latched onto Luna, who was now spinning in circles while starting at the ceiling to keep herself entertained.

"Hi, Luna." Bethany waved. Luna turned to her and approached. Bethany crouched to Luna's level, examining her clothes. "I'm glad to see the clothes fit. Look—" She dug in her department store bag. "I brought you something." Bethany plucked out a stuffed animal. I froze in place as she pulled out a grey wolf with a blue t-shirt. If life was trying its luck as a standup comedian, I was the punch line to most of its jokes. "This is Harry," Bethany introduced while handing Luna the toy. "I had one when I was a little girl. When I heard they recreated his show, I had to get you one." Luna hugged the wolf, clueless to the irony, and then stared into the remaining contents in Bethany's bags.

"Oh." Bethany handed Luna the bags. "These are just some more clothes and other girl's things I thought Buck might not have thought of."

"Please tell me there're no Disney pink pajamas in there?"

"No, but there is some underwear, brushes, and other

necessities. I'm pretty sure you didn't get her any," Bethany jabbed while poking a finger in my arm.

"Hey, I feed her. Isn't that enough?"

"Seriously, though, how's she doing?"

"About as well as a kid in her situation can be." I rubbed the back of my neck. Luna looked bored with adult talk and took her stuffed animal to the stairwell, where she made Harry the Wolf dance along the front step. Bethany watched, the trace of a smile along her lips.

"Still not talking?"

"No."

"Well, give it time." We watched Luna as she bent the wolf's head to imitate a howl. I pursed my lips.

"So." I cleared my throat. "Thanks for this. I honestly don't know what to say."

"Don't say anything. Honestly, I wish I could do more."

"Oh, Bethany, you're one of the good ones." Bethany's stare slipped onto the big red letters along the envelopes.

"Buck." She kept her eyes on the mail. "Are *you* doing okay?"

This was embarrassing. I tucked the bills deeper into my grip. Social navigation wasn't really my thing, but I tried to sway the conversation elsewhere.

"Oh, these," I stuttered. "They're old. They're not even mine, actually. I think it's the neighbors. Mailman must have messed up. Hey," I hurried. "Did our characters level up last session?" Bethany tilted her head to the side, paused, and then answered the question.

"Yes, but it didn't go without issue. Nicolai's barbarian misinterpreted a half-orc chief's singing as a war cry and attacked the entire Blood Reaver tribe." I belted into a laugh. Bethany joined in, choking on her words. "It gets better," she snorted. "In order to make amends, the paladin forced Nicolai's barbarian to marry the half-orc's daughter."

"I don't know who loses on the deal." I held onto my gut, roaring a laughter that let out all of the stress I'd been holding back the last few days. It felt good.

Bethany updated me on the rest of the game, gossip at *Gamer's Pair-of-Dice,* and the next scheduled game day. I told her about meeting Terminator on the Green Line, and she countered with a unicycle rider on the Eisenhower Expressway. We joked about the White Sox and topped it off with Bethany's thoughts on the latest Mandalorian episode. We'd lost track of time when Bethany's cell phone went off. The caller face read *Tim.*

"Whoa," she called out while staring at her phone's face. "Look at the time. I should go."

"Yeah, besides, Luna's probably starving."

Bethany put the phone to her ear. "Hi, Tim. Give me one second, I'm in an echoey hall." Bethany looked up at me. "Give me your phone," she demanded. I dug in my side pocket and pulled out the device, using my thumb to unlock the interface before giving my phone over.

Bethany balanced her own cell phone on her shoulder and ear while programming her number into my contacts list. "Call me if you need anything." She leaned in and returned the phone before giving me a light hug. She smelled like lilacs and vanilla.

"Okay," she whispered. "See you at game day." I watched her make her way out and waited until she was safely in her car before I turned to gather Luna. Luna shook her head at me, her eyes drooped, and her mouth was in a half frown.

"Hey, when you're an adult you have to talk. It's what we do. You should try it." Luna rolled her eyes and then we made our way up the steps.

I slid my key into the front door. Luna and I entered the flat, our hands weighed down by Bethany's gifts. The streetlights colored the dark apartment in a soft blue light. I shut the door, locked it, and then flipped on the lamp. To my surprise, sitting statue still on my couch were three figures. On instinct, I stepped in front of Luna, dropped the bags and final notice envelopes then dug inside my coat. My thumb flicked the holster's guard strap, making a snap sound.

"No need for violence, Mr. Palasinski," the woman with the Idaho birthmark on her face declared. Her voice sounded as crisp and orderly as when we first met. She was dressed in a burgundy business suit that was a size too large. Her eyes remained fixated on the cell phone she was thumbing. She patted the open cushion next to her without looking up. "Please, come sit." I took in her friends. To Idaho-Face's immediate left was a brawny man in a tuxedo. He had a dirty pair of two-toned shoes and white cotton gloves. His face was completely covered with his long, wet black hair. He was stock still, void of breath. But it was the figure slacked in my secondhand recliner across the coffee table that surprised me the most.

Sitting with their skinny fishnet stockinged legs was the green haired stranger I'd seen on the Green Line. The androgynous creature lit a cigarette and brought it to their brightly painted red lips. Their yellow cat eyes were painted with runny mascara spoiled by dry tears. They wore a candy-striped coat that was accented by a flickering light bulb chained around the neck. The stranger's sex-pink pencil skirt matched their stiletto high heels. What frightened me the most though was the smile. It was wide and curled at the ends as if they knew a sick joke that no one else would appreciate.

"You're right." I gripped Luna's hand. "There's no need for violence. Luna and I are leaving."

I unlocked the apartment door once more and opened it, keeping my eyes peeled on the strangers as I guided Luna out. I could feel her tug me into the hall before squeezing my hand and screaming. I turned to see what the matter was, only to find that my apartment hallway was filled with children. Only, they weren't kids at all.

They were the height of early grammar school students, wearing old fashioned frilled dresses and little sailor suits. Their faces though were anything but youthful. They were the cadaverous cockled glowers of elderly men and women. They had puckered lips, wrinkled skin and milky white eyes. A few mouths gaped open, showing serrated buttered teeth spaced like a Jack O'Lantern. They were at least twenty strong, holding hands and spinning like devils let out for a night. I tugged Luna back into the apartment and shut the door.

"What the shit are those," I called out to my surprise party. The man with the tuxedo remained still and green hair's already-wide grin grew bigger. Idaho-Face kept her eyes on her cell phone but pressed her lips together as if ready to speak.

"The children won't hurt you." She combed her black hair behind her ear. I could hear a zoom from her phone as if she just sent an e-mail. "They're just here to ensure that you talk with us."

"Oh, that's nice," I said dryly, trying to mask any anxiety. "Luna needs a play date."

"Mr. Palasinski," Idaho-Face said with a lifeless tone. "I'm here because you never completed your contract."

"Luna," I warbled in a soft voice. "Cover your ears, kiddo." Luna took her fingers and cupped the sides of her head. "Fuck you, lady. You set me up."

"Oh," Idaho-Face said frankly. "How so?"

"Hmm," I hummed. "Let's see. You sent me to kill an immortal vampire. You forgot to tell me that he was *the* John Dillinger. He suspiciously somehow knew the stakeout location you suggested. Oh, then when he visited me in this location, the guy shot me down in a hail of gunfire. *I should be dead.*"

"You're upset, Mr. Palasinski," Idaho-Face spoke flatly. "I understand. Perhaps I should have chosen my words more assiduously. The point I'm trying to make is that our organization couldn't help but notice that you're still pursuing Mr. Dillinger."

"Yeah," I grunted. "That's for personal reasons."

"It will still benefit our organization, Mr. Palasinski," Idaho-Face continued to thumb her phone while a text bell rang from it. "So our contract seems to remain valid."

"Oh spare me, lady," I interrupted. "I know all about your stupid undead rebellion and I don't care." Tuxedo Man's head jerked in a sudden chiseled motion, locked in on Idaho-Face. She clicked the side of her cell phone and placed it into her suit coat. For the first time, she raised her chin and made eye contact. I could see that besides her strange birthmark, Idaho Face had two different colored eyes.

"Very good, Mr. Palasinski," Idaho-Face complimented

with her same unaffectionate voice. "I assume that Mr. Dillinger attempted to recruit you for his Undead Union then?"

"Not exactly," I responded. I didn't want to tell her that Dillinger only informed me of the ridiculous war because he was likely about to kill me. It couldn't hurt if Idaho-Face thought that I possibly had a dangerous ally. Meanwhile, I was trying to figure out how the hell I was going to get out of this one. Let's consider that while my current house guests didn't have any supernatural vaporizing powers, I was still in a bind. First, Luna and I would either need to go for the high-rise window nearby or fight through the army of Benjamin Button monsters in the hallway. Luna's scream might have been ignored, but shattered glass or gunshots would likely draw police. Still, knowing my off-putting track record, violence might be better than trying to talk my way out of this one.

"Whatever do you mean, Mr. Palasinski?" Idaho Face questioned in a monotone voice.

"*Lady.*" I slapped my thigh. "Please stop calling me that. It's Buck."

"Okay, *Buck.*" She squared her posture to my own.

"And what should I call you?" I asked.

"Whatever you'd like, Buck." Idaho Face pressed her hands to her lap.

"Ms. Boise, it is." I smiled. The green haired stranger snorted. Tuxedo man stretched his gloved hand and placed it on Idaho-Face's thigh. Idaho-Face pushed it away quickly, causing the hand to retreat.

"Sure, Buck." She straightened her cuffs. "Now, please, elaborate."

"Dillinger," I sighed. "Wanted to know who was trying to kill him."

"And?" asked Idaho-Face. I watched as Green Hair savored their cigarette and decided I wanted one of my own. I took the time to remove a smashed cigarette from a crumbled pack in my back pocket, all the while keeping myself in front of Luna. I patted myself down for a lighter, keeping the cigarette hugged on the corner of my lips as I answered.

"*And*," I said through the side of my mouth. "I told him some crazy bitch with Idaho tattooed to her face."

"Hmm," Idaho Face hummed. "I see, Buck."

"Ms. Boise," I said as I found my Zippo in a side pocket and flicked its spark wheel. "What the hell did you expect? Like I said." I lit the end of my crooked cigarette. "You screwed me."

"Blame will get us nowhere, Buck." Idaho-Face folded her hands together. I watched as her cheeks twitched as she struggled to press her lips into a smile. It was as creepy as Mickey Rourke's plastic surgery. "I would like to be honest with you. We are navigating a war between usurping dictators and those with enough temerity to stand against their tyranny. We are few, but formidable. Since we don't have the numbers to complete all of our tasks alone, we outsourced. Now, I'm unsure who else hired you to destroy Mr. Dillinger, but clearly your new employer and I have similar mindsets. Perhaps we can come to some sort of arrangement?"

"What about tipping Dillinger off to my shooter's perch?" I argued.

"Deception, Buck," Idaho-Face bit back. Her voice was so vanilla that I couldn't tell if she were lying or just bad at stirring plausibility. I took another deep puff of my cigarette. This was a delicate negotiation, which made me a bull in a China shop. I needed to remain calm. I ignored the shuffling feet outside my apartment door and gripped tighter on Luna. She clutched my leg.

"I don't think my employer would be open to it." I shrugged. "Seeing that he likely wants you dead as well. He's not a big fan of undead."

"Perhaps, that's not as distressing as you believe Buck," Idaho Face objected. "He should at least hear our offer."

"Sure," was all I could muster. "Fire away."

"In return for your employer's assistance," Idaho-Face returned her hands on her thighs. "We would offer them a position at the head of our table once we reclaim the Necrotic world of Chicago. They could administrate the direction of the necrotic population as they see fit. If they truly despise the undead, they could even have you dispose of them."

I recognized the word necrotic from role-playing games. It was a form of the word necromancy or the forced manipulation of dead. Creating armies of skeletons, forcing lost souls to do your will and siphoning the life out of victims were all forms of mainstream necromancy. It was exactly what Death was ticked off about. I tried to hide my disapproval by looking over Luna again. She was breathing heavily, her face strained into a grimace. I patted her on the back before tucking her deeper behind my leg.

"What's in it for the messenger?" I asked, pretending to care.

"I've noticed quite a few bills in your mailbox, Buck," Idaho-Face replied. "Perhaps we can assist by ensuring that you never have to worry about a bill again." She examined my walls and ceiling. "Perhaps even assist in an upgrade to your home?"

"Just say it," I bit back. "You mean my shit-hole."

"Your words, Buck." Her expression dulled. "Regardless, your reputation as a sharpshooter is celebrated within the underworld community. We could use a permanent commodity like you and that rifle within our organization."

"I'll pass along the message," I cut in. "Now, can I please have my damn shit hole back?"

"Certainly, Buck." Idaho-Face nodded and stood. Green Hair leaned back in the recliner, combing a hand through their widow's peak.

"I need a minute with our host," Green Hair called out. Green Hair's voice was heavy and masculine with a grind like old clock parts. My ear caught a hint of an Irish brogue. It didn't fit the stranger's sharp and smooth features. Shockingly, Idaho-Face gave Green Hair a black look before moving out of the living room. Tuxedo Tim, who'd been motionless to this point, followed as she approached the front door. I pressed Luna to move away. Idaho-Face nodded, opened the door and waved Tuxedo Man out. I pressed on my toes and leaned outward to peek into the hall. There was a line of hag-children waiting like trick or treaters. They reached their talonlike hands out. Tuxedo Man gripped one of the children's clawed fingers and then reached out to Ms. Boise. She sighed and closed the door behind them. I took Luna by the shoulder and lightly guided her toward my room. Luna gripped Harry the Wolf and hurried to safety. If Green Hair, who seemed to be in charge, wanted to talk, then it would just be the two of us.

My Millennium Falcon ashtray was docked on the coffee table, its pool filled with crushed cigarette butts. I added one more to the collection before digging in my pocket for a replacement. I sat in the center of my couch and drifted into a relaxed position while plucking a new cigarette from the pack, but there were none left. I tried to give a careless shrug, but I knew that I opened up negotiations on a ridiculous note.

Green Hair pulled out a pack from inside their striped coat, removed two filtered cigarettes, and extended their hand. I looked at Green Hair's fingers, which were long and spidery. Green Hair's black slits stared at me as a lunatic smile spread beneath. Green Hair dug in their coat. Before I could react, they removed a matchbook with a gold octopus on a plum cover, folded their fingers over one match and flicked it all in one motion so that the tip was aflame. *Okay, cool.* Green Hair extended the burning match to the tip of my cigarette and then their own. I took my cigarette, examined it, and then placed it in my mouth before puffing the smoke.

"Not bad, aye?" asked Green Hair with a gravelly voice. I reveled in the sweet taste of the tobacco.

"Not bad." I flicked ash into the Millennium Falcon.

"Should I start with an introduction then?"

"That would only be proper."

Green Hair's lips stretched wide. "We are not proper men, Danny Boy."

"No, we are not."

"Where should I begin? My real name is Dothur, though I've earned a dozen nicknames within my few centuries. Most fellas call me The Mad Knight." He paused and smiled. "Trust me, I didn't make that up. I've always considered myself as quite calm, plus I don't save princesses. The manky lad in the tuxedo is my foolish brother Dub. We're the two remaining sons of the ancient Irish witch, Carman."

"Wow, you're oddly forthcoming."

"I don't like to waste time on polite ceremonies. Manners are—" he paused, rolling his head, "—exhausting."

"I get it. Nothing worse than holding in a fart."

"You said it. Nevertheless, centuries ago, our mother slept with a devil, fair folk, and Death himself to have us. It was a vie for power that helped Mother get hanged and had us running for our lives. For the last few hundred years, the three of us separately went our own way stealing, murdering, and plotting for power. However, when our oldest brother, Collin-Dian, was murdered recently, Dub and I decided to have a little family reunion. You see, Collin ruled the supernatural community in Chicago and when he was slain, a silly new hierarchy took over. Your *Ms. Boise* was one of Collin's most loyal subjects and when he died, she solicited Dub through her powers of seduction. She and Dub gathered those loyal to my brother's memory and organized, and I've just been along for the ride."

"Wow. That's a hell of an info dump if I ever heard one. So let me guess, you're helping this rebellion to retake the throne for yourself?"

The Mad Knight's lips parted into a beam, showing a strange set of tiny teeth that I'd only just noticed. They were perfectly set, but as small as a child's and twice as many.

"No, lad. I could give two shites about the rebellion."

"Uh," I buzzed. "You might want to tell that to your brother's girlfriend because I'm pretty damn sure she's ready to give her life for the uprising." The Mad Knight chuckled. It was guttural and genuine, which made it *genuinely* creepy.

"I know." He puffed. "They all would."

"Uh." I smashed my cigarette into the ashtray. "Why are you telling me this?" The Mad Knight shrugged.

"Not sure. Maybe I like you. Maybe I'm bored. Perhaps I'm showing what's up my sleeve in hopes that you present me with what's behind your back." The dead light bulb around his neck flickered momentarily.

"Behind my back?"

"Yes, like the fact that you're working for Death," he plopped on my metaphorical lap with a smile.

"Wait, how do you know that?"

"The quick version? I was spying. I always spy. It's my thing," he said while wrinkling his nose and snickering. "You see, there's three big powers in this world that keep me from doing all the fun things my heart desires. The Big Honcho is one, Satan another, and finally Death himself. Anytime I try to do anything meaningful, I run into one of their brick walls." The Mad Knight crossed his legs. I tried to look away.

Sharon Stone he was not.

"Let me tell you," he continued. "It can be really annoying."

"I'm playing a tiny violin for you." I rolled my eyes. "What is exactly *meaningful* to you?"

"If I'm being honest, sheer chaos."

"Like the Butterfly Effect?"

"No."

"Like Deus ex Machina?"

"No."

"Hey, Alex, do I have to answer in the form of a question or are you going to tell me?"

The Mad Knight laughed. "Let me ask you a question. When has society's system ever profited you? I mean truly."

"Oh, Jesus," I sighed. "I'm going to need another cigarette for this." The Mad Knight protruded another cigarette from his pack and handed it over. He lit it with another match while going on.

"Think about it, Danny Boy," The Mad Knight said in a tone as soft as shattered glass. "Knowing your profession, as I do, I'm assuming you had a tough upbringing?" I smacked my lips together but remained quiet. "You see, the dotted lines that most people try to follow in order to get their slice of happy-pie is broken. Whoever made the map drew those lines crooked on purpose. They go nowhere. *We* go nowhere. Once it is realized, we're in too deep, prisoners of the substances and lifestyles we are used to. It's an infinite loop." I thought back to my alcoholic father, overworked mother, and inmate brother. The Mad Knight either did his homework or was speaking truths.

Possibly both.

"And?"

"It was never our fault. The system worked us. It has for a few millenniums now. Worst yet, it's just a squat reflection of a bigger order. Go straight to the top. God made a structure so he could exist. Satan needs that structure so he can thwart it. Death needs structure so he can end it. No one wants to admit that the bricks are lain crooked because that means it'll have to be bulldozed, disregarding that the house will eventually fall."

"And you are going to be the one to knock it down?"

"Shite if I know. What I just presented to you, Danny Boy, are just cliff notes. In its truest, most raw form, this information has driven wise men mad. I've thought about it until I thought a hole in the ground. I spent decades wondering if there's ways to stop the cycle, and if doing so is worse than allowing the shit pile to stack higher."

"Won't it just collapse upon itself?"

"Of course, only to start again. The circle always continues. Unless—"

"Unless you stop it?" I cut The Mad Knight off.

"*Unless*, true chaos, not this organized anarchy masquerading as discord, rears into the cycle."

"You're nuts."

"That's very true. It's an occupational hazard that comes with thinking."

"Okay, full circle. Why are you telling me this?"

"The randomness of what I do is a stranger to even me. However, now that I have told you this, let's work with it. Why don't you give Death your two-week notice and join me? Come on, we both know the guy is a self-centered egotist. He'll likely turn on you eventually."

"Well, since he controls my existence, that's probably not a good idea."

"Such a safe answer. Come on, Buck. Shock me, say something less predictable," he sighed. I stayed mute. "Fine, we'll kill him together."

"I don't know what your problem is, but I'll bet it's hard to pronounce."

"Or am I starting to make sense? After all, you *do* have his scythe, don't you?"

"So?" I tried to play it cool.

"That'll do it."

"And then what?"

"I don't know," The Mad Knight laughed. "I don't think that far ahead. It's too much like..."

"Order?" I crushed my cigarette onto the hull of the Millennium Falcon. The Mad Knight beamed.

"Ah, you get it, Danny Boy." The Mad Knight dabbed the butt of his own cigarette into the ashtray. "Maybe we'll use the scythe to go after the Devil or God. Maybe we'll cut a hole into the fibers of the Universe. The world is our oyster."

"I don't know, Mr. Crazy. I just have so much on my plate already. There's this new internship plus Luna. I'm just not in a position to deal with world-ending uncertainties right now."

"We'll work on that."

"Maybe."

"Oh, okay. Think about it though, would you?"

"Sure."

The Mad Knight slapped his hands on his thighs. "Well, I should be going. Good luck with my brother's girl-friend. She's been cooking up things for you for some time."

"Yeah, I'll think about the offer. For now, though, it's late. Plus, I never invited any of you over in the first place."

The Mad Knight smiled. "No, you didn't."

He stood up and strode with long crooked steps to the front door, flaunting his backside as he sashayed. He opened the front door, turned to me, and gave one last horrifically wide smile. I short waved him goodbye and then watched him exit, shutting the door behind him. I immediately ran to the entrance, peeking through the peephole. The Mad Knight paraded to the spiraling stair-well banisters, and without looking down, he leaned in over the handrail and fell over. I was taken aback by his apparent suicide, but the thump at the bottom never came. Instead, there was only a strobe of light followed by silence. My hands quickly locked the door latch as my heart thumped out of its chest.

This was *really* bad.

Within the span of ten minutes or so, my nightmare had become a damn Netflix full fifteen-episode series. Saying I was cornered was an understatement.

Ms. Boise wanted me to betray Death. She'd been all calm and professional about her proposal, but I knew a snake when I saw one. She'd bitten me once, and I assumed she was slithering back to finish off the job. The only question was, what the hell did she want with me?

Now there was this Irish lunatic, The Mad Knight, who wanted me to betray *everyone*. I didn't think he was testing my loyalties to either party. It seemed like something different entirely. From what he was blabbing about, it seemed like he had some vast knowledge that obligated him to fix the entire world through a storm of disarray. Sure, it may have felt as if he was offering me a partnership in his bizarre heroics, but it came with a lot of catches. For starters, it sounded like I'd make enemies with Death, the Devil and, oh yeah, *God*. It was a classic bait-and-switch deal.

Sure, if I joined him, I'd finally have an ally when it came to killing Dillinger, and there was a chance I could

give Death the slip, wiggling out of my ominous circumstance, but at what price?

I had no answers. While I hoped The Mad Knight was
just some immortal psychopath down on his luck, his
words haunted me. It was the mention of Death turning on
me that lingered, making me fear that I was doomed
without The Mad Knight's help. Perhaps making a deal
with him was my only hope. Perhaps it was a big trap.
Whatever the case, for that night, and every night thereafter, I'd make sure to fasten each lock, secure each
window, and sleep with Old Lilith nearby. Ms. Boise, Dub,
and The Mad Knight were coming back for me, and I
didn't know how it would end.

15

I'd been sitting in bed drinking thoughts for breakfast. I was drowning in speculation and needed somewhere to clear my head. This is what happened when you're fresh out of Zoloft and didn't have money for a refill. I'd done a bit of internet research and found that The Mad Knight's story checked out.

Ancient Irish mythology stated that there was a legendary witch named Carman with three wicked sons. Though stories contradicted one another, folklorists agreed that she'd created a great blight in Ireland that had only ended when some ancient fairy race known as the Tuatha Dé Danann had stepped in. After Luna woke up, I checked under the bed for real monsters before crisping elbows of raisin bread for breakfast. When we were done eating, we packed the van and headed to see Denise. Now that Ms. Boise, and more importantly The Mad Knight, knew where I lived, I decided to take provisions for a few days just in case. I brought a change of clothes, the last of the food in the cupboard, and tap water in a milk jug. We made our way southwest to Resurrection Cemetery.

It was a sunny Friday in Chicago, which meant that come four o'clock, everyone would be outside enjoying the only three months of warmth in the Midwest. No one in the three-one-two area code knew exactly what we had done to offend nature, but it was clearly unforgivable.

Luckily, it was early so Luna and I had a few hours to spare. It took three cigarettes and an hour of driving to get to Resurrection Cemetery. The famous rust stains along the gate's bars were known throughout Chicagoland as the grip marks of Resurrection Mary, resident ghost.

Legend had it that the famous vanishing hitchhiker was struck down by a car along Archer Avenue in the 1930s. Since her death, she's terrorized motorists by asking for rides to Resurrection Cemetery. Most folks said that she was a beautiful young woman in her early twenties, and appeared very much alive, clad in period ballroom clothes. It's only when she vanished at the entrance or singed the bars with her grip to release the lock that witnesses realized she'd been a ghost. The story has inspired other tales across the country, but it all started here.

I told the Luna the story as we approached and watched her gaze narrow and follow the gate stains as we drove through. It was funny to think that a vicious were-wolf would be afraid of a ghost, but kids will be kids. We swerved through acres of cemetery road, pulling over underneath a tree near Denise's grave. I turned the key, letting the engine rumble idle while staring at the steering wheel's horn. A murder of crows balancing on the oak's arms above us cawed their cemetery hymn. It was never easy to visit Denise's grave. Although I tended to leave with peace of mind, it was not without awakening feelings and regrets that I'd rather let sleep. We lumbered up a small hill toward Denise's grave, and the memories that I just couldn't wash out started to blacken my mind.

It had been Christmas Eve. Denise was supposed to work the late shift, but the December snow caused for slow business and cut hours. I had spent every holiday by myself, and although I pretended it didn't bother me, Denise knew it sucked. I had planned on dragging my recliner to the apartment window while helping myself to antidepressants and a glass of twelve-year single malt Aberlour until I fell asleep. As I'd let the caramel burn set in, the door burst open and a caroling Denise, donned with gifts under her arms, told me that this Christmas would be different. I still remember the smell of her vanilla lotion as she had leapt in my lap, watching me open my future-favorite black Prada tie and silver dress watch. *For your next job*, she had told me. Little did she know, it would be. We had spent the rest of the night watching creepy clay animation, ordering Chinese, and finishing off the scotch. It doesn't sound like much, but it was everything.

That story is just one of many that I could tell. And *that's* why I'm so damn angry. How is it that a girl like Denise, the only star bold enough to twinkle in an otherwise black sky, is the one that's snuffed out? She was the needle in the haystack. She worked all the soup drives and took in stray animals. She was the only one that sympathized with even the lowliest wretches of society, wretches like me. So, who will put flowers on a flower's grave? I decided long ago that it would be me. I'd do it by making people leading blameworthy lives hurt.

Justice masked as revenge? Maybe, but it worked for me.

Luna and I made it to the grave. I stood mute while Luna dusted off the headstone, tracing her finger over each letter and wordlessly mouthing the name *Denise*. I saw Luna's index finger trace over the date of death, glower, and look up at me while squeezing her doll. I didn't cry anymore, but the stone in the pit of my stomach caused me to tuck my lip up tight as I searched for something to say. Luna inspected my face as if it were a crossword puzzle.

"Yeah," I forced out through an exhaled breath. "She was my sweetheart, kid."

Luna didn't flinch. She moved to my side and just stared down at the headstone with me.

The crows continued to call as we stood in green grass. The sun gleamed down, heating our backs while shaping a gold shimmer across Denise's name. I watched the sparkling sheen skate across the marker and wondered if it was something more. I wanted to pretend it was a sign from Denise, but the levelheaded voice in my mind, the one that had remained silent out of respect for the dead, finally spoke up. It was the sun, nothing more. Now that the mystery had been solved, there were bigger issues that deserved my attention.

Whether I wanted to accept the absurdity of my predicament or not, the fact remained that I had been killed by John Dillinger while doing a job for Ms. Boise. My life was spared by whatever fate awaited me in the afterlife in return for working for Death. He was taking time off and expected me to help him kill anything that was trying to cheat him. First stop was John Dillinger, my former murderer and vampire.

However, while trying to finish the wily bastard, I'd stumbled upon a civil war going on in Chicago's undead community. It appeared that Ms. Boise had hired me to kill Dillinger because he was part of a usurper group of undead that took over the necrotic throne, and after an unwelcome visit to my home, confessed that she was hoping I'd finish the job. Not to mention the problem that was possibly the biggest wild card: Ms. Boise's boss, a bizarre elven lunatic known as The Mad Knight.

He didn't care at all what happened. Instead, he was interested in a bigger picture, trying to break the dysfunctional system that made everyone from the mouse to the lion miserable. He narrowed down the source of the problem to God, the Devil, and Death, and wanted to use my inside position to thwart the fat cats of fate. Or so he said. How he planned on doing that was anyone's guess.

That left me here. With my place compromised, a little girl to protect, and a job unfinished, I had decisions to make. My first priority was keeping Luna safe. I had to decide whether she was safer with me or somewhere else. Maybe I could pawn her off on Bethany for a few days, but then again, I didn't exactly have Luna's condition figured out. If the girl changed into a toothy grinned werewolf, it could be bad for Bethany's babysitting career. I'd have to keep Luna with me, one eye peeled at all times.

If I wanted to keep our squishy parts intact, I'd need to make a decision on the undead rebellion. Ms. Boise and the ghoul gang surprising me at my home had been a power play. They'd offered the olive branch but had also been flexing their clout. If I didn't play ball, they knew where I lived and had the resources to hurt me. I didn't appreciate it. Would tricking the rebellion into a room rigged with explosives get me bonus points with Death? I also wondered how that might affect my relationship with The Mad Knight, who suggested he couldn't care less about the uprising.

At times like this, my military background reminded me that the mission came first. Killing John Dillinger was the assignment. Ensuring Luna's safety was my personal charge. Ms. Boise was a distraction. I started to think about how I'd go about locating Dillinger again. He would stay away from The Violet Hour if he was as smart as I knew he was. As I strained to think how this mission could be any more demanding, the mission called for more.

My cell phone gave a short buzz in my pants pocket; I pulled it out. There was a single, simple text that said *Is he dead yet?* Jumbo, who was house sitting for Death while supervising my job, wanted results. I didn't have any. I texted back *Pending*. Alright, new plan. I'd stop at The Violet Hour and kidnap one of the creepy-smiling host and hostess duo. Then, torture. I didn't like it, but I didn't have much of a choice at this point.

I took one last look at Denise's grave and blocked out any disapproval she might have about what I was up to. If I was ever going to see her again, it wouldn't be in Hell, which was where I was going if I didn't get this job done. I took a deep breath and looked to Luna. She took notice of the white-haired statue that was finally moving and stared up at me.

"Ready to go, kid?" I asked. Luna nodded. "We've got work to do."

We rolled out of the sprawling cemetery toward the

scarred gates. I was trying to wipe the solemnity off my face for Luna's sake when a glint from the intersection between the cemetery road and Archer Avenue caught my eye. I slowed down the van and made out a visitor fixed at the corner. I could hear Luna's breathing speed up as we gaped at a woman adorned in a glossy embroidered white dress. She was young with a porcelain face and honey colored hair. She looked up at us with a melancholic moue and raised her hand. With a single flick, she jutted out her thumb. *No, way. This couldn't be.* Luna squealed. The noise caused me to press down on the gas, swerving past the hitchhiker onto Archer Avenue as fast as I could.

"No," I said aloud. "Hard no."

The shock of our little encounter helped shake off the gloom. We were an hour into Chicago traffic when my phone rang. It was Nolan, our Dungeon Master. I was an advocate for phone safety while driving, but the fact that we were at a standstill on the Stevenson Expressway made Nolan's call an exception. I put the phone on speaker, letting the white noise from the audio fill the van.

"Hello. This is Jack Burton in the Porkchop Express," I greeted in my best Kurt Russel voice.

"Mr. Burton," Nolan's voice called out in a terrible Egg Chen imitation. "Where is da' six- demon bag?"

"Oh, man," I sighed while beeping my horn at the truck trying to cut me off at two miles an hour. "Our imitations are awful."

"Da' worst," Nolan agreed. "But dats not why I'm calling."

"What's up, Mr. DM?"

"Hey, buddy, I just had a strange encounter with Freddy, and I wanted to make you aware." "Nolan," I laughed. "It's still morning. Do you live at the hobby shop?"

"Don't you judge me. I wanted to pick up da' new wizard's book before work so I could read it on my lunch break."

"Okay, nerd. What did Freddy the Vampire Slayer have to say?"

"He was asking if I knew where you were. He wanted to talk more about vampires."

"Well, he's weird, so I guess that's not so strange."

"Well, yes and no. That's not what was strange. What was strange is the fact dat' he said he'd already stopped at your house, but you weren't home." I waved my hand at Luna, who had helped herself to the radio buttons. "Last I checked," Nolan continued over the obnoxious pop song. "You weren't about giving out your address." I turned the volume down and cleared my throat.

"Yeah, it's the whole stereotypical ex-military conspiracy theorist thing," I joked to disguise any concern. "They give us a whole speech about expectations before we're discharged." Nolan laughed. "Seriously though, that is bizarre, but I'm going to bet Freddy got it from that dip shit, Darren. He gave it to Bethany, too. It wouldn't shock me if he was passing it out like candy on Halloween. The guy hates me."

"Yeah," Nolan cut in. "But Bethany is a chick. Let me clarify, Bethany is an attractive woman. They don't usually talk to Darren. He's susceptible to fold like a lawn chair. Otherwise, Darren takes his job pretty seriously. Too seriously to be exact."

"True. Maybe Freddy was there when Darren gave it to Bethany?"

"No, Buck. I was der' when Bethany asked. She was super concerned about Luna and asked me if it would be weird tah' ask Darren first." Luna eyeballed the phone. "I gave her da' thumbs up. Freddy was gone fer' the day though."

My Chicago accent translator took a moment to process. "Hmm, well that is definitely out of the norm. I appreciate you letting me know."

"Yeah of course, buddy. Alright, I need to get tah' work. Are you going to make next week's session?"

"I should be able to," I said with a delay.

"Dude, that will be in two weeks."

"I know, I know. Sorry, life is crazy."

"Alright, well, I'll cross my fingers. The party needs you."

"Well, until then."

Nolan said goodbye and then I pressed the off button. Luna studied me biting my lip as I thought about what Nolan had to say. How did I go from having a secret Bat Cave to running an open house?

Careless paperwork, that's how.

All things considered, Freddy was the least of my worries. As offbeat as he was, the guy was harmless. If he showed up at the doorstep of my apartment sometime in the future, I'd scare him away with an empty threat and then endure the awkwardness of his glares at *Gamer's Pair-a-Dice.* That is, if I ever had an apartment again. If I didn't solve all my little dangerous issues soon, I might not be able to return home.

We rolled down the littered streets of Damen Avenue shortly before lunch to scope out The Violet Hour again. I was just going to do a quick drive-by to see if the delivery trucks and cleaning crew were still on schedule. It's funny that I was so resolute in returning to the place where I had nearly been killed, but such is the burden of my profession. I slowed down just enough to take in a red sign posted on the front of the establishment. I strained to read the letters as I slowed down the van.

CLOSED FOR RENOVATIONS. CHECK OUT OUR WEBSITE FOR MORE DETAILS.

Son of a bitch.

Dillinger knew he was exposed. Staying there would have been a big mistake. He wasn't going to reopen until he solved his little hitman problem. I recalled all the jobs I did in the past. Collectively, none of them had given me as much grief as this one. Apparently tracking down supernatural monsters was tougher than I'd thought. A car behind me beeped, forcing me to return to the regular speed. I kicked the van forward and thought about my backup plan.

You win this one, Dillinger, but I have an ace up my sleeve.

16

The groan of my mobile office's engine caused a stir in the donut shop's drive-through. A look of horror came from every driver in the stretched line of economy vehicles. My pollution machine grumbled over the environmentally friendly clown cars. I had asked Luna what she'd wanted for lunch after putting a few miles between us and The Violet Hour. She'd pointed at an over-the-top bakery's mascot smiling along the street. He was a stereotyped Italian man with a puffy mustache and chef's hat balancing a plate of donuts on a tray. The building's white eaves and pitched Italianate roof architecture were tastelessly cliché, but if the girl wanted racist donuts, then racist donuts was what she'd get.

After crawling through the line, paying with car toll change, and receiving our order, we found a parking spot in the donut shop's lot and turned off the van. The pair of us took our overly frosted donuts into the back cab to let the van's engine cool down. It was hot out and I noticed that the summer humidity made me ripe. I felt naked nowadays when I wasn't armed, a rabbit's hole of piled psychological issues that I didn't care to get into, so I wore a jacket even in the ninety-degree weather. It was a Chicago Bears windbreaker, with enough room in the chest to hide Thing One and Thing Two. I'd earned it for buying an economy case of cigarettes. I sipped my super-sized black coffee while watching Luna chow down on a chocolate puff with a parading protest of animal candy on top. She poked at the sugary creatures so that none escaped before glancing up with a chocolate smile.

Luna seemed happy enough tagging along and I enjoyed her company, *a lot*. I didn't know much about children, but her go-with-the-flow demeanor seemed pretty rare for a kid her age. It was nice. It had a way of keeping my blood a degree cooler through the recent excitement. Plus, for as much as she didn't talk, there was an air of good nature about her. You just had to read between the lines. I wondered how I would sort everything out with Luna in the upcoming months should I untangle this mess. One step at a time, I guessed.

I needed to give answers to Jumbo quickly but was hesitant about how I'd talk to Luna regarding my new plan of action. After she was good and sugared up, I put down my coffee while sitting directly in front of her atop a construction helmet that I had used as a disguise. Luna picked up on my awkwardness, grabbed her doll, and scooted away from me until her back was across the cab wall. She puffed up her frosting covered cheeks and squeezed Harry tight.

"Yes," I confessed. "I have bad news." Luna furrowed her brow. "We need to go back to the place where I found you." Luna shook her head violently. "Please, kid, I need

you to roll with this because if you don't, I won't do it."
Luna held her breath and gave me a narrow-eyed death
glare. "I need to find the bad man that bought you from
the other bad man who delivered you in a crate. If I don't,
there is a very good chance that I won't find him at all.
And that would be bad." I paused and thought about
what would happen if I didn't kill Dillinger. "I mean,
really bad." Luna gave me a once over but didn't say
anything. "Like, *I'll-be-dead* bad." There was a long
moment of silence as Luna squeezed onto Harry while
staring at her light-up gym shoes. I didn't have any clue as
to what I'd do if she refused, so it all came down to this.
After an excruciating pause, Luna stared up at me and
nodded.

"Thank you," I sighed in relief, duck-squatting through
the back of the van to hug her. It was instinctual, but it felt
good. It felt even better when she squeezed back. I pulled
away and looked her in the eyes. "I'm not going to let
anyone hurt you, kid. Once this is over, we'll talk about
new books, school, and possibly a bedroom."

We cleaned up after our dextrose invasion and headed
back to the westside toward the old, abandoned factory. I
was on the verge of my second wind from the caffeine
overhaul as we started crushing gravel along the path to
the converted storage facility. I could see Dillinger's
building from a half mile away. It looked untouched. The
delivery dock's door was still gaping open from Adam's
quick semi-truck getaway, allowing sunlight to pour in.
From above, the pair of gargoyles seemed to stare at the
intact paved tire tracks from our last visit. Dusk was still
hours away, so I had time to kill. Keeping that in mind,
Dillinger wasn't just some dumb apex predator, he was

cunning. Just because he wasn't here didn't mean that I wasn't in danger.

I reversed the van, kicking up a cloud of gravel dust. If we needed to make a quick getaway, we'd be ready. The car sat fifty feet away from the door. I didn't feel comfortable leaving Luna alone knowing that police, security, or Dillinger's thugs would likely explore the mystery vehicle if they arrived. Luna was instructed to follow close behind me. I took Old Lilith as a precautionary measure, though I saw no reason to use the long-range weapon if close quarter combat ensued. I just didn't want to explain to the Grim Reaper that I lost his instrument of total destruction because I didn't have proper locks on my van.

There was hesitation as I took that first step toward the warehouse. I gave myself the briefest second to examine why. I'd never been afraid on a job before. Hell, part of me thought that being gunned down a few days ago was over-due. *Why am I so nervous this time?* It had to be Luna. I couldn't help but feel if in the event we were caught, she'd pay the price and that scared me. If I became bullet food that was fine. It would suck, but it was an acceptable professional hazard. Luna, on the other hand, might be tortured for answers, thrown back into service, or worse.

The thought of that killed me.

So, as we hurried our way into the broken dock doors, I knew that being careful was an understatement.

We used the broken door to gain access. The first thing I noticed upon entering was the missing bodies of the two old were-women. There was still shattered crate wood and dried blood on the cement floor, but no corpses. Someone had cleaned up the crime scene.

That isn't good.

I quietly scouted out the remainder of the lower floor, but everything had remained untouched. With the bottom floor cleared, it was time to go upstairs. Luna and I crawled up the industrial steel steps, trying to tread lightly on a staircase engineered to thunder with a cat's gait. The second and third floor mezzanines hugged the four walls, supporting a handful of glass office doors. Luna and I stalked along the catwalks checking each abandoned office for clues.

There were moldy shipping boxes, rusted desks, and rat droppings. After an hour of searching, we gave up on the middle levels. That left only a narrow stairwell to the fourth floor. The flight of steps led to a single worn oak door of a main boss-like office. My imagination went wild as we approached, traveling back in time to when this place had been an active worksite. I envisioned some cock-strong manager in a cheap suit sipping coffee while inspecting scurried employees below.

The faded gold letters along the door read *Ex-blurred-letters-ice*, which I assumed spelled Executive Office. I tested the doorknob. Bizarrely, it was locked. My chagrin turned to optimism. I couldn't see the point in locking a door to protect moldy paperwork. The lock was traditional. I removed the warder's key in my pocket and inserted it into the keyhole. I applied slight torque to the wrench, scrubbing the key back and forth until I heard a distinct click. I pulled the knob and the door opened.

Bingo.

Luna threw me a suspicious look and I gave her a toothy grin in return. Luna shook her head. I pushed the door and was met with a reserve of heat from the sunbaked walls. The room had been well kept compared to all others. While the office's wallpaper was tired and the ceiling tarnished, the furniture inside was organized. The desk was something fashioned out of the forties, but it was polished and free of clutter. There wasn't any filth, and it was void of vermin. A cedar rolling chair with green crushed velvet cushions sat at the desk with twin gunmetal grey filing cabinets tucked under the workspace. I closed the office door behind us but motioned for Luna to stay near the exit momentarily. I didn't put it past Dillinger to booby-trap anything. Sure enough, as I flicked on the amber light from an antique bronze library desk lamp, I spotted a thin red wire snaking from behind a pinup of a scantily clad bob-haired flapper along the wall. The cable coiled under the desk and into the back of the hutch drawer. Red wiring meant "live" universally, so I asked Luna to step back into the hall. Luna wrung her hands together and inched into the lonely stairwell.

I removed the poster one tack at a time to find a hollow in the wall. The red wire's top had been inserted into a car battery sitting in a drywall nest. I pinched the rubber insulated wire and tugged. A spark spat out. Like a matador, I sidestepped the waste drawer and prepared to open it.

"Alright, funny man," I said underneath my breath. "Let's see what you're hiding."

There was a snap and pop before several random items violently flung from the desk. The drawer had been rigged with a miniature catapult that triggered upon opening. I took a second to study the pile of scattered ammunition along the warped wood floor. Alongside a broken glass vial of clear liquid were silver pellets, rock salt, and an assortment of crystals. The red wire had been bound to the handle. Anyone who wasn't aware of the booby-trap would likely be shocked still as they pulled the drawer, and then pelted by mystical ammunition. Dillinger was protecting the contents from supernatural forces.

I rifled through the proverbial junk drawer of mystical items, from twined sage to dried chicken's feet. The leftovers seemed harmless. I called Luna back in as I dug up a few file folders tucked under the treasure trove of leftover Happy Meal witch toys. Luna entered gingerly, taking bite-sized steps before stopping to study the pile of broken catapult armaments on the ground. I dissected each file as she fixated on the junk. There was correspondence between Dillinger and a DuSable about organizing an Undead Union. On the top of the letterhead was a sigil that matched Dillinger's signet ring.

Details in the letter included proposed voting rights and requests for fair representation based on individual undead needs. I didn't know the first thing about the modern vampires, ghosts, and revenants mentioned in the various transcripts, but the Undead Union's ideology didn't sound half as malicious as Ms. Boise made them out to be. In addition, there were several blueprints for the Field Museum's Egyptian exhibit. There were specifics on transforming a long- established warlock's nightclub into lodging for supernatural refugees. Most importantly, there were details about an Operation Shackled Moon, an initiative to free, *drum roll, please*, paranormal prisoners.

I flipped through the pages. Each document gave specifics on rescuing ghoulish house servants from aristocratic fiends, dispelling voodoo zombies from priests, and liberating lycanthropes from werewolf fighting pits. Every objective had assigned names to them.

Designated to werewolf recovery duty was none other than John Dillinger and Adam Frankenstein.

Son of a bitch.

I peered over my shoulder to Luna, who was arranging magical rocks into a mosaic masterpiece while kicking away silver pellets. Dillinger had tried to save her. Could a ruthless vampiric gangster also be a superhuman Hallmark sweetie who rescues enslaved kid-werewolves on the side? I imagined the shoebox card with one of those bigheaded Precious Moments kids in the likeliness of Dillinger, his clawed fingers over the chest. The interior read, *You turn my cold heart into a gold heart.*

The cocky smile he'd had when I was tied up slipped into my thoughts. Wait, what was I thinking? This was the same man that had gone on endless crime sprees in the early twentieth century. He'd murdered a cop in East Chicago. He ate people for food. Oh, and let's not forget, Buck, this guy had shot me down in cold blood. No, there was only one place for this man, and it was on the business end of Old Lilith's barrel. The job was still Dillinger.

I collected the files and decided to slip out of Dillinger's factory before it was too late. Luna and I didn't waste time cleaning up our mess. I couldn't give a damn if Dillinger knew we were here. The man was astute enough to know he was being hunted. Having a mess to clean up was the least of his worries. We hurried down to the bottom floor where we left from the broken dock door. The heat was getting unbearable and as we headed to the van, I struggled to air out my sweaty stomach by fanning my shirt. Luna tugged my pant leg. I gave her the quickest little glance and noticed that she was staring behind us. I spun around expecting Dillinger or his goons to be behind us, but there was no one there. Luna pointed up to the top of the factory and I noticed that the gargoyles were missing.

I'm ready for some blessings that aren't in disguise.

Those pieces of granite sculpted shit had several windows of opportunity to do something, and it was only *now* that they decided to go fly off and tattletale on me? They were likely mid-flight to Dillinger of the Undead Union. However, unless they had the speed of a Grumman F-14 Tomcat, we had a little time. I wrote their disappearance off as a learning experience that came with amateur undead killing and made a mental note to shoot every damn gargoyle, fountain statue, or garden gnome I came across in the future. I took Luna by the hand and tugged.

"Okay, kid," I said as I picked up the pace. "Speed it up. Those oversized Halloween props might be rushing to get backup."

Luna followed my pace, hopping into the back of the van as I checked beneath for explosives. Once I saw the coast was clear, I jumped into the driver seat, shoved the key in the ignition and put the car into drive. We kicked rocks as we sped out of the factory district and onto real streets. Luna stared out of the window to the sky. It was midafternoon and, naturally, we hit Friday evacuation traffic. We were now on the Eisenhower, surrounded by Mercedes and BMWs. Every driver wore a business suit. They were presidents, vice-executives, and any other upper management title that had the luxury of dictating their own schedule. I half wanted to ram them off the road but told the Emperor Palpatine in my head to relax. Instead, I fiddled with my phone to get it to share music with my car radio. This would all be a lot easier with a little Tom Waits.

I chose the *Orphans: Brawlers, Bawlers & Bastards* album and turned it up until the speaker static kicked in. Luna glowered at me as Tom's shattered glass smothered in smoker's cough voice cried throughout the van. She wiped the sweat from her creased forehead and drew her lips into a hard line. I flicked my eyes between Luna and the road, jaw drawn. As we drew to another sudden stop, I decided to make my stand.

"Kid," I spoke up. "Listen hard. We might die fighting vampires or babysitting demon toddlers, but it will be for naught unless you respect the Tom Waits. You get me?" Luna looked at the radio as if it were spewing earwigs, covering her ears with her hands. "I get it. He has a—" I hummed while searching for the right words. "—distinct style. It's deliberate. Do me a favor though and listen to these dang lyrics." Luna shook her head. "One song, come on. If you hate it, we can play whatever you want." Luna sighed, crossed her arms, and leaned back in her seat. We listened to Tom. One song became two and then two became four. By the time we reached our exit, we'd listened to the entire album. I never looked at her. No, that would only thwart my intentions. I've learned that Luna wasn't the kind to take crap if she wasn't happy. Tom had jammed his broken fingers into her werewolf heart, singing razor lullabies that milked the darkest minds with ardor.

We pulled up in front of *Gamer's Pair-of-Dice* as the Earth bled the last hours of the sun's fury for the day. I prayed that Darren wasn't there, as I was so hot I could drink iced Windex and ask for seconds. Today's visit could end with a Darren fatality. Luna and I trotted into the cooled air of the hobby store. The register was unmanned. We headed straight to the back looking for Freddy. I had vampire questions to ask and death threats to administer. No one gets to visit me at home. Well, except Bethany, but she had clothes for Luna. Then there's Ms. Boise's freak show, but I had no real options on that one. Anyhow, all others must die.

I pushed to the back but was sad to find Freddy and his usual table of outcast gamers were missing. Wendell, a teenage Warhammer player who frequented the store, must have seen my boiling expression. He waved me down with his stick arms and pointed toward the closed off back hall. I knew what he was trying to say. Past the hall and to the left was an emergency exit where smokers like me went to feed their chemical enslavement. I nodded, waved Luna to follow, and stomped toward the door. I was mentally poking at my frustrated embers in hopes to provoke them into a frenzied fire as we entered the lonely white hall filled with storage. I needed to remind myself that someone, as harmless as they might be, looking for my home was bad in my line of work. I kicked the handlebars of the emergency door and stomped into the alley.

A pack of Goth maniacs in pleather pants and trench coats were speaking in bad British accents along the tight lane that bridged the alley to the main road. Freddy, who was at the front, donned a pair of plastic quarter machine fangs in his mouth as a trio of dark dorks pointed finger guns at him. A pudgy woman with cropped hair and scratch marks painted on her cheek howled like a wolf, her chipped purple fingernails curled into imaginary claws. Darren hid in the back near the street outlet recording the action on his phone with a satisfied grin. Luna leaned on me as she pulled her brows together, blinking rapidly.

"Don't worry, kid." I tucked her behind my leg. "These scary looking people are just LARPers. They only pretend to be dangerous."

"Dang it, Buck." Darren dropped his camera angle. "You ruined the shot. We're trying to record a promo video for the store here." It was time to center my inner-asshole. Time to shine.

"Listen up, children of Morpheus," I shouted. "Your Monster Mash is over. Freddy and I need to have a chat about his attempt to visit me at my private residence." The Buffy cast froze, their eyes darting between my glare and Freddy's reaction. Freddy grimaced and swallowed hard.

"Come on, Buck," yelled Darren. "Can't this wait?"

"Oh," I gasped with false bravado. "Would the representative of Confidential Information Sharing Brigade like to take the stage? I have a few choice words for you too, you fat piece of—"

"Okay, okay." Darren lowered his head like a scolded dog and scurried along with the other LARPers inside. Luna followed behind them, posting next to the entrance. Meanwhile, Freddy puffed out his man-boob chest, pushing the bridge of his moon shaped sunglasses farther onto his nose. It appeared someone had a backbone to break. I approached him with a John Wayne gait and waited for the nerds to completely disperse.

"Hey, Freddy." I crushed a discarded pop can that littered in the alley. "I heard you stopped at my house." Freddy flipped a drape of long bangs over his glasses, combing his fingers through his mane. His trench coat lapel was covered in cheap Spencer's iron on patches of

Jack the Pumpkin King. It was the sort of tacky decor that screamed *wanna-be-lost-soul.*

"I did," he said with a straight face.

"Freddy," I sung while wagging my finger like a parent at their sock chewing puppy. "I want to warn you as a man that hasn't taken his PTSD medication, your next answer needs to be spot on. Why did you think it's a good idea to come to my home?"

"You wanted to know about vampires, didn't you?"

"I can buy the Requiem book."

"No," he snarled before taking a breath. "*Real* vampires."

"Freddy, from one crazy son of a bitch to another, there's no such thing as vampires, man. Let it go."

"Oh no?" he snapped back, his nostrils dilated. "Then why have you been going to The Violet Hour?"

A torrent of Mount Doom level magma erupted inside me. This nut bag had been following me. I could feel my face get red as my mental playlist blared the Godzilla theme song.

"Oh hell, no," I hollered, getting into Freddy's face. I was at least a half foot taller, which made my stare down that much more excessive. "Freddy, have you been following me?"

Freddy opened his meaty jowls to speak. He hesitated for a moment before balling his fist. I looked down and noticed a familiar looking *Hello Kitty* key dangling on a wrist coil around his cuff. Just as he did, the screech of brakes signaled the quick stop of tires from along the street. I heard the rumbling of a heavy engine. I spun around to see the cab of Adam Frankenstein's truck blocking the main road. It choked out black fumes. The block shaped head of Adam sat behind the driver seat, the scar from my bullet still mauve along his forehead. In the passenger seat was orange flannel Charles Bronson, his wounds still covered in duct tape.

Charles Bronson pushed open his door and leapt out into the street.

I turned to warn Freddy, but he had already run to the backdoor of the hobby store at peculiar speed for a fat man. Unexpectedly, he grabbed Luna and jolted her up into a fireman's carry. Luna's eyes bulged. I dug for Thing One, but before I could draw out the gun, Freddy pushed the door open with his free shoulder and entered. As if kicked by a mule, Freddy came hurling back out into the alley, dropping Luna as he fell onto his butt. Freddy's sunglasses shattered against the hard alley ground. For the first time I could see Freddy's eyes. They glared red over his clenched jaw.

Stepping out from the emergency exit were The Violet Hour's host and hostess duo. The dark-haired hostess wore a cobalt leather jacket over an ivory dress and thigh high boots. The blond Ken Doll dressed in a striped V-neck t-shirt with skinny jeans and deck shoes. Both were armed with iron gauntlets etched in Norse or Celtic runs daubed with glue and salt. They held the salted steel gloves up in a boxer's guard. It was strange to see such normal looking people appear so out of place. I released my pistol and instead wrapped my arm around Luna's waist, scooping her up. As I withdrew from Freddy, a hand grasped my shoulder. I clenched my open hand's fist, readying to strike, as orange flannel Charles Bronson shook me. Before I could take the first swing, Charles Bronson shoved me out of the way, moving toward Freddy.

"Shaw," the thick accent of Adam Frankenstein cried from over his booming engine. "Get in ze 'truck."

I couldn't believe what I was hearing but as I turned back to look at Freddy, he was on his feet and wrestling Charles Bronson. Surprisingly, Freddy was able to wiggle free from Charles Bronson's grip and used one fat arm to lift the orange flannel warrior by his neck. Ken Doll secured the hobby store door while the dark-haired hostess circled Freddy from the rear.

Meanwhile, as Freddy clamped Charles Bronson's neck, the fat man looked out into the sky and shrieked a horrible melody that was a symphony of dying cat, tea kettle, and a lion's roar.

The sound ripped through my eardrums as if I were standing next to the stage side speaker of a Slayer concert. I couldn't think straight. I cupped my ears to plunge out all sound. When the racket finally stopped, my watery eyes and ringing ears made me feel as if I were spinning in circles. On cue, strange vapors of milky white fog spewed from my eyes, ears, and mouth, instantly refocusing my senses. I could see that Ken Doll and the hostess were having a harder time recuperating. They were writhing at Freddy's feet with bleeding eardrums.

A static crackled in the air as a gust of wind pushed alley garbage and muddy water. The faint murmur of singing children and soft-soled shoes echoed between the buildings. Shadows flickered above us. I searched the skyline and made out a hundred pairs of eyes arched on top of *Gamer's Pair-of-Dice*. It was the hag children donned in their old-fashioned Little Orphan Annie outfits. Their alabaster eyes fixated on us as they opened up their maws to reveal yellow, crooked teeth. Some of the hag children salivated while others curled their talons.

I looked down at Luna. Her eyes were still rolling in the back of her head. It was executive decision time. I mustered my strength and carried Luna toward Adam's truck. Adam Frankenstein was still in the driver's seat. Beryl ooze dripped from his earlobes. I scurried around the massive grill of the truck and then made like Spiderman, using one arm to climb up into the passenger seat while dangling Luna under my remaining bicep. Adam groaned as I shut the door. He shook his head hard and then started shifting gears. I looked over his wide chest to see Ken Doll and the hostess stumbling toward us as hag children climbed down the walls like roaches. Looking out the window, I could see Freddy was now pummeling Charles Bronson, spurting maggots from every one of the orange flanneled defender's orifices. Charles Bronson continued to wave his arms, futilely but fervently trying to fight back.

I'll never watch Death Wish one through five the same again.

The tractor truck kicked forward as Adam pressed hard on the gas pedal. Ken Doll and the hostess gritted teeth while giving one last spurt of speed. Ten or more hag children skipped and giggled in pursuit. One at a time, Ken Doll and the hostess leapt onto the driver's side of the moving truck, landing on the cab's driver side step. They gripped the handle while Adam picked up speed. The hostess crawled in through the open window.

"Stop, you fool," roared Adam as he nudged the hostess onto Luna and me. The bang of metal rang from the semi-trailer behind us. Tiny footsteps clanked on top. Ken Doll dangled from the door while he looked atop the truck toward the clamor. His lip quivered and his eyes went round. He hurried into the window and over Adam.

"Shut the windows," Ken Doll bellowed as he rolled along Adam's python arms on to the hostess. I could feel their pressure shove me into the passenger door as Adam straightened out the truck. I looked through the magnified side mirrors and saw five of the hag children smiling at me as they surfed on the trailer top. They began clawing onto the side of the truck, closing in on the cab.

"Shake and bake, Adam," I shouted. "They're on the sides."

Adam didn't hesitate. He used a Giordano's delivery truck parked on the corner of an upcoming intersection to smash and scrape the hag children off. *That's what you get for illegally parking along a corner.* I watched the grinning hag children turn to geriatric pâté. The truck swayed for a moment before Adam could gain control. All five of us stared at the street in front of us without saying a word. Once we put at least five miles between us and *Gamer's Pair-of-Dice,* Adam pulled off to an abandoned supermarket's lot and stopped the truck. I hurried out with Luna, putting space between Adam, Ken Doll, and hostess. I could see a smear of gore along the truck's trailer. Ken Doll and the hostess followed me outside but froze once I dug my hand through my zipper into my breast. Adam's heavy footsteps could be heard along the other side of the truck. He made his way around the front and paused when he saw the standoff.

"Seriously," Adam sighed.

"Start talking, freak show," I demanded.

"I am not a talker, Shaw," Adam groaned. "Nor are you

a listener. So instead, I'll show you." Adam stomped to the rear of the trailer, seemingly uncaring of my James Bond action pose. Ken Doll and the hostess followed, keeping an eye on me. I looked to Luna. Her eyes fluttered open.

"Well, hell." I carried a waking Luna and followed the group. We gathered at the back as Adam pulled the boat-tail's safety bar. With a single thrust of his arm, Adam opened the trailer fairing's steel door. It was dark inside, but I could hear shuffling. The mechanical sounds of turning wheels emanated as a short shadowy figure rolled forward. The stranger reached the lip of the truck, allowing the sun to paint him. I took a step back once I recognized the person perched on an apple-red electronic scooter. It was Jumbo, and he was staring at me like I was the stranger.

17

There's a certain look that inspires the saying "ridden hard and put away wet." It's a grocery list of features that involves frayed hair, tattered clothes, and a threadbare complexion. It's pit stains, an unkempt beard, and food splotches. It's cracked glasses, untied shoes, and coffee-stained teeth. Jumbo, who I hadn't seen in a few days, was a poster boy for the hard and wet campaign.

It was concerning to think that Jumbo could get this low so fast. The timeline between when I'd seen him last, all perky and clean, and now, drained and shabby, didn't add up. Even the guy's wheels downgraded. Jumbo sported some state-of-the-art moon rover wheelchair complete with custom foot rigging, monster truck wheels, and multi-button joystick. Now he drove one of those scooters that senior citizens ride or die on through the grocery store. What did the Addams Family do to him?

"Jumbo," I asked slowly, "have they hurt you?"

"What are you talking about?" Jumbo struggled to straighten the wheels of his aisle blocker.

"Jumbo," I enunciated louder, "blink twice if they've touched your privates."

"Well," Jumbo drooped his shoulders and sighed, "I see why they chose him."

"Come again?" I asked. Jumbo straightened out his back.

"Hey man, tell me something." Jumbo combed a clumpy braid from his eye. "How do you know my name?"

I paused and pursed my lips. "Uh, this is awkward. Are you ashamed to know me? Because if so, I throw shade at you, sir."

"That's the thing, dude," Jumbo replied. "You don't know me."

"Jumbo, you're making me look bad in front of the kid," I said while helping Luna get to her feet. Luna rubbed her eyes. "Come on, don't you remember the party at the Grim Reaper's place? You hired me to be Death's intern while he was out? I killed Zombie Pete for you? Any of this ringing a bell?"

"Oh," Jumbo said with a blank stare. "It's not ringing a bell, man, but it all makes sense."

"Hey, Ugly." I shook my head at Adam. "It's against the Geneva Convention's regulations to beat your prisoners."

"I'm not a prisoner," Jumbo spat out. "And you never met me. You've been duped, Mr. Shaw."

"Thank God." I held my hands over my head. "Please show me where the hidden cameras are because you got me good. I mean, Death's intern? Come on. Also, Jumbo, you know my real name. Come on man, we're tight."

"No, Mr. Shaw." Jumbo plucked a dented can of open Coke from the handlebar cup holder. He took a sip, pushed his scooter as close to the edge of the tractor trailer as possible, then returned his attention to me. "I don't."

"It's Buck," I said as if it was obvious. "Alright, this is getting lame. Jumbo, can we skip the regular questions and get straight to Final Jeopardy?"

"Yes, please." Adam rubbed his economy sized fingers over the scratches on the corner of the truck trailer.

"Buck," Jumbo called out with sincerity. "I'm about to let you in on a few truths. You can choose to believe them or not, but they're true nonetheless." Jumbo shut his eyes, breathed, and opened them again. "Buck, you are bait for a war involving life, death, and everything in between. There's a civil war going on that I'm sure you are aware of. About a year or so ago, a band of concerned supernatural creatures within the Chicago community took power from a tyrant warlock dictator who wanted to rule people like slaves. The victors divided power into a fair system that included a witch democracy, undead union, yada-yada. However, the remnants of the warlock's forces reorganized and came up with a Hail Mary plan to steal Death's domain from him, even though the Boss man was never involved in any of the rebellion, giving them the ultimate wild card for retaking Chicago."

"I'm with you so far." I leaned my elbow on Luna's head. I'd heard bits and pieces of this story already, but it was important to fact check. Luna looked up at my arm pressed on her head and growled.

"Good," Jumbo complimented. "The warlock's old forces, led by his former business director—"

"Oh, yeah." I snapped my finger. "Idaho-Face." Jumbo smiled. "Yes, Rosita."

"Ha," I snorted. "I call her Ms. Boise."

"Stay with me, man." Jumbo put his hands together in prayer. "Anyhow, Rosita, fueled with vengeance, petitioned for the warlock's brother, Dub, a powerful doppelgänger that's also the bastard son of the Grim Reaper, to join her in her diabolical plan to steal Death's scythe." I put my hand over the satchel hiding Old Lilith. "Together, they tried to murder Death's trusted computer programmer and replace the handsome devil with Dub, who is fantastic at impersonating people. They abused Death's domain to kill off important figures in the supernatural community while persuading Death to go on a vacation. Here's where you come in, Buck."

"You can't just take an all-powerful weapon from a divine being. There're protective measures and complications beyond belief. Death had to willingly give it to someone that has zero intentions of abusing its power for personal gain. So," Jumbo crooned as if mid-thought, "Rosita and Dub must have talked Death into hiring someone that was just as clueless to their intentions as Death. They found you, and once they convinced Death you were capable of killing Unmentionables while he was away, they assigned you to kill their Undead Union enemy, John Dillinger, while planning to recruit you for their cause."

"Whoa." I rubbed my chin. "So, I'm like a double agent of epic proportions. James Bond with magical nuclear codes."

"No," Jumbo objected. "More like Double-O-Twelve-and-a-Half. They needed someone desperate and clueless. You fit the bill."

"I liked the old Jumbo better." I crossed my arms.

"No, no, no," Jumbo argued in a cool tone. "This is good, man. See, Rosita and Dub thought they'd disposed of me, but unbeknownst to them, one of the Undead Union's big dogs rescued me." I read between the lines.

"You mean Dillinger?" I asked.

"Duh." Jumbo shrugged. "Don't you see, dude, if we can use my knowledge of Death's domain and your position as the keeper of Death's scythe, we have Rosita and Dub right where we want them. We can finally put down their rebellion."

"Hold on." I held my hand out. "You've been a mildly interesting storyteller when you weren't insulting me, but there're a lot of assumptions being made here. For starters, who says I'm going to help you?"

Adam clenched his fist. The Ken Doll and hostess exchanged gape-mouthed stares.

Jumbo scratched at his head.

"Why wouldn't you, man?" Jumbo lifted his pop can and slurped it empty.

"Oh, I don't know," I said dryly. "Let's start with the fact that there're a lot of holes in your story."

"Like what?" Jumbo crushed his can back into the cup holder.

"First," I tried to rebut. "How do I know that anything you're saying is true? For all I know, you're the bullshitters trying to get me off of Dillinger's back or something. Why shouldn't I trust the rebels instead?"

"Alright, man," Jumbo bounced back. "How about the fact that your fat role-playing friend was Dub in nerd clothing, and that he used the chubby Lestat guy to spy on you? Which also means that he likely killed your friend in the process."

"Okay." I cracked my knuckles. "Well, sad to hear Freddy might be dead, but he was not my friend. Freddy had no friends."

"Likely why he was chosen," Ken Doll stepped in. "Dub does his research. It's a lot easier to impersonate someone with minimal daily maintenance."

"Oh." I cocked my head back. "Look at you being all smart." Ken Doll smiled. "From now on, please shut your mouth when you're talking to me. I can only concentrate on one piss wizard at a time." Ken Doll frowned.

"Also, man," Jumbo piggybacked. "How about the part where Rosita set up your murder?

She anonymously tipped off Dillinger in hopes he'd kill you. That way you were dead and furious with John. It's a win-win for the guys that want John dead and a resurrected fool to trick into stealing the scythe."

Rosita had danced around a lot of facts in my apartment. She'd lied to me and tried to kill me on several occasions. Hell, even The Mad Knight had confirmed her shaky motives. Stealing the rifle while setting me up to kill John sounded like an evil genius's plot. Meanwhile, Dillinger's boys here had moved heaven and Earth just to connect with me to explain.

"Fair point," I conceded. "But there's still like ten thousand other loopholes that I need answers to."

"Probably, dude." Jumbo licked his braces. "And I'm willing to answer them. However, let's just frame this for you. Think about all that's happened the last few days. Harvest every fact you've received from our perspective, Rosita's side, and everything in between. When you put it all together, it points to Rosita and Dub's rebellion being really scary for all of us."

"Yes, it doesn't look good for them, that's for sure."

"Where there's smoke there's fire," the hostess kicked in.

"Not you, too." I shook my head at her. She held her Sears catalog smile. "What about The Mad Knight? Where does that guy fit in with all of this?"

"Who?" Jumbo buzzed.

"The elf dude in heels." I sucked my cheeks in to give my best David Bowie face. "You know, light bulb necklace, cat eyes, and Cheshire Cat smile." The group looked to me with an array of raised brows, twisted mouths, and wrinkled noses. "Dub's *brother*. Hello."

"Oh." Jumbo cleared his throat, "Dothur? That guy hasn't been seen in ages. He shouldn't be a problem."

"The guy shared a cigarette with me at my apartment," I shouted. "He confessed his crazy plan to thwart God and shit on my damn recliner." Jumbo looked to Adam, who was picking at flakes of loose paint from the truck. Adam shrugged.

"Not sure what to tell you, Buck." Jumbo smacked his lips. "Rosita has a lot of scary allies. Whether Dub's brother is involved or not, it doesn't change the circumstances. It's them versus us. They want to use you to steal Death's dominion and we don't."

"What about my mark?" I pushed back. "You forget I'm a damn professional hitman and Death hired me to kill your friend Dillinger."

"Let me handle that," Jumbo brushed me off. "I think Death will understand once I explain."

"Wrong'o buddy," I hissed. "I might be new to the

game, but I know that Dillinger is an Unmentionable and he screws up Death's system. Guess what? I've been hired to kill him on pain of an eternity in Hell. That won't change."

Jumbo sighed. "Buck, are you really going to ignore everything I told you."

I took Luna's hand. "Not sure yet," I tried to say without sounding as frustrated as I was.

"If you're serious, you'll spare me some time to think."

"There is none to spare." Adam punched his truck. "We are in overtime already."

"Take it or leave it, Red Skull," I bluffed while trying to ignore Adam's hostility. We were all a bit frustrated, and it was so damn hot. *Could someone shut off the sun already?*

"Let him go." Jumbo waved me off. "I think Buck here is in grave danger and he could cost the world its natural balance, but if he needs time to think, we'll give it to him."

"I'm no stranger to sarcasm." I narrowed eyes. "From my perspective, you're all a bunch of shit pouches. Jumbo, you're helping a damn vampire and undead construct," I said while thumbing to Adam. "There're entire Victorian novels packed with their documented murder sprees." Adam creased his brow but remained mute.

"This is beyond morality, dude." Jumbo massaged his temple. "We have a counter plan to stop the rebellion but will likely need you for it."

"Pray tell what this plan is?" I queried.

"With this." Ken Doll stepped forward and presented the *Hello Kitty* key once on Dub's wrist, handing it to Jumbo. Jumbo reached out and retrieved the key, pumping his fist.

"This is a start," Jumbo breathed in relief.

"Maybe for you, ya dingus," I snapped. "But not Buck Palasinski."

"Dude, you are a damn professional killer," Jumbo jeered.

"Yeah." I guided Luna away from the assembly. "Maybe I am, but don't expect me to just help you because you have a few valid points. In fact, don't expect much out of me at all. Now, can I go?"

Jumbo shook his head. "Stupidity is not a crime, so yes, you're free to go."

"Good," I barked. "Come on kid, we're leaving." I looked over my shoulder while Luna and I walked away. "Goest and fucketh thyself."

The van was parked in front of *Gamer's Pair-a-Dice*, a red zone at the moment, and I was on the tougher part of the westside. *I didn't think this through.* I continued to walk through the decayed parking lot asphalt. I could hear hurried footsteps behind me. It was the hostess. She jogged in front of me and blocked my path.

"What?" I demanded. The hostess held out her hand, which was pinching a white business card. There was a twenty-dollar bill folded under it.

"Here, please," the hostess said, her pitch high and hopeful. "Use this to get back to your van. The number on there is in case you change your mind, friend." I took the card and tucked it in my pocket. I had to admit that Team Dillinger was far more courteous.

"What's your name, anyhow?"

"Selena," she said through her red lipstick grin. "My mom was a big fan."

"Well, Selena." I pulled up Uber on my phone. "I'd ditch Dillinger and crew while you still can. They're a bunch of douche canoes."

"They're the only douche canoes I have."

"Well, not me. I have me, myself, and I."

"Okay, friend. I'll have the phone on me. Call whenever." She smiled. I tugged Luna's hand. "Have a great day."

I gave her an over-the-shoulder middle finger.

I was a baller on a budget. I had no money. The credit card I'd been using should have declined a few swipes ago. The cash Selena gave me could hardly afford Pam the Uber driver, who would pick us up in seven minutes. A hotel, motel, or worse was out of the financial plan. The van was too risky to retrieve just yet. The few friends I had would be in danger if we stayed on their couch. There was only one option. I had to go back to our flat.

I thought about how I could secure the apartment while peering out of the window of Pam's foreign SUV. The vehicle's air conditioning still had that new car smell. It felt good. Luna dozed off next to me, using my arm as a pillow. Ms. Boise had said that she would give me time to think, but Dub had breached the unspoken cease fire by attacking me. I wondered if this would change our arrangement, putting us in danger. Then again, Dub had never actually attacked me. In fact, the only reason he and the hag children had attacked at all was because Adam and the gang had showed up. Could Dillinger and the Undead Union have tried to press Dub's hand by exposing him in front of me or were they just in it for the key?

Dub may have killed poor Freddy. If he did, then that took our deal off the table. The ping-pong game of points and counter points continued until we returned home, but ultimately it came down to one thing. I'd need to learn Freddy's fate for myself. Before I did, I had to set up the apartment like it was a dwarf fortress along with Home Alone traps, occult wards, and a panic room. So, when we arrived back at the apartment, I hurried Luna up the stairs.

The apartment appeared to be unmolested. I pushed the ruddy couch against the front door, my only entrance, and closed all the drapes. I went online and read a few doomsday prep forums for trap ideas. I skipped explosives and went straight to the swinging weights and nail spikes. After securing the windows with spring-loaded spears made from mop handles and butcher knives, I scoured Google for magical protection tips. I was flooded with anemic sites that suggested positive attitude and meditation, but eventually found blogs with more tangible measures.

I used some of my role-playing miniature paint to mix up a batch of Haint Blue, a popular shade that allegedly deterred malevolent spirits. I then removed my couch barricade and painted the outside threshold of my apartment door, surrendering my security deposit in the process.

Next, I was instructed to hang garlic, but because I didn't have any fresh cloves from the garden at the moment, I did the next best thing. I dangled a half bottle of garlic seasoning and a frozen garlic pizza on shoe strings over my front room window. Finally, I read about the power of salt against dark magic and remembered that Dillinger had some prepared in his booby trap. I collected all of the McDonalds salt packets in my junk drawer and made a line near every room's edge.

Once that was complete, I organized the bathroom into

my panic room. I placed pillows in the bathtub for Luna to hide in and then reinforced the cheap white cedar door with a solid maple one that had been lingering in the building's laundry room. I nailed a two-by-four pried from my bed frame into the bathroom wall to be slid down behind the washroom entrance as an extra barricade. Finally, I placed the hammer and a softball bat in the washroom. If I went down, Luna could hide here and make her last stand.

The house looked like an obstacle course. I made peanut butter and jelly sandwiches and then joined Luna on the couch for what I hoped wasn't my last meal. We ate while watching public access cartoons. Luna gave the apartment a once over, her eyes locked on the garlic pizza and seasonings dangling from the ceiling. Her nose crinkled and her mouth turned into a near flat smile. Luna must have had her doubts about my ADT system for vampires. I bided my time until the show's happy ending to break my newest line of bad news. I was about to break and enter Freddy's home. If I took Luna and we were caught by the police, they'd take Luna to a foster home. Plus, if I went alone, I could be quicker. It was best if she stayed here at Fort Knox.

"Hey, kid," I said with my hands delicately gripped on her shoulders like one of those TV dads. "I have a favor to ask." Luna's brows knitted. "I need you to stay here by yourself for an hour." Her expression hardened. "Just listen. Have I ever steered you wrong?" Luna puffed her nose. "Exactly. I haven't. I'm going on a dangerous trip that could get me in trouble with the police. If I'm caught, they'll take you away." Luna's expression dulled. "Once again, that's bad." Luna put me through another one of her torturous intermissions. "So, what do you say?" I sat there with my hands on her shoulders like an idiot. After an eternity Luna nodded and shooed me away with her little hand. I smiled.

"Thanks, kid. I'll be back in no time."

18

I drove the sedan to the address left on Fredrick L. Waters, Occult Expert's magnet. He lived in a suburb called Oak Park. The area bordered Chicago's west fringes, and in some ways appeared to be nothing more than an extension of the city with its busy streets and tightly packed commercial buildings. It wasn't until you continued west into the residential pockets of Oak Park that you understood that this is where the wealthy went to enjoy a taste of city life while basking in Victorian mansions, eating at fine local restaurants, and accessing plush public parks. Freddy didn't live in that part, though. He lived in the butthole of Oak Park near the highway that the wealthy drove on to get to their estates.

A weight saddled my shoulders as I scouted Freddy's building. I shrugged off the antsy feeling within as simple precautious awareness but deep down, I knew I felt naked because I didn't have Luna. After finding a parking spot nearly three blocks away, I unruffled my tie in the rearview mirror. I'd changed into my suit in hopes to blend in with the struggling upcoming hopefuls of Oak Park. They'd be coming home from work around now, and I hoped I'd easily be ignored. Once I thought I looked like a regular office Joe, I grabbed a few unopened bills from the glove compartment, Old Lilith's satchel, and then headed toward Freddy's address.

Freddy's block was filled with heather precast brick buildings with tall bay windows along their faces. There were small decorative panes of stained glass running up the centers. The whole neighborhood looked like mass-produced Frank Lloyd Wright knockoffs. The green door to Freddy's complex had one of those buzz entry systems with key fob access. Since my custodian key wouldn't work, I waited near the short front lawn, pretending to open up bills while absentmindedly fidgeting with my ring of keys. When a young couple complete with new baby in a stroller pushed toward the front door, I came ambling after, my nose still in my mail. The couple were using the buddy system to open the door with their key fob while removing their daughter from the stroller and collapsing the cart to squeeze it through the entrance. The father took one look at me with my nose in a final notice, frowned, then held open the door. I gave an inattentive *thanks* before entering; a feigned look of concern washed over my face while I tucked the bills in Old Lilith's satchel.

Once I put space between the young family and myself, I scouted the bottom floor for additional exits in case my errand went sour. I found a back door between the maze of narrow gold painted walls with chess pattern tile that led to the alley dumpsters. There was also a single outdated elevator complete with an accordion-style gate and round buttons. A few garden apartment windows that led into bushes if I was desperate. Once I designated my emergency exits, I used the stairs and went up to Freddy's unit.

The fifth-floor carpet smelled of mildew. Every door looked the same except Freddy's, which had a tacky sign that matched the magnet under the knocker. I looked over my shoulder to ensure the hall was clear before listening. *Quiet as can be.* Luckily, his door lock didn't match the key fob system. It gave a guy with a custodian key complete access. I gave one last glance from my left to my right before sticking my key inside and entering.

The unmistakable stench of bad milk emanated from Freddy's little place. Where my cheap apartment sacrificed location for size, his tiny studio flipped the script. There was a garage size room complete with a convertible futon, tiny entertainment system, and computer desk covered in gaming books. A small archway led to a tightly-packed kitchen with enough walkway for a single person to get stuck between the miniature fridge and oven. On the opposite side of the studio was a beaded curtain that led to an awkwardly exposed closet bathroom complete with pink out-of-date tile and stained porcelain.

What a shit hole; and I should know. I'd lived in every cheap shack and shanty Chicago had to offer. This place screamed *temporary, while I sort out my divorce.*

I wasn't a detective, but I read a lot of grimdark noir, which practically made me an expert of one liners and clue searching. I followed the standard spiral technique, searching the outer rims of the shoebox apartment before getting to the deeper little crevices and drawers. Beyond the scattered dice and pornography expected of a thirty-year-old role player was one obvious indication that the worst may have occurred for poor Freddy. All of his clothes were still neatly folded in his drawers and his bumper sticker covered luggage was in his closet. There was a half-gallon of milk with a week late expiration date and leftover Chinese takeout with the receipt stapled to the pint box. The purchase had been made ten days ago and was the only food for Freddy to live on. Poor people ate leftovers for breakfast, lunch, and dinner.

I tried to get into Freddy's computer but was locked out after several failed attempts to guess his password. I searched his drawers for tips that could help move along my sinking investigation. Hidden under a copy of a Codex Gigas was an obsidian stone dagger complete with an ivory bone handle. I was no historian, but an apparent Mayan snake had been engraved into the grip of the weapon. The creature's rattle-tail started at the pommel and slithered up as if its hissing mouth was regurgitating the blade. I filed the blade under *badass* and then pocketed it in my coat.

I slunk along to the bathroom in hopes that Freddy might have hid something in the bog.

Clever folk concealed valuables in plastic baggies taped inside toilet tanks. Such was not the case. All I found was a ratty flush valve. I was about to give up when my eye caught an unsettling piece of evidence. Bespattered on the inside of the shower curtain and along the pink tiles inside the tub was the lightest spray of what could only be dried blood. I crouched down near the stains and made out thin incisions within the fiberglass molding, the kind that are accidentally made when chopping vegetables on a kitchen carving board or hacking up a corpse. I shut my eyes and sighed.

Suddenly the buzz of voltage pursued by a strobe of yellow light flashed behind me. A throaty hum over my shoulder crooned an old Irish song I recognized as *The Black Velvet Band.*

"Tsk, tsk. I cannot believe you bit the bait, Danny Boy," a granulating voice called out behind me. I leapt up and removed Thing One. The Mad Knight smiled as he looked down the barrel of the silencer. "Jumpy, are we?" He leaned on the wall. The rawboned man had slicked his fern-flushed hair back into a ponytail, giving his cat eyes that much more impish definition. He wore an eighties style letterman jacket, red chested with white sleeves, over a dress shirt clipped to a leopard pattern tie. His taut leather pants clung over white high socks and dark loafers.

"How did you slip past the beaded curtains? They're impregnable alarms for teenagers smoking pot since the sixties."

"And her hair, it hung over her shoulder," he sang. *"Tied up with a black velvet band."* The Mad Knight paused, straightened out his back and stared at me. "I get around," he quashed before moving to sit on the closed toilet. "Buck, seriously, you are so much better than this." He stared down as his feet. He frowned, licked his thumb, and rubbed it along a scuff on his toe cap.

"What are you babbling about now?"

"Come now, laddie. Dub obviously wanted you to come here, and you fell right into his poorly spun trap. You should have known that's what the entire dog and pony show at that hobby store was about."

"Wait, so is Freddy actually dead?"

"Of course he is. My brother *always* kills his subject. It's like..." He shrugged. "...his thing."

I hung my head. *I'd killed poor Freddy.* "Come on, keep your chin up, Danny Boy."

"Why would he do that?"

"I don't know, the guy isn't all there." The Mad Knight tapped the side of his noggin.

"No, I mean why did your brother want me to come here?"

"So he could separate you from Luna, of course."

"Dothur, what are you talking about?"

"Ugh, I hate that name."

"Stop buying time, asshole, and answer the freaking question," I ordered. The Mad Knight straightened out. His face went blank.

"Oh, there we are. That's the Buck I like." He hesitated, wiping his lips before grinning. "I told ya before, *I spy*. My brother does too. It's why he took Freddy's face in the first place. He watches everyone like they're pieces on a chessboard."

"And you don't?"

"Nah, I'm a spontaneous voyeur. I like to shoot from the hip."

"You're seconds away from being shot in the hip, then the chest, and then your smirking face if you don't keep talking."

"Dub knew you had a soft spot for the little werewolf girl you stole from his rebellion. Once you packed your van like a mobile home this morning, my brother's girl-friend calculated that the statistical chance you'd join them deteriorated into the one percent range. They couldn't have that, so we wove a last-minute plan to press the matter by showing you fake Freddy in order to tempt you into making a mistake."

"Go on." I thumbed back the hammer of Thing One.

"I was supposed to post up here. I doubted you'd come

by, but if you did, I'd nab the little girl while you were rifling through Frederick's porn and take her to the safe house."

"But I didn't bring Luna."

For the first time, I saw The Mad Knight's eyes glimmer in true excitement. He leaned in and stared at me from the tops of his cat eyes. I could hear the slather of spit from his mouth as his lips stretched up to his dagger sharp cheekbones. The light bulb on his chest flickered.

"Exactly."

I pulled the trigger, firing three times. Silencers aren't like in the movies. There's no little chirp. The action of the gun calls out, but it's muffled. The faint echo hit my ears almost as quickly as The Mad Knight blinked out of existence. The trio of bullets cracked the pink tile behind him. I guided the pistol throughout the room but there was no one there. The son of a bitch had vanished.

I looked at the cracked ceramic. If Thing One was ever recovered by authorities, I'd be inculpated for Freddy's murder, but I could care less at the moment. Luna was in danger. Rosita, Dub, and the hag children were coming for her. The hairs on the back of my neck stood up.

I had to hurry.

I scooped up the hot shells in a weak attempt to clean up my trail and bolted out of Freddy's apartment. The lyrics from The Mad Knight's tune haunted me. I hightailed it from the complex to the sedan and sped home. I was fifteen minutes from the apartment, ten if I drove like Mad Max. I finally understood what that weight saddled on my shoulders was when I first arrived. My gut was trying to tell me that I was falling for a trap and that Luna was now in trouble.

19

The front door stood cracked open, and the salt line had been split in two. There was no one in my floor's hallway. Though even if there were, it wouldn't have stopped me from removing Thing One and Two before storming inside. I cleared the front room. I could see creepy little footprints along the salted carpet from tiny Oxfords. It appeared the spring-loaded spears had done their job. Vibrant red blood colored the tip of a butcher knife duct taped to a mop handle. A trail of the same candy apple gore dribbled into my kitchen. There were tiny bloody handprints on the linoleum kitchen floor accompanied by drag marks. I tried not to slip on the puddle and moved into the hallway toward the bedroom and bathroom. The trap near my bedroom window hadn't been triggered, which means that they'd only entered near the front of the apartment, the same section Dub and Rosita had explored during their visit.

I spun around to the bathroom. At first glance it appeared shut, but a light push on the surface revealed that the lock had been smashed and the door hem pried open. Someone, or something, had applied enough pressure to slip their little fingers into the pleat between the threshold of the wood and then pushed hard. I nudged the reinforced door with my foot hoping to find Luna huddled in the tub but fearing I'd only find her remains. I didn't know how I'd cope with the latter, but I found neither. A discarded hammer saturated in bright blood rested atop the pillows I'd softened the tub with, but Luna was gone. She'd put up a fight, but had been taken nonetheless.

My eyes welled with tears. I leaned on the bathroom wall and slid down into a heap. A stockpile of anguish soaked within my bones let go, pouring acrid heartache into every bit of my body. I planted my face in my hands and wept. Crying was foreign to me, especially the blubbering I was letting out. I didn't know how long it lasted, but when I finally came to, my knees were in my chest and my hands dug into my armpits. Evening shadows had fallen over the apartment. I cowered in a half-trance for another minute before coming to my senses.

My knuckles, which trembled on the stash of assorted items beneath my breast coat pocket, rubbed against a sharp paper corner. I dug inside and removed the business card from Selena. It was a handout for The Violet Hour complete with business hours and a general line. There was a management extension underlined in red pen.

Am I really about to call one enemy to deal with another?

I simmered in the idea. I'd been doing nothing but making enemies my entire life.

Enemies were easy. They couldn't betray you. If I really wanted Luna back, I'd have to earn it the hard way. I pulled out my phone and dialed the number.

"Hello," Selena's perky voice greeted. I wiped my eyes and took a breath.

"Selena," I said hoarsely. "I'm ready to talk."

"That's great, friend. I've talked to John earlier. He'd love to meet with you. How about you come by—"

"Tell John to meet me at 400 North Lake Shore Drive."

"Uh." Selena hesitated. "There isn't anything there."

"False. There's a half-block hole for the Chicago Spiral Tower. Funding died. Construction stopped. It's a metaphor for the hole that I'm in."

"Oh," Selena hummed. There was another pause. I assumed she'd put me on mute. "Okay, that will work, Mr. Shaw."

"It's Buck."

"Yes sir, Mr. Buck. Will midnight work for you?"

"Yes."

"Fantastic," she said with a giggle at the end. I wanted to smash her lips through the receiver but reminded myself I was making friends. "Anything else?"

"I'd ask for him to come alone, but I know that won't happen."

"I see. I'll let him know."

"Great. I'll see you tonight then."

"See you tonight, friend."

I pressed the red button that ended the call and tossed my phone on the bathroom floor. I felt like shit. The apartment was so quiet that it hurt my ears. There were no cartoons on the television or talking toys. I remembered this pain. The vacuum of nothingness that sucks out any other glint of life. It was the same silence after Denise had been murdered that had broken me quickly and driven me temporarily insane. There was only one way to escape. I needed to fix what I'd done.

I dragged myself off the floor and went into my room. I took inventory of everything that was even slightly considered an instrument of war and placed it along my bed. Along with Old Lilith, Thing One and Two, I added my old M40A3 long range rifle, a .22 revolver I kept beneath my pillow, and the Mayan knife I'd recovered from Freddy's studio. I grabbed the modern fit trench coat I'd bought myself for my birthday and packed it with every clip I'd stashed in the alcove under the closet. I shoved parts of the M40A3 on top of Old Lilith and in my jacket and then put the entire ensemble on. It was heavy, but manageable.

When I was done, I went back into the bathroom and pulled my electric clippers out of the drawer. I stared at the bedraggled collection of pillows in the tub while I plugged the shaver into a socket. The clippers buzzed. I brought it to my head and started shaving hair off my scalp. I turned to my reflection. My milky eye and bomb scars were more definite, as if they'd been highlighted with neon. I stared down the fool with a fresh buzz cut, dignifying that I'd gone all 2007 Britney Spears.

"*It's Britney, bitch,*" I jeered at my reflection and threw the clippers in the sink.

Shortly after, I grabbed the keys for the sedan and left into the summer night. The drive downtown was tolerable for a Friday. Maybe time passed quicker because I was so preoccupied fantasizing about bludgeoning Dub, Rosita, and The Mad Knight to death. The screams they'd shriek would be heard in Kankakee.

Once I arrived in the Loop, I made my way toward a quiet parking lot where Lake Michigan and the Chicago

River met. The parking lot was rarely used and sat on the opposite end of the river, directly parallel to my target, The Chicago Spiral Tower's pit. The abandoned cars and illegally docked boats coated in dust were a testament to the parking lot's seclusion.

The day had caught up to me. I had a few hours before the meeting, so once I ensured that I wasn't being watched within the parking grounds, I lowered the driver seat and tried to fall asleep. My mind raced to Luna. She was a tough kid, but it hurt to think how scared she might be. I took solace in knowing that they didn't want any information from her. Luna was a bargaining chip, *a hostage*. She shouldn't be harmed. Still, I wouldn't put anything past monsters like Rosita and Dub.

I don't know when I faded into sleep, but there was no dreaming. My body was too tired for that. There was only blackness and purpose. I woke up to my phone buzzing. I fumbled to answer but was too late. The alert told me I'd missed a call from Jumbo. *Fake Jumbo.* I thought about calling back and telling Dub that I was going to hang him with his own intestines, but then it dawned on me. Dub didn't know that the real Jumbo lived. Dub also didn't know that I'd been told the truth about the imposter. Dub was likely calling to play an angle. I needed to avoid a knee jerk reaction and think about how I'd respond. For now, I'd text and buy time.

Minor setback, I texted. *In the field. Call you soon.*

Please do, Fake Jumbo replied, adding an emoji sad face.

I checked the time and realized that I'd been out for hours. The harbor's parking lot was still empty. I decided to make my way to the Chicago Spiral's hole and scout it out before I met Dillinger. I used the Lakefront Trail along

Lake Michigan to access the bridge spanning over the
Chicago River. The overpass was mostly for cars but had a
thin pedestrian walkway that few people knew about. I
crossed the platform sitting above the spinach green
waterway and stopped at a blocked off stairwell that led
down to the construction site. I ignored the trespassing
signs and made my way down. The hole was still
surrounded by a block-long construction fence. It had
been years since the wired barricade was cared for. There
were multiple gaps one could widen or slip past to gain
access. The only complication was the various residential
skyscrapers encompassing the abandoned development.
Any spectator from the fifth-floor gym to the fifty- fifth-
floor office of the neighboring high-rises could see me
should they just so happen to be gazing down at the
barren development. I couldn't risk it. Luckily, I'd thought
ahead.

I removed a set of clothing kept blanketed over Old
Lilith's satchel. After I pet out the wrinkles, I donned the
yellow CPD traffic vest complete with a peaked cap. I
completed the look with a long metal Maglite. Once my
master disguise was complete, I left the cover of the lot and
made my way to a large gash in the fence. I pretended to
inspect the incision, knowing anyone from a high-rise
could be watching. The gate looked as if a truck had
backed into it, stretching a hole wide enough for a person
to fit. I made my way through and walked to the hole.

I'd found the place on Google Maps during a particu-
larly boring night. The man-made crevice was at least six
stories deep and wide enough to land a football field in it.
There were steel crates, a rusted bulldozer bucket, and
grime-covered construction helmets scattered throughout

the bottom. It was as if the crew had just never returned from a lunch break. A twenty-foot-tall silo-shaped structure that looked like a water tower sat inside with an abandoned toolbox on top. I had no idea of the steel cylinder's purpose, but decided to meet Dillinger at the bottom of its legs. There was a bar ladder built in the cement crown of the Spiral's hole that reached the full six stories down. I carefully descended, trying to balance all the weight from my Punisher arsenal. The climb took five minutes. I lit a cigarette in celebration. A swarm of fat rats scurried away from the light. Even Midwest vermin were overweight here.

I'd used to have one bad eye, but the other one had always compensated for its twin's faults. I was a terrible shot with pistols but put a rifle with sights in front of me and I was as accurate as hindsight. The same was true when I was scanning distances. I'd been trained for years. Even now when I closed my formerly impaired eye and used my strong one to compare landmarks, motion, and subtle idiosyncrasies, I could pick up on a fly playing hide and seek.

I spotted Dillinger's silhouette standing on the lip of the hole almost immediately. The guy was dead, but it was still unnerving just how still he could be. The soft lakeshore air wavered his hair and coat ever so slightly. I gestured with my cigarette hand, creating a dancing firefly in the night. Two pinpricks of light flickered from Dillinger's eyes. There was a blur and then Dillinger was gone. I remembered that he was lightning fast when he wanted to be. I felt the hairs on the back of my neck stand up. I reeled around with the Maglite and, as expected, Dillinger stood at arm's length.

"New haircut?" Dillinger jabbed as we exchanged glances. His dove-colored suit was custom tailored with a red Prada stripe on the vest. His irises shone an eerie hue of gold, the way candlelight flickers off of coins, and a set of mauve veins webbed around his neck. Tense with anxiety, I clicked back the hammer of the .22 hidden in my pants pocket. Dillinger must have known that I was edgy because he hurried to speak again. A set of jagged teeth protruded from beneath his thin lips. "It appears you're not in the joking mood."

"No."

"You and me both, Abercrombie." He pointed to his face. I narrowed my eyes. His skin was taught and sallow. The corners of his nostrils were painted with dark dry blood. It appeared Dillinger didn't take his vitamins this morning.

"What the hell is wrong with you?"

"My clip joint is on lockdown." Dillinger spat something black on the ground. "I don't want to risk my volunteers, so let's just say I'm going on a hunger strike."

"Why don't you just eat some of your staff?"

"I don't do that, *Buck*," he articulated. "It's bad for business. Besides, Dub has been doing a good enough job knocking off my associates without any help."

"Huh?"

"Jumbo told me you're up to date. Dub has been using Death's computer program to kill off all of my mortal allies. It's making it tough to continue my operations."

"My heart aches for you," I lipped while puffing my filtered killing machine.

"I know I'm not your favorite, but maybe we can put it past us."

I grimaced in response.

"If only temporarily." Dillinger casually stretched his back. "You see, we're at the height of a major predicament. Letting someone wield the power of death is bad business for everyone. Sure, at the moment Rosita and Dub are knocking off people that help keep my outfit operational, but it's only a matter of time before they start doing worse."

"Not really my problem, *John*."

"No, it's not, is it? You're what we used to call a gunsel, a reckless gunman. You only care about your work. I can respect that. That is." He halted, combing his hands through his greased hair. "Unless you're not doing your job."

"Are you trying to scare me?"

"I'm trying to tell you that we have a common set of enemies that need to be dealt with. They have me on the ropes, but you're not far behind, Abercrombie. When your boss returns from his vacation, I'm sure he won't be happy that you've helped give up his bailiwick."

"That is unless I join Rosita and Dub." I dropped my cigarette and smashed it with my heel.

"Okay, then why are you here, tough guy? Last I checked, you called us."

"They took Luna." I frowned. Dillinger winced.

"The little girl?" I crossed my arms and nodded. "That's terrible." I fluttered my eyes to push back tears. Dillinger's forehead creased. We stood and listened to far off police sirens, waiting until they died down before continuing our conversation. "No matter what you choose, I'm honestly sorry. I hope you get her back."

"Yeah, well that's why I'm here. You're a resource. You seem to have an edge when it comes to numbers."

"It's a slight edge, but it's shrinking quick. A lot of our supporters are going dark. They just got through with a war. They don't want another."

"Great."

"We do have one edge though that's even more valuable than numbers."

"What's that?" I asked while watching John remove his phone. His cold, dead finger was having trouble moving the interface, so after a few failed tries he removed a Stylus pen from his pocket. He chose the name *Wheels* from his contact list. He looked me over as it dialed. "We know more than they do."

The sound of Jumbo's nasally Midwest voice answered the phone. "Yo, dude," he greeted. "Bring the vehicles topside," Dillinger said plainly.

"Aye aye, Captain," Jumbo replied.

Dillinger put his phone in his jacket and began walking toward the bar ladder cemented to the wall. He took a step up before I interjected.

"Wait," I asserted. "I never said I was going to help you."

Dillinger smirked in the way historical photos had captured throughout the years. "You didn't have to."

I followed the vampire to the top of the Chicago Spiral's hole. There were a pair of vehicles with dimmers on when I reached the surface. Both were black Mercedes C-Class sedans. Their windows were darkened to a shade of black that made it impossible to distinguish any passengers. Dillinger gave a carefree wave and walked to the C-Class closest to us, opening the back door and holding it open for me. I could hear the air conditioning inside blowing out.

"Care to get some dinner?" Dillinger asked, his brows raised deviously. I closed my eyes and took a breath. I was between a rock and vampire. It was time to make a choice that for once didn't make enemies. I opened my eyes back up and headed to the sedan.

"I need to come back for my car," I blurted like a helpless tween being picked up for a sleepover.

"If you want, we can wait for you while you get your vehicle?"

"No. I'd rather cry in a Mercedes than a Ford."

20

The Chicago Water Tower was a historical landmark along the Magnificent Mile.

Nowadays it's the backdrop for expensive downtown shopping and site seeing, but in the nineteenth century, the eight hundred and fifty-nine foot building was vital for spotting fires. Boy, did they spot one. On October tenth of 1871, the Great Chicago Fire destroyed over three-square miles of the city. The Chicago Water Tower was one of the few buildings in the red zone left standing. Legend had it that when the flames reached the tower's grounds, they'd parted and went around the building.

It was after midnight when we rolled along 806 Michigan Avenue. The Chicago Water Tower roosted at the feet of the seventy-floor Park Tower, a skyscraper action-packed with fine dining, shopping, and the five-star Park Hyatt resort. We pulled up to the face of the hotel where two doormen in immaculate charcoal uniforms complete with kepi hats stood sentry. I'd never tried to pull up under the gold framed canopy lurched over the hotel for fear of rejection due to my car model alone. When Dillinger's cars rolled in, the doormen leapt from their posts with the same eagerness as dogs greeting their masters.

"Good evening, Mr. Lawrence," the smug voice of a smooth-faced doorman greeted.

"Oh." He ducked his head back, taking in that I wasn't Dillinger. "Apologies, sir."

"It's okay, Jacob," John called out from his side of the car as a second doorman opened his door. "Can you just hold the cars for a few? We won't be long." Jacob tipped the brim of his cap. Ken Doll, who'd been driving our Mercedes, exited the car, dug in his jacket, and handed Jacob a large brick of neatly stacked bills. Jacob and his partner traded glances before Jacob tucked the money in his breast pocket.

"Of course, Mr. Lawrence," Jacob saluted. "We'll park them in the front."

Dillinger's entourage exited the second car. Selena withdrew from the driver's seat, adorned in a flowing gown with a plush scarf and expensive looking boots. Her arms and neck were littered with loose jewelry. I didn't know a lick about fashion, but she seemed to be crushing the Bohemian thrown-together look. With her was a tall man in a double-breasted camel plaid suit. He wore a beret and sunglasses. He had graphite skin with shades of rotted pickle along the creases of his Van Dyke beard and a nose that looked as if it had been gnarled by dogs. On his finger was a large gold signet ring that matched Dillinger's. I couldn't tell if he was staring at me but I *could* tell that he wasn't good at disguising his undead condition. He looked like an undercover boogeyman.

Dillinger pressed his hands into his pants pockets and swaggered his way to the water tower seeded across the sub street, whistling as he did. I rolled my eyes before catching up to him. We crossed Tower Court, the small plaza of trees, grass, and planted flowers, toward the limestone walls at the base of the water tower. The castle-style building had been adapted into a boutique art museum for tourists. A sign across the door read *Closed* with the hours of operation below it. Ken Doll, Selena, and the mystery cannibal caught up to us as I peeked inside the window, pushing up on the tips of my toes. From the dim light of the security lamps were the framed original paintings of author and artist, Dr. Seuss.

"Please tell me we aren't here to see *The Cat in the Hat* exhibit," I lamented.

"No, Buck." Dillinger combed his sharp fingers through his hair. "Though I'm sure that's about your reading caliber." I frowned. Dillinger snickered. Everyone else stood quiet. "I, too, am running out of safe places to talk given the circumstances." Dillinger placed his index finger under his large canine tooth and bit down. There was an uncomfortable crunch. Dillinger traced his now bloody finger over the doorknob of the Tower's entrance. "So, we are going to a place where measures have been taken to keep out every copper, stool pigeon, and wet sock there is." A click came from the knob's lock. The dim interior lights glowing from the Tower's windows went dark. Dillinger turned the knob and the door opened. "Quickly now, Jumbo and Adam are waiting." The group entered the blackness without a care in the world. I stood outside by myself.

"Time to stop making enemies," I murmured under my breath. "Time to get Luna back."

I stepped inside and like some haunted horror movie, the door shut behind me, leaving me bathed in darkness. I was half tempted to dig into the satchel and remove Old Lilith's scope for its night vision but before I could, a cold hand took mine. It was small and soft. It tugged me and soon our feet were clapping on hard tile. I took note of our steps and the directions we turned as I trudged blindly. There was shuffling, the groan of metal, and the hiss of an air seal. I was tugged again and pulled toward a pinprick of tangerine light flickering at the bottom of a descending hall. I tread carefully, my heel finding a declining step. Soon the speck of light grew until it spread out along an arched doorway cascaded in Halloween orange. I followed the guiding hand through the threshold, where my eyes adjusted.

I didn't know what I'd been expecting, but it wasn't this. We were in the foyer of what appeared to be a knockoff Parisian cafe. Orange light gleamed from globe-shaped bulbs crowned on chandeliers along the baroque-trimmed walls. The distant whoosh of an espresso maker and bad bistro accordion reverberated from the long coffee house. The distinct bouquet of coffee filled the air, though there was an odd trace of a metallic tang. There were round, walnut coffee tables running parallel along a polished mahogany bar. Two ceiling-high bookshelves shouldered a cramped, abandoned stage. Despite the grand décor, it was the patrons that I paid most attention to. Dressed in business suits and hipster garb alike were *freaking* vampires.

There was a gaggle of wan-skinned emo types caked in

dark mascara with spider black apparel and brightly dyed hair. They had colorful tattoos inked on pale flesh, brightening their tortured art. Their eyes were brilliant shades of sapphire, emerald, and blazing white with pinprick pupils. A few had paint or clay stains along the fingers. All of them were frightfully beautiful like a belladonna bloom. Scattered between them were smaller bands of business types who waded in the dining hall like hungry crocodiles. Some read newspapers while others swiped tablets over steaming coffee. In the shadowy corners were twisted creatures with rubbery skin, bald, malformed heads, and bulging yellow eyes. Each had a grotesquely long pair of fangs protruding from the centers of their bat-like lips.

Dillinger led us to the back of the cafe toward a well-lit corner table surrounded by the Legion of Doom. Along with Adam, who was doing a terrible job of blending in with his worn leather jacket, ripped jeans, construction boots, and truck driver hat, was Jumbo. Jumbo had shaved and wore a t-shirt that read "*Sorry I'm late. I didn't want to come.*" He perched on top of his scooter, balancing his laptop along the center of the handlebars. The trio looked up from their conversation, making room as we pulled up spare chairs from another table.

I moved my chair against the wall and studied the fastest route to the exit. I knew that I was already in the wolf's den, but the soldier in me insisted. I scanned the group from left to right. They looked as excited as teens at a Barry Manilow concert. I stared back with my poker face. A distracted Dillinger peered near the register and waved someone over before rejoining the tension. He bit his bottom lip with a sharp canine, placing his twitchy palms on the tabletop as if to calm himself. He looked like he had fleas. Before I could fit a good one liner in, I felt the hairs on the back of my neck stand up. Ken Doll and Selena stared at something next to me. I turned to see what it was, only to find a stock-still barista appear out of thin air.

"Mr. Dillinger," the pasty woman caped in a green smock greeted. "Welcome back." She had a streak of turquoise dyed into her pixie-styled haircut and a pin-sized nose ring. "We were excited to hear that you'd be joining us. The usual, sir?"

"Please," Dillinger retorted. "Quickly if you could. I'm a little hungry."

"Of course," the barista responded. "Anyone else?" The hour was late, and I hadn't eaten dinner. A good cup of joe and a muffin sounded divine.

"Is there a menu?" I butted in. The barista gave me a healthy dose of side eye, dug into her smock's pouch, and planted a little black book into my hands. I ignored the judgment and read the list. There were typical categories like Espressos, Blended Beverages, and Cold Brews, but after reading the descriptions I quickly caught up to the horror novel set before me. There were blonde roasts, Americanos, and South American blends complete with blood types and ages. A sidebar promised that this cafe worked with farmers for one hundred percent ethically-sourced blood-coffee. It continued to blabber on about its commitment to pay fair wages for every organ harvester to build a better farming community. I must have had a distinct look on my face because everyone gawked, glared, or smirked.

"Do you just have regular coffee?" I clapped the menu shut and handed it over.

"Uh," the barista hummed. "I'll have to check the back."

"Great," I said dryly. "If there is, I'd just like a regular coffee, no blood or guts."

The barista didn't dignify me as she asked again, "Anyone else?" Everyone stayed quiet.

"Great, I'll be back shortly."

"Buck." Dillinger waved a hand at the undercover boogeyman. "This is DuSable. Together we run the Negative-One Union." DuSable bowed his head.

"*Bonsoir*." DuSable bobbed his head.

"DuSable runs the Rigor Mortis Society," Dillinger continued. "While I handle Algor Mortis."

"Crud and blood," DuSable piggybacked.

"That's very nice," I fussed, thinking of Luna in a trunk. "But this isn't a book club. I now know who you all are. We all hate the crazy rebels. You don't like them trying to topple your authority, and for me, they kidnapped my—" I held my tongue as I was about to say daughter. "Luna. That's the main reason I'm debating helping you. So, what's the plan?"

Jumbo straightened his broken glasses. "Dude, you really suck at introductions. Nonetheless, you're right. There's no time to waste. Let's recap. John here, elder local vampire, used his resources to help other undead like DuSable dethrone a warlock who was running Chicago's supernatural community with an iron fist. Since then, John has made enemies with the remnants, in particular a bruja named Rosita and her doppelgänger boyfriend Dub."

"Bruja?" I hesitated. "What's a bruja?"

"Central American witch," DuSable warned.

"Yes," Jumbo concurred. "Anyhow, in a desperate move

to regain power, the pair tricked my boy Death by killing me and replacing me with a Dub imposter that could control my *flawless* computer program from the boss man's apartment. A program that organizes mortal deaths. Meanwhile, the rebels arranged for Grim to go on vacation, but not before giving his power to kill everything to you, Buck. Their plan: trick you into willingly giving over the all-powerful scythe in order to circumvent protective measures set by the All Mighty. However, as you stumbled along, you learned the truth. They're a bunch of assholes. When you saw past their charade, they tried to force your hand by stealing your kid. And now, that about catches us all up."

Jumbo's words hit me like an uppercut. Outsiders saw what I felt. Luna and I had a bond. I would move mountains to keep her safe. A voice inside wondered if Jumbo intentionally used the words *your kid* to get my help. He didn't have to. I was already hard pressed. Maybe he sincerely thought that Luna and I were a mini family. That thought woke me up.

"Great." I knocked on the tabletop. "So what do they have going for them?"

Adam cleared his throat. "To start," he said with his Hans Gruber accent. "They have an army of soulless children at their disposal."

"Yeah," I cut in. "What the hell are those things, devils?"

Dillinger snorted as he traded glances with DuSable. "No, devils are much worse. Trust me, I know one." DuSable shook his head.

"It's complicated," Jumbo added. "We're still trying to work out the details, but dark magic perverted these

Unmentionables into monsters with an insatiable hunger for flesh. Murder keeps them going, making them fast and hard to kill. They're not undead. They're what we classify as aberrations."

The barista reappeared out of nowhere, placing a saucer held mug in front of Dillinger. "One Romanian dark," she declared. "Negative O with a hint of nutmeg." I stared disgusted at the latte art spread like a skull over his amber colored drink. The barista gave me a glance and in a passive aggressive manner said, "Yours will be up shortly, *sir*. We found a bag of *regular* in storage." She walked away with a counterfeit smile. Dillinger eagerly sipped at his cup, leaning his head back as he savored the flavor. Color returned to his once pallid flesh and his mauve veins abated.

"Does no one see the irony in this?" I asked.

"Anyhow," Jumbo cut in with an amused tone. "Besides the army of evil children, there are the evil geniuses. Rosita is a powerful witch that has studied Brujería under her Master and former head of Chicago, Collin, for decades. Dub is not only a shapeshifter, but Death's love child, and is immune to every conventional type of dying."

"Uh," I hummed. "Did Death go out for a pack of cigarettes and not come back?" Ken Doll and Selena chuckled like a laugh track.

"Opposite," Jumbo answered. "Dub's mommy seduced Death."

"Noted," I blurted.

"Don't forget," Dillinger added as he licked his lips of foam. "That Dub and Rosita have the power to kill off all mortals and have been killing my human support with their *flawless* program."

"We're working on that, dude," Jumbo asserted.

"There's Dub's brother, The Mad Knight." I tapped my finger on the table. It all started to sound pretty insurmountable.

"Yeah, man," Jumbo dove in. "I've been doing my research on Dothur. He was said to have disappeared into Arcadia centuries ago. Rumor has it that he died or lost his mind."

"Guys," I proclaimed. "I am telling you that I've had several conversations with this guy. He's nuts for sure, but very much alive."

"If that's the case." Jumbo rubbed the back of his neck, "then he has an arsenal of fairy powers."

"Oh fantastic," I aired and wiggled fingers in a mock celebration. "Yay, I'm so happy."

"Dude." Jumbo shrugged. "We never said it would be easy."

"Well." I rubbed the top of my freshly buzzed head. "What do we have going for us."

"You're looking at it." Dillinger waved his hand to the group. "A tech guy." Dillinger pointed at a typing Jumbo. "A revenant." Dillinger's hand moved to a waving DuSable. "Frankenstein's monster." Adam growled as John directed his hand to him. "Two blood thralls," Ken Doll and Selina gave a glamor shot pose. "And an old vampire bank robber."

"Ugh," I gasped. "What about the Undead Union?"

"We've been over this. They're afraid," Dillinger scoffed. "Cheating death has serious consequences in the afterlife. Those that survived the uprising are terrified to risk their immortality again. Rosita and Dub are scary."

"Guys," I shouted. "Please tell me we have something going for us."

"We do, man," Jumbo objected. "We have information they don't. For starters, they think I'm dead. I'm not, which is great because I know the interworking of Death's domain. We also were able to obtain the key to Death's place, which could help us stop these random deaths."

"Oui," DuSable verified. "I've reached out to Mary. She may be willing to help us with a boat, but her asking price is steep."

"Cool, brother," Jumbo complimented. "That's a plus. Another advantage, Buck, they think you're clueless. You're really good at it."

"Thanks," I lauded in a plain tone. "So is that it?"

"Well, then there's your powers," Jumbo said nonchalantly.

"What powers?" I chastised. "I don't have any powers."

"No?" Adam barked. "How about when you coughed up ectoplasm in The Violet Hour's bathroom?"

"Oh, that." I clucked my tongue. "I don't know how that happened."

"Do you really not know about your deathly privileges?" Jumbo questioned.

"I have no clue," I admitted. "What's with the smoke? I just assumed it was excess lung butter from a lifetime of tobacco abuse."

"Buck." Jumbo leaned into his scooter. "You're going to start to feel some changes in your body. This is natural and means you're growing into a man."

"Are you going to tell me or not?" I pleaded. "It kind of seems important since we are fighting an insurmountable war."

"Does no one appreciate good humor?" Jumbo cleared his throat. "Okay dude, when you were killed by Dillinger," Dillinger winced, "the boss man denied your death."

"So I'm undead?" I blurted.

"Not quite." Jumbo pinched his fingers together as he explained. "Vampires, wights, and ghosts are undead. They walk the line between mortality and oblivion. *You* are bound by the fundamental forces of Death. You've been returned to life and are anchored by Mr. Grim's very essence. Spiritualists in the Victorian era dubbed it as ectoplasm and used to take weird ass pictures of it coming from psychics' ears and crap."

"The smoke?" I guessed.

"Good," Jumbo complimented. "It's the energy of the afterlife. The electric that charges us as we pass over."

"So." I looked at the palms of my hands. "The Grim Reaper blocked my death, but he also made me a living generator for whatever makes up the afterlife?"

"While that's likely the most dumbed down explanation possible," Jumbo said through his stained teeth. "You're starting to get it. The boss man had to in order to keep you alive."

"Okay, great, so I can make cool smoke rings," I bleated. "How's that going to help us?"

"Well." Jumbo leaned back in his scooter. "Until the boss man removes the anchor, it's not easy to kill you. The threads of ectoplasm will always try to sew you back up. Also, interns before you have been able to manipulate the ectoplasm to create dope as hell manifestations, but that's before my time."

I gave Jumbo a blank stare for longer than I should have. After I felt I'd made him uncomfortable enough, I spoke up. "Okay, so we have a small band of volunteer undead, a few secrets, and I can cough death fog. Not the best sell, but I'm in nonetheless, so what's the plan?"

Dillinger leaned back in his chair, staring at me from the tops of his sockets. He cracked his neck before speaking in a low tone. "They want the scythe, plain and simple. They tried to pretend they were your allies, but that didn't work, so now they've taken a hostage. It won't be long before they reach out to you and give you their demands."

"Humor me," I pleaded. "What should I do when they demand Old Lilith?" Dillinger gave his signature smirk. "Give it to em'."

Dillinger explained his idea. I had to admit I liked it. It involved a bit of caution, some subterfuge, and a lot of guts. I gave my input, sprinkling a bit of Buck Palasinski into the design before agreeing. I heard the video game level up sound effect as I did. Much like all arrangements, this could all go sour very quickly, ending in death and destruction for us all. Still, it was my best chance of getting Luna back. We went over the second and third draft until finally wrapping up the plan into one solid blueprint. The vampire barista finally delivered my plain coffee just as we put the final touches on everything. I took a sip of the bitter coffee, giving me the much-needed boost I desired to depart back onto the streets.

"I had no idea that happens to werewolves." I finished my cup of coffee and clapped my hands together. "All we need now is for them to contact me."

"I'd expect it to happen shortly," DuSable predicted. "They're getting antsy."

"Great." I stood up. "Well then how do I get out of here?"

"Ardicus will see you out," Dillinger declared while pointing to the Ken Doll. "Ardicus?"

"Your name is Ardicus?" I laughed.

Ardicus' face went flush. "Yes, Buck." He looked down at his feet. "Now please, come with me."

I waited for Ardicus to scoot out of his chair and approach the exit. I gave Dillinger one last glance.

"John," I announced. "If this works, I'll be a very happy man. As a courtesy to you, though, I'm going to warn you now, don't expect a pass should Death still want your head." Adam pounded his fist on the table, Jumbo murmured, DuSable groaned, but Dillinger stood stock still. He looked off into the distance, either pondering or brooding. As if snapping out of his trance, he lifted his head up and traded stares with me.

"I'd expect nothing less," Dillinger said calmly.

Ardicus took me back into the darkness, guiding me with his chilled hand. I followed closely until we were outside the water tower. A party bus full of drunk baseball fans singing 'Go Cubs, Go' along Michigan Avenue welcomed me back to the surface. Ardicus and I waited for their chants to fade away.

"Can I offer you a ride back to your car?" Ardicus offered.

"What the hell is a blood thrall?"

"Oh, it means that I'm part of Dillinger's trusted entourage."

"What does it really mean?"

"It means that he shares a drop of blood with Selena and I every few weeks for a little taste of his power.

Nothing crazy, but we can mimic diluted versions of what Dillinger does on a whim. In return, we're loyal to him."

"And you like that?"

"I like being liked."

"You really trust your boss, don't you?"

"Oh, yes," he cooed. "I know what people think when they hear his name, but he's not that man anymore."

"You sure?"

Ardicus' plastered smile faded. "Oh, yes," he echoed.

I removed a new pack of cigarettes from my coat, twisting the plastic wrap off of it and crumbling it into a ball. I used my lips to remove a cigarette from the pack with one hand while handing Ardicus my trash with the other. He took the crumpled plastic and stared hard at it like it was a murder weapon.

"I'll walk," I told Ardicus, cutting through the plaza toward the sidewalk. I didn't look back to see his reaction.

I trudged south along Michigan Avenue to retrieve the sedan. It was a little over a mile and I thought the hike could do me good. The city doffed its gray, morning work suit, adoring itself in an evening gown. Chicago was elegant at night. Her buildings twinkled with gold lit windows and ruby radio antennas. Her steel turned shades of brunette, and her glass polished into sapphires. She smiled on her guests, brandishing modern art and gardened parks. It had a way of easing my mind. The streets were calm and still cooling from another summer day. Even night was bright in Chicago due to light pollution from streetlamps, high rise windows, and passing cars. It caused the Chicago River to sparkle red, yellow, and orange as I crossed Dearborn Street Bridge. I didn't know why I couldn't contain the venom inside me, but Dillinger's

ghoul-gang had done their best to tolerate it. They must
have been desperate. Luckily for them, I was too. I
lumbered to the sedan and reminded myself that I needed
to try harder to be a team player. I'd been a lone wolf for
too long and I wouldn't survive the wild much longer if I
didn't join a pack. Neither would Luna.

21

The apartment waited up for me but refused to clean up any of its mess. My traps bent over crooked furniture. Strewn kitchen magic crunched under my feet. Dry blood pooled along fractured glass. I stumbled from room to room like a drunk ghost taking inventory of what needed to be cleaned up in the morning. Part of me hoped I'd find Rosita, Dub, or The Mad Knight hiding in a closet, but all I discovered was that I had roaches again.

I looked over my phone. There were no new messages. My stomach turned at the thought of Luna spending a night alone with these monsters. I took a deep breath and shook out the image. My body was tired. If I wanted our plan to work tomorrow, I'd need my rest. I draped Batman's gadget-filled jacket over my nightstand and flopped onto my bed.

Sleep took me quickly and before long I was suffering from nightmares of abandonment, forgotten failure, and let downs.

WHEN MY EYES opened back up it was morning. For the first time in years, I hadn't jolted up to the three o'clock missiles.

After rechecking my phone, I rallied to the coffee maker and waited for it to brew a decanter of black. The cheap mud tasted like dirt, but shook me awake nonetheless. After my third cup, I climbed over debris and baptized myself under the lukewarm water of my Lunaless shower. Complacency let you forget how bad things can get again. Typically by this time I would have hit the gym, filled myself up with breakfast, and started researching my next job. This morning, I felt hollow.

I'm not sure how long it was before the water turned icy, but it was my signal to move on. I dressed in my funeral blacks along with the twenty-pound jacket and left to do my part of Team Dillinger's plan. I headed to the hardware store to pick up a can of silver spray paint, an eight ounce can of Kona wood stain, and a hand-sized carton of industrial duty rock salt. When I reached the counter, my card declined. The pig pink man with a face like a possum and name tag that read "Hank" gave me a stare that told me I was useless. A line of uniformed janitors and commercial painters behind me balanced supplies in wait.

"Wife must have gotten a hold of my work card," I explained. *You wish you had a wife and job, loser.* Hank pursed his lips. "I'll just put this all back."

I pretended to put back the wood finish before checking over my shoulders. When the coast was clear, I pocketed the items and headed for the door. Hank didn't take note. I cringed as I exited, fearful of a hidden security scanner, but no alarm went off. I hurried back to the sedan like a child who stole candy and turned the key to get in. The low fuel symbol on my dash flashed. I pressed my forehead onto the steering wheel and tried to get a grip.

Buck, this is stupid and awkward, but it will pass. Focus.

I straightened up and headed to the closest gas station. I scoured the car from cup holders to floor mats in search of spare change. I came up with a dollar and ninety-six cents. I walked into the pay station with my head low and handed over the coins. The young woman behind the counter forced a smile, removed four pennies from the spare change bowl and rang up two dollars. I felt my face go flush at her mercy. I returned to the sedan and pumped my half gallon of unleaded. The gas needle crawled a centimeter forward as I started the car. It would be enough to get to *Gamer's Pair-a-Dice*.

I circled the hobby store before pulling into the parking lot. The alley looked like it had before a Mortal Kombat scene broke out, and the van sat in front of the store in one piece. I had no desire to go into *Gamer's Pair-a-Dice*. I wasn't certain how everything had played out after my escape, but it wouldn't help me at the moment to find out. I took what I needed from the sedan, locked the doors, and hurried to the van. Before I could unlock the driver side lock the jingle of the hobby store's door rang out behind me.

"Buck," a soft female voice called out. I cringed with the van key over the lock. "Hello," the woman sang. I whirled around. Bethany wore dark business casual clothes. Her usually curly blonde hair had been straightened. She'd highlighted her eyes and lips with makeup.

She looked extra lovely. "What are you doing here so early?" She ogled my suit, "and so dressed up?"

"I, uh, have a job interview." The weapons packed into my coat felt a hundred pounds heavier. Bethany, who was carrying a bag with a freshly purchased gaming book, closed the distance. She extended her open hand and rubbed the top of my head.

"Wow, haircut too, huh?"

"Uh, yeah." I straightened out my satchel, subconsciously tugging it so it hung over my stomach. "I went a little too short."

"No, no. It looks good. You look intense."

"Intense?"

"Yeah." She grinned. "Like a secret agent, sexy but dangerous."

"I've never been a martini guy." I tried to sound natural. Bethany snorted. "Question for you. Is Darren inside?"

"Of course. Why?"

"We had a…" I hesitated. "Weird exchange last time we saw each other."

"Oh, he told me."

"He did?"

"Of course he did. All I wanted to do is pick up the new adventures guide to read on my lunch break, but Darren pounced."

"What did he say?"

"He droned on about you ruining his promotional video. He said you had some sort of army flashback and started going off on everyone for sharing your personal information."

"Is that it?"

"Eh, I wish. He went on and on about the legality of

sharing customer information. I tried to defend you, but the guy loves to talk about you. I think he's just jealous because—"

"That's all he told you?" I interrupted.

"Well," she stammered. "He said you may have lost him some customers. Apparently, Freddy never came back after your rant. Darren thinks he's scared that you'll call the cops on them, but I assured them that you aren't that kind of guy." A current of relief released my body from its stiff posture. Apparently, no one had seen what happened.

"Hey, wait." Bethany's voice climbed two octaves. "Where's Luna?"

"Yeah," I quavered. "I need to pick her up soon."

"Oh? You found a babysitter?"

"Something like that."

"You know I can watch her if you ever need. I wouldn't charge you."

"Hey, Bethany, I'm running late."

"Oh shoot, I'm sorry."

"No worries, I just have to go."

"Yeah, of course. See you for next game session?"

"Uh." I thought about everything I still needed to do to get Luna back. "Maybe."

"Okay, well good luck with the interview."

"Thanks." I hurried to unlock the van. "See you soon."

I jumped into the driver's seat and woke the beast up. Bethany gave a wave from the sidewalk before heading to her car. I smiled then checked the dashboard. I nearly cheered when I saw the gas tank was three-fourths full. I kicked the vehicle into drive and headed downtown.

The weekend brought much needed rest to the roads. It was the tail end of a hot summer and the first signs of respite were in sight. A parade of rain clouds blanketed the sun. After a short trip down the Eisenhower Expressway, I was back at the lonely harbor parking lot that rested under Lakeshore Drive.

I climbed into the back of the van and removed the stolen paints. I read the can of wood stain, which promised a quick one hour dry, before using a shammy cloth lying near a spare tire to spread varnish on my art project's wood. Afterwards, I drenched silver spray paint over the metal. The fumes in the van forced me to retreat. I gasped between parking spots and ditched boats. As I did, I saw a sign for *DuSable Harbor* pointed toward the nearby docks. I was embarrassed to admit it, but I never knew the pier had a title. I relished in my static paint high and thought back to the undead boogeyman at the coffee house. Could Dillinger's partner be Jean Baptiste Point du Sable, founder of Chicago? Doped on fumes, I wondered if he had quite the same odor in the 1780s.

Seagulls squawked above. I looked up at the clouds; they warned that there'd be rain soon. I gave it another minute before reopening the van's rear double doors. The bitter perfume of the paint was intense, but far less potent than before. I kept the back of the van open and leaned on the vehicle's wall. The phone in my pocket buzzed. I hurried to peel it out of my too-tight dress pants and saw that I had a text from an unknown number.

Shall we discuss an exchange? The text read. I leaned my head back, took another breath, and navigated the phone's buttons to take a screenshot. I sent the photo to the number on The Violet Hour's business card. Not shortly after I received a response.

Perfect, my friend, the reply read. I assumed it was Selena. *Try to coax them into meeting tonight at the location.*

How the hell do I do that, I wrote back. I read my draft, deleted it and then texted *Cool.* I stared at my phone for a moment. Just staring at the text from Rosita or Dub irked me.

This was my only chance to get Luna back. One mistake and I could give our entire plan away. I hung my thumb over the digital letter pad for what felt like an eternity before finally putting words down onto the text line.

I'm not playing games, I texted. *Tell me how to get Luna back.* The goal: advertise my temper while playing into a feigned ignorance. Or at least I hoped. The three periods of an ellipsis told me someone on the other side was texting back. My phone rang with an answer.

Listen carefully. If you want the child back unharmed you will give us the rifle Death bequeathed you.

I blew air from my nostrils to let off steam and phase out the mental noise. I tried to think happy thoughts, like my wizard, Sarsicus, casting a fireball spell at mind flayers or Tom Hanks dancing on a giant foot piano. Finally, when I felt the time was right, I answered the text.

Fine. We exchange tonight.

Excellent. We will text the meeting spot shortly.

NO WAY, I wrote in all caps. *I choose the location if you want the rifle.*

There was a delay before the next message came through. *Tell us the place and time.*

The hole where the Chicago Spiral Tower was supposed to be built. Midnight.

This time, the reply was quick. *We'll see you then.*

In a last act of defiance, I answered. *Bring Luna and*

leave the bullshit at home. I checked my sentence while it sent. My eyes went wide as my phone turned the word bullshit into emojis of a cow's cartoon head and a swirl of brown smiley poop.

"Damn it. Who ever invented emojis needs to die in a sharknado."

I took the path that led north to the bridge, crossed the river, and hurried to the abandoned construction site. Once past the fence, I descended the ladder to the subterranean play land and went to work. I placed the Mayan knife, .22 pistol, and extra ammunition for Thing One and Two in the designated areas. I took the carton of industrial duty rock salt used for melting ice and poured it in a closed circle around the silo's foundation. Finally, I climbed the bar ladder along the silo wall and placed my last item on top, balancing it on a canopy bar used as welder's perch. When I was done I returned to the surface, soot covered, but finished.

I wondered how well my planted tricks and traps would hold up against the rebellion's supernatural abilities. Jumbo told me that Death's mysterious anchor not only kept me from dying but gave me powers of my own. Death's past protégés were able to manipulate the ectoplasm stirring inside of them. I wondered how they figured out how to wield it in the first place. Was it a serendipitous sneeze that caused an intern to shoot an afterlife lightning bolt from their nose or did it take eons of deep concentrated coaxing to release, like the morning after Taco Bell?

The viscous substance patched me up well enough, but otherwise, it didn't seem too handy at the moment. If sliming people with pearly puke was the next lesson in ectoplasm class, then I'd bring a doctor's note. First things first, I needed Death to promote me. That meant cleaning up this mess I was in. I ignored the self-deprecating futilitarian in me and decided to get back to saving Luna.

It was nearing lunch time, and a chill cooled the air. The sky looked like secondhand smoke. My stomach rumbled, but my wallet remained anorexic. If I wanted to stay sharp for tonight's meeting, I'd need food. *Being poor sucked.* I remembered that there was one last pack of Vienna hotdogs in the fridge at home with my name on them. So I loaded everything back into the van for what might be my last trek home.

I climbed to the stairs of the apartment door, only to be met by an envelope taped to my door that read "*Eviction Notice.*" I snatched the envelope and read it. The letter inside informed me that I had one week to vacate the premise unless I paid back rent, late charges, and taxes. The total bill read like something out of a Final Jeopardy score. I crushed the paper in my hands and entered the apartment.

I put a pot of water on the stove before opening up the fridge. There was a lot of real estate inside. The condiments along the door stared at me in disapproval. I collected the frankfurters and threw them into the pot to simmer. I logged onto my laptop, searching for Jean Baptiste Point DuSable. A list of historical threads pulled up on my browser. I leapt between links, reading up on the boogeyman's life before his wiener shriveled up and fossilized into retirement. *I must be hungry.* I collected the warm hotdogs from the boiling water, placed them in the cradle of partially stale sesame seed buns, and began my feast. Somewhere out there a dietitian was crying.

Little was known of Jean Baptiste Point DuSable's past

prior to the 1770s. Born of African descent, the handsome
and well educated du Sable had started his career as a
supply trader, traveling from French Louisiana north to
French Canada. He'd boldly taken his trading business
down the uncharted Mississippi River where he'd sold to
travelers. While in Illinois, he'd married a Potawatomi
woman named Kitihawa, and later settled along the mouth
of the Chicago River in the 1780s. There he'd sold bread,
flour, and pork out of his log cabin at inflated prices to
make a mint. Decades later, he sold his property and
moved south until his documented death in 1818.

However, according to *IgotStonedinSalem.com*, an occult
website for practitioners of magic, there was a Bokor priest
in New Orleans that claimed to be the student of Jean
Baptiste Point du Sable. The article went on to say that
Jean Baptiste Point DuSable had been a powerful voodoo
priest in life, which helped bring him his fortune. Later, he
ascended from death to seek revenge upon those that
wronged him through a powerful voodoo ritual. How he
was wronged or who his student had been, wasn't
mentioned in the article, but if any of this was even slightly
accurate, it would explain the rotted man I had coffee with.
Jean Baptiste Point DuSable was a voodoo revenant.

I finished the last of my third hotdog. My traps had
been set, my projects completed, and stomach filled. There
was nothing more for me to do but wait. So long as
Dillinger did his part, this plan just might work. I thought
about how I'd warned him before I left the coffee house.
Men that dealt in death tended to respect honesty, no
matter how brutal. I hope he'd taken what I'd said as
advice and not a threat. Otherwise, Dillinger might have

been tempted to backstab me tonight. *Probably not the best idea you've ever had in retrospect, Buck.*

The apartment's calm was deafening. I smoked another pair of cigarettes, staring at a grain in floor's wood until a listless daze fell over me. I really needed Zoloft. A cool breeze blew through the broken window. Distant thunder foretold an omen I couldn't interpret. All I wanted was to save Luna. The only people I planned to kill were monsters. I was the good guy for once. *Right?* Puzzled, a voice rang out in my head. It was the words The Mad Knight uttered.

We are not proper men, Buck.

22

It was the clap of thunder that woke me. It had been so loud that, for a second, I thought I was back in Afghanistan. I stood instinctively, knocking the ashtray off my lap. The light drizzle outside matured into a proper storm. The apartment was dark. I pulled out my phone to see what time it was. The clock on the wall read ten minutes past eleven. I was cutting it close. I saw I had one text. It was from Fake Jumbo.

Updates? It read. I slid the display and cleared the text.

"I have a date for you." I tucked my phone into my coat pocket. "With five pretty little ladies in jackets." I kept egging myself on as I collected my car keys. "They've been good little girls all week, but today ain't no school night." I gave myself one last glance in the bathroom mirror. I was disheveled and pale. Was this really how I wanted to look when I died? I ran my face under some water, straightened my tie out, then slapped color in my cheeks. I stared at myself again.

"Redemption time, you piece of shit."

I returned to the dining room, squeezed on my leather gloves, grabbed my coat, and marched out of the door. It was game time. I flicked my coat's lapel up as the rain trickled down my neck. I gave the sky a stare that said *don't push me*. There was a flash of lightning but no thunder. I took my time walking to the van. Getting my head right was far more important than being prompt at the moment. I had to convince myself that I was the baddest man on the block. I hopped in the van, let the engine call out into the night, and then pushed the pedal down with purpose. The beast kicked up mud. I flipped on the playlist titled "*Walk Like a Badass*" on full volume. By the time I neared downtown, I felt brazen enough to drink honey straight from a damn beehive.

I parked in my usual spot under Lake Shore Drive. I had fifteen minutes left on the clock.

This was the first time I was going unarmed to anything. I felt exposed. Anxiety tried to rise to the surface, but I kicked its gasping head back under water. If circumstances called for violence, I'd just have sore knuckles in the morning. I collected the briefcase used for businessman disguises and trading Punisher comics. It was heavier now with Old Lilith in it. By the time I tightened my mental bootstraps, there were ten minutes left.

I sang Louis Prima's *Just a Gigolo* to calm myself while walking north along the Lakefront Trail onto the steel bridge and crossed the Chicago River. I noticed a long barge docked alongside the construction site stacked with cargo crates the size of semi-trailers that hadn't been there before. I took note, used my backdoor path to sneak near the construction site, and approached the slit in the Spiral Tower's fence. There were five minutes left.

Rain clouded my vision with blends of pewter, slate, and charcoal from the hazy concrete backdrop. I slopped through the gravel's muck. Five figures stood at the lip of the Spiral's hole. A petite form matching Rosita's held up an umbrella. Huddled beneath it was a small silhouette with slumped shoulders gripping a doll. *Luna.* On Luna's opposite end was a hunched body with the build of a professional wrestler. A soaked tuxedo clung to their thick shoulders told me it was Dub. Adjacent to him was a wiry figure flushed in shadow. They held a heavy pistol at a fifth person perched on their knees. I closed the distance and saw that the man with the gun was none other than The Mad Knight. He wore a fisherman's slicker and had his green hair braided into twin pigtails resting on each shoulder. At the bottom of his barrel was a wincing Dillinger.

I tried not to show signs of shock, swaggering up with my hands in my pocket.

"*When the end comes I know.*" I planted myself a few yards away. "*That I'm just a gigolo. Life goes on without me.*" The group stared at me. "Oh, hello," I greeted with my best crazy eyes.

"Mr. Palasinski," Rosita announced. She had painted her face with a Día de Muertos skull complete with webs along her forehead and flowers over her brows. A necklace made of animal bones hung from her neck. "Thank you for your promptness."

"It's Buck," I corrected.

"Apologies," Rosita conceded. "I'd nearly forgotten. Now, if you don't mind, my associate here will now frisk you for security reasons." I shrugged. Dub plodded over to me, his hair flung over his face. His white Mickey Mouse gloves patted my chest, ribs, and underarms with authority. He was strong. Luckily, I wasn't armed. After fondling my thighs, Dub straightened his back and returned to his post alongside Luna. "I'm sure you may be asking yourself why our friend Mr. Dillinger decided to join our little meeting."

"Not really." I shrugged. "Luna, you okay?" Luna nodded.

"He was caught surveying our meeting place," Rosita explained. "You wouldn't have any idea as to how he knew where we were meeting, would you?"

"Sounds like our phones are bugged or something," I deflected. "You should probably use a burner. Now do you want the scythe or not?"

Rosita narrowed her lips under a sterile stare. "Yes, let's complete the transaction. The child for the scythe. Show us the merchandise please." My hands hesitated. I flicked the brass hasps and opened the briefcase. A disassembled Old Lilith greeted them. Dillinger shook his head. "Excellent. Now, please, assemble the rifle, Buck."

I flung a suspect look, but no one budged. After a long pause, I pulled the stock from the briefcase and connected it to the remaining parts. Even in the rain I could put a rifle together in seconds. When Old Lilith was complete, I showcased it to the group. Rosita looked to Dub. He grunted.

"Excellent, Buck," Rosita applauded. "Now give it to Dub."

"Absolutely not, Mrs. Potato Head," I chided. "I get Luna first." Dub cracked his neck. "There're only five bullets in the chamber. I have no other weapons. You hold all the cards. The least you can do is assure me that I'm not going to be double crossed. Send me the girl."

"Agreed, Buck." Rosita pulled the umbrella over her head so that the storm showered down on Luna. Luna cringed. "Dub, please escort the little one to Buck." Dub did as told, and guided Luna by her shoulders. Luna picked up her pace and hugged my leg. I pet her cheek then tucked her behind me. "Now hand the rifle to my associate, Buck."

I remembered what Jumbo told me. Unless I did this willingly, Old Lilith couldn't be taken. It was up to me now. I closed my eyes, weighing everything one last time. Giving them the rifle meant we might be able to get out of here. It was super bad though for the future.

"No, you twit," Dillinger muttered. In an instinctive reaction, I held out Old Lilith.

"Take it," I commanded. Dub hastily tugged the gun out of my hands and backed away. An emotional weight stirred in my stomach. Dub took several eager steps backwards. Dillinger lowered his head. The Mad Knight gave his T-rex grin. Even the ever-frigid Rosita's hands trembled. It was done.

Rosita cleared her throat. "We'll need to ensure that Buck truly has given us the firearm willingly. Dothur, please stand up the prisoner."

"Stand up, laddie," The Mad Knight commanded in his junkyard voice. Dillinger glared at me before coming to his feet. He'd warned that these creeps were as cliché as two-timing villains could get. Greed warps logic. The Mad Knight motioned his pistol toward the edge of the hole.

"Hold on there, tiger." I pointed to The Mad Knight. "This wasn't part of the deal."

"No it wasn't, Buck," Rosita agreed, her lips slithering into a hard line. "However, Dillinger is not just a liability.

He's our sworn foe. Punctuating his skull with a bullet is necessary. That is," she delayed. "Unless he's your ally after all."

My spine stiffened. I traded a stare with John, whose copper eyes waned. "I warned I'd likely have to kill you, John." I shrugged, secretly studying the foreground for an escape route for Luna. Dillinger's nostrils flared. Dub lifted Old Lilith and targeted Dillinger through the scope, ignorant to the measures needed to properly aim a long-range rifle. Still, he'd need to be blind and rocking on a speedboat to miss Dillinger from this range. Dub checked the safety. I covered Luna's eyes.

"Last words, traitor?" shrilled Rosita.

Dillinger grimaced at Rosita. Rain dripped from his nose. He showed her his sharp, clenched teeth before returning his attention to me. "Buck, I told you, these people will betray you. Don't let them do this."

"Ugh," Rosita snarled in disgust. "Shoot him, Dub."

Dub fired. The bullet hit Dillinger straight in his heart. A blemish of red colored his dress shirt as the impact jolted him backwards down the crater. A splash echoed from below. I'd seen a lot of people get shot, but this was different. John Dillinger had spent his entire life trying to escape death and now his dead body lay at the bottom of a six-story hole. It was like watching a monument bulldozed. Still, better him than Luna.

"Something catch your eyes, brother?" The Mad Knight jested. "I'd have gone for the noodle."

"It doesn't matter," Rosita corrected. "The scythe kills all as long as it hits its mark. So ends the reign of Dillinger."

"Okay," I announced over a crack of distant thunder.

"You have what you want. We're going now." I guided Luna in the direction of the fence's gash.

"Incorrect, Buck," Rosita uttered. Dub flipped the barrel toward me. I locked in place.

"What are you doing?" I chastised.

"Tying up loose ends," Rosita declared.

"You bitch," I cursed.

"If it's any consolation, you never stood a chance, " she continued. "Every step has been calculated from your early hiring to your internship with Death. The odds have always been in our favor."

Dub's face slurped and wrenched until it took the shape of Jumbo. The tiny head on Dub's burly body was outlandishly spooky. Jumbo's false face smiled like a Jack-O' Lantern, mocking me with his blue-dyed braces.

"If you want Luna to stay safe," Rosita urged. "I suggest you walk toward that ledge." Luna squeezed at my jacket and squealed. "I assure you, we'll take good care of her, Buck. After all, we've had plans for her from the begin-ning. That is, until Dillinger broke her free."

I squeezed Luna tight. This was the inevitable finish I feared. Rosita, Dub, and The Mad Knight would double down, claiming Old Lilith, killing off anyone that opposed them, and taking back Luna. I was powerless. It only took me a second to decide that this fate, one where Luna survived, was still better than us trying to escape, and getting killed in the process. I'd suffer so Luna could thrive.

"Please, just take care of her," I begged, prying Luna's clasped fingers from my coat.

Luna tried to readjust, but I pushed her away. "Kid," I looked directly at Luna, "I'm glad I got to say goodbye.

Now, don't do anything stupid. You have a long life ahead of you." Tears welled from Luna's eyes. Her grief gave me long-awaited purpose. Drops from the sky rolled down from my scalp to my cheeks, masking any tears. I trotted to the hole, rolled my neck, and halted exactly where Dillinger had.

"Trust us," Rosita consoled with a barren voice. "She'll make a powerful soldier with enough training. Now, say goodbye, Buck."

I opened my mouth to speak, but nothing came out. Dub wasted no time. He shouldered Old Lilith and squeezed the trigger. Whiplash kicked my neck back as the bullet struck my temple. Ringing cried in my ears. My numb body tumbled into the Spiral's bedrock hole. There was a weightlessness. I plunged down with the rain into a pool of cold water. I heard my spine crack before what was left of my head slopped to the side. My last vision was Dillinger's body, his mouth gaped open, and his arms flung next to me. I thought of Luna as my vision faded.

23

A gurgle bubbled in my ears. The sharp pressure in my temple eased. My back popped and fingers curled. A torrent of warmth shuddered through every limb. The ectoplasm was doing its job.

I pried my eyes open. A helix of gauzy film coiled around my head, unaffected by the rain. The halo of vapors corkscrewed along my bullet wound. I tried to remain still, letting the hocus-pocus do its thing. The wafting ectoplasm curled to a billow of cloud that I inhaled into my mouth. I raised my hand and felt my temple. It was smooth and unblemished. I sat up. My body felt brand new, refreshed like I'd had ten hours of sleep on one of those fancy foam beds that no one can afford.

"That was creepy to watch," Dillinger muttered faintly. I turned to face him. He sat squat in a puddle of pooling rain and blood. The hole and red stain over his heart lingered, but Dillinger seemed uninjured.

Vampires.

He used a pinkie to dig water from his ear while he

stood. "Looks like everything is going as planned. I told you they're predictable."

"Yeah, well," I whispered. "They still have Luna up there so let's stick with the plan."

"Take it easy, Abercrombie. You got the real rifle?"

"Yeah." I stood up and ogled the silo. "It's on the top."

"Great. Get into your position. I'll call the cavalry."

"Remember what we agreed on, Luna first, not the rebellion."

"Yeah, yeah, I got it."

Dillinger dug in his soaked coat and removed his phone. He sent a text and then set the device on a crate next to him. He combed his hands through his slicked hair before nodding to me. That was the signal. I slopped to the silo and climbed its barred ladder. I summoned my inner ninja, creeping up the slippery rungs as softly as possible so that Team Evil, who were still up on the surface, wouldn't hear me through the storm. Once on top, I opened the rusty toolbox, removing my satchel. One by one, I extracted the real 7.62 caliber bolt-action rifle pieces from the man-purse and assembled Old Lilith. I'd done my best to paint the earlier M40A3 to look like Old Lilith. Apparently, no one could tell the difference.

Dillinger took cover behind the collection of steel construction crates. I heard the groan of corroded metal from his ambush point. Dillinger protruded an old fashion Thompson 1918 submachine gun from a chest. Apparently I hadn't been the only one who planted toys. I stared as Dillinger fidgeted with his Chicago Organ Grinder's ammunition drum. He must have sensed eyes on him because his jaw set as he looked back at me.

I wagged a finger and mouthed. "Cheeky monkey."

He grinned, bobbed his brows, and then hardened his expression again as he raised his Thompson.

Calm struck while we waited. I adjusted the scope's optics to the low-light setting, coloring everything in dull green. Denise's watch glittered from rain and outlying high-rise lights. If there *was* a Grim Reaper, Devil, and God, then there had to be an afterlife. Maybe it was just my psyche trying to ease my mind, but I decided Denise could be watching, and if so, she might be proud. Using that thought as motivation, I readied for battle.

The silo quaked beneath me before I ever heard the truck above. There was the cacophony of bangs and booms, from a far-off crash of the construction fence to the grinding of engine gears from the surface. Gunfire from The Mad Knight's pistol rang, and then Rosita's voice called to run. I saw headlights brighten the lip of the Spiral's hole. Suddenly, two silhouettes appeared along the crater edge up above. Rosita glanced down before flashing her head back to the speeding vehicle chasing her. The rumbling disrupted any clean shot. I aimed my shaking sights at her forehead but pulled away when I spotted Luna clutched under Rosita's arm.

The violent orchestra crescended when the squeal of brakes revealed the front of Adam's semi-trailer truck just ten feet away from the hole, blocking Rosita's escape. The front grill girded with flowers, iron spikes, and a mounted pig's head covered in Norse ruins. Adam, Selena, and Ardicus sat in the cab dressed like commandos. Along each side of the cab was a pair of welded bars stretched out like eagle wings with wired mesh for feathers. Adam was herding the group into the pit.

From the darkness, a large bird of prey flew over the

truck, descending down the hole and landing at the bottom. The creature shifted into a hulking humanoid figure. The transition was rigid with the cracks of bones, jerks of body parts, and a wail of agony. When the transformation was complete, Dub stood at the bottom of the hole clutching the fake rifle. A split second after, a hum of electric followed by the tungsten flash of an antique camera blinded me. When my vision adjusted, The Mad Knight stood shoulder-to-shoulder with his brother, the bulb along his neck flickering. The pair seemed unaware of John's and my missing corpses.

"Hurry down, my love," said a voice with enough resonance and base to bewilder James Earl Jones.

Rosita bit her lip while clutching her bone locket. Her skull makeup had been partially smeared from rain. She took one last glance behind her, whispered under her breath, and then her feet lifted off the ground like Mary Poppins. Luna tried to run, but just as I was about to fire, Rosita tugged the child up to her chest and hovered down six stories to her allies.

"It's the Flesh Golem," Rosita hollered while landing. She tugged Luna by her hair. Luna squashed her eyes in pain, grabbing futility at the top of her head. I tried to block out any emotions as I slowly and carefully readjusted my shot.

"He's a clever Holy Joe, ain't he." The Mad Knight checked the remnants of his clip.

"You better watch your backside." Dub grunted.

"Is everything a joke to you?" Rosita sneered. The Mad Knight beamed with his hundred tiny teeth. The rap of a truck door thudded above. "Just buy me time and I'll cook up a spell for that stitch-faced fool."

"Shall I call our children?" Dub's husky voice bellowed.

"Yes." Rosita raised her chin.

Dub parted his hair, revealing a maw of angler fish pin teeth. The jaw opened and a screech like hot steam from a kettle punctured through the storms. The cry pierced at my eardrums just as it had in the alley of *Gamer's Pair-a-Dice*. I stuffed my head under my arm in a daze until the noise ended. Stunned, I moved the barrel toward Rosita and aimed at the base of her neck. I controlled my breathing, trying to refocus while following the jittery woman wave a hand over her head. She spoke in broken Spanish as an amethyst glow twinkled along her fingers. Luna's eyes shined with tears as Rosita grasped the girl's collar, moments later Rosita stopped.

"Wait," she called out. "Where are the bodies?"

"Right here, doll face," shouted Dillinger from his rusted bunker. A barrage of bullets from the Thompson pierced into Dub, forcing the doppelgänger to dance the full-auto boogey. Dub fell to the ground in a steaming heap. His body twitched and snapped along the wet gravel. From there, everything happened almost instantaneously. A chrome light flashed, and The Mad Knight vanished. Rosita released Luna and dove for cover, disappearing behind the leftover bulldozer bucket.

Luna was free, but in harm's way. Dub lurched to his feet, now a towering grizzly bear. Blood spewed from his wound, but the holes were tiny in comparison to his sheer mass. Another flash flared behind Dillinger, and The Mad Knight pounced from John's backside. Dillinger spun in time to bat The Mad Knight's pistol with his Tommy Gun. Both firearms flung to the floor, forcing the men into a grapple that knocked over crates. Meanwhile, the huffing

Grizzly-Dub reared its lips to reveal enormous teeth and charged Luna. I focused on the bear's center of mass.

Relax, breath, squeeze.

The rifle gave a soft kick. Old Lilith's silencer created a spitting sound as a fluorescent bullet ripped into Dub's heart. I drew my eye from the scope just in time to watch the bear's massive head let out a bellow before it fell face first onto the ground, nearly missing Luna. *Never piss off a man that can end you from another zip code.* Rosita stood up from her cover, wailed, and, with a hand blazed in periwinkle flame, threw her spell at me. The purple tennis ball sized energy grew into a meteor, its heat causing me to wince. But just as the fireball should have crashed into the top of the silo and melted me like wax, it instead smashed into an invisible curved shield. The salt circle had worked.

Rosita's eyes burned with fury. She flicked her fingers and another twinkle of fire flickered in her palm. She glared at Luna, who was now starting down at Dub's corpse as it returned to its original form. I plugged my eye back into the scope and tried to take aim. My magnified vision rebounded just as an anvil of flesh and muscle slammed down between Luna and Rosita. It was Adam.

His open leather vest revealed medical electrodes patched between a bare, jutting mishmash of scarred muscles across his chest. He charged Rosita, tackling her before she could release her spell. I heard a crunch as they went prone. She coughed blood before giving a sick red smile. Adam hung over her with the same confused stare I was likely wearing.

Rosita pointed to the top of the hole and gurgled out two words. "Mijos."

Static crepitated along the atmosphere. A swarm of

hag-children poured from the surface and spider climbed down at an alarming rate. Some, seeing their mother's plight, leapt reckless from the walls, smashing into Adam. Their gnarled teeth bit into Adam's shoulders and back.

Rosita rolled out from under Adam and floundered to her feet. I aimed but Adam, who was fumbling with a handful of soaked monster children, was too close for comfort. Rosita clenched her bone necklace, whispered, and limped away. Her skin began to fade into diaphanous cobwebs. I fired at Rosita, but the bullet passed through just as the bruja faded into nothing.

A baseball team's worth of hag-children reached the base of the silo. They clawed up, faces frozen in broken grins. I aimed Old Lilith at the lead creature and fired. The sapphire bullet bore through its forehead, rupturing it into cherry jello. The headless hag-child fell backwards onto its siblings, causing several to tumble. A trio of remaining exorcist-girls continued to clamor up. I slung Old Lilith by her strap and took a leap of faith toward a cluster of devil-kids circling Luna. Groans called from under me as the hag-children broke my fall. Pain seared from my elbows and back upon impact, but I used it as rocket fuel. I planted my feet in agony onto the ground and pushed off my pile of involuntary crowd surfing partners. Luna raised her arms. I lifted her up and hurried to my closest planted weapons. I kicked the parts of a withered cement mixer over, grabbed the knife, and gun, then hurried to the pit's wall ladder.

Luna twirled to my back, clinging. The hag-children were fast, crawling like apes with their hands and feet. There was too much going on to know how Dillinger or Adam were, but I assumed they weren't faring well. The plan was falling apart. I reached the ladder and started climbing. The hag-children clawed up the sides. I was struggling to ascend with a knife and pistol in my hand, so I stopped, unloaded the .22 on the closest horror until it fell. From the opposite side, a small wrinkly hand of a bald child donned in overalls clasped my foot. I put the Mayan blade between my teeth, held onto the ladder with both arms, and gave a short hook kick. My heel connected with the creature's temple, sending both the hag-child and my shoe back down to Earth. I continued upward.

The slippery bars took time, allowing more hag-children to catch up. I wasn't going to be able to reach the top, so I scaled to a wide balcony along the fourth-floor rim. Luna rolled off me. There was a legion of hag-children scattered throughout the pit, but I was more concerned about the throng trailing me. I gave a crescent kick to a mutant Eloise lookalike, forcing her to topple onto her family and down the pit.

Near the silo now on the opposite side of the hole, a supernova of electricity from a swarm of little monsters told me Adam lived. He smashed a hoary boy in a striped unitard through the bedrock. From a third-floor ledge above him, a gang of harpy-toddlers pushed a huge scissor lift to the ledge. I flipped the rifle, aimed through the scope, and fired a precious bullet at one of the hag-children pushing the lift's tire. A blue blaze pierced the creature and popped the rubber. Adam looked up and stampeded out of the way, crushing several hag-children under his boots. Automatic gunfire helped me locate Dillinger. He was at the center of the hole's floor unloading his recovered Tommy Gun. There was a break in fire; John threw down the smoking submachine gun and retreated.

He was just steps away from Thing One and Two. I removed the Mayan dagger from my mouth.

"Under the orange cone," I shouted as loudly as I could.

Dillinger flicked his stare to me, nodded, then hurried to a construction cone and kicked it over. The silver .45s greeted him. Dillinger picked them up and fed lead into his pursuers, giving him a temporary escape route.

Crack.

I felt a hard blow on the back of my head. The impact drove me forward onto my face. My ears rang as I rolled posterior to see my assailant. The Mad Knight stood over me, water leaking from his yellow slicker onto my face. He held the pistol in his hand like a hammer.

"Stand him up," Rosita ordered from nearby. Her voice sounded low as if played in slow motion. My brain was trapped in La-La Land. The Mad Knight grabbed my tie and choked me to my feet. I wobbled but remained standing.

"A fine ruse, Buck," Rosita complimented. My eyes finally managed to focus on her. She held Luna at the edge of the pit, ready to push her. "It won't be enough though. Now, you will be giving over the real rifle or else the child dies."

A graduating class worth of kindergarten fiends clattered up onto our perch. I was outnumbered, overpowered, and disorientated. *Sucks to be me.*

"You shot me last time we did this," I slurred.

"Yes." Rosita concurred, "and I will again, Buck. You must know already that it ends the same as before, only this time we leave with the real *rifle.*"

"I'm guessing *'please'* won't help?" I said through ground teeth, my head throbbing.

"Buck, you just assassinated my lover," Rosita said flatly. "So, *no*." She tugged Luna in front of her, "but I give you my word. Hand over the weapon by your own free will and I will honor our bargain. The girl lives."

Luna sobbed. I was getting good at making the poor kid do that.

"Fine," I conceded. "But please." I removed the silver watch Denise had given me for Christmas. "Give her this to remember me by."

The Mad Knight took the watch, examined it, then pitched it toward Rosita. With one hand on Luna, Rosita caught the watch awkwardly.

"Sentimental nonsense," she condemned, "but you have a deal." She handed the watch to Luna, who moaned and sobbed even louder as she huddled over the time-piece. Rosita stared at Luna. I broke into song.

"When the end comes I know." I slung the rifle from my arm, locating the knife by my feet. *"That I'm just a gigolo, life goes on without me."*

I extended Old Lilith to The Mad Knight. He tugged, but I didn't let go. The Mad Knight's smile flipped upside-down.

"Release the rifle, Buck," Rosita barked.

"I can't," I said in singsong.

"Why?" Rosita sizzled.

I smiled. "Because this is Luna's verse."

Luna reeled around, her face covered in wolfish fur. Her eyes glistened green as a pair of sharp fangs protruded from drooled lips. The watch in her claws steamed. She grabbed Rosita's clasped hand along her collar and flipped the bruja over her shoulder like a rag doll. Rosita gasped as she was flung over the edge, barely managing to grab onto the ledge at the last second before falling to her death. Several hag-children leapt on Luna, who swelled at an exponential rate. Muscles stretched and her height extended. Luna swatted them off her like flies, hurling them into the gaping hole.

I didn't hesitate. Ectoplasm fumed from my mouth. I ducked, grabbed the Mayan knife from the floor and plunged it into The Mad Knight's knee cap. He gave a screaming laugh. I spun around and swept The Mad Knight off his feet with my hooked leg. He tried to hold on, but I used my leverage and a shoeless foot to his face to pry Old Lilith from his body. I backed off to get a better shot with Old Lilith just in time to watch Luna reach full size. She had grown two feet taller with fur-covered muscles. Her head now looked like a timber wolf. Luna ran her claws through another hag-child, splitting it in twine. I had to admit that I didn't exactly think this through. I had no idea whether Luna might murder me next.

A flash shimmered in my eyes. I aimed the rifle down at The Mad Knight, but he was gone. More and more hag-children crawled to the party. I put my eye back in the scope and aimed at Rosita, but one of her children gave her cover in an attempt to lift her from the ledge. I fired into the creature's back. The creature fell, but Rosita's painted skeleton fingers still gripped the cliff brim. Then from behind me, pistol fire started to clear the hag-children between us and Luna. Dillinger joined the fray, smattered in blood.

From the surface, a high frequency pitch called out. My ears rang and I felt nauseous. I searched for the source and found that Selena and Ardicus had set up and deployed the LRAD device like planned. They pointed the sonic weapon down on the minions, causing the Sesame Street parade to hiss and double over. What was mildly discomforting for us caused severe disorientation in anything directly under Selena and Ardicus' aim.

Luna howled, but continued to smash heads. She ground meat with her claws until there were no moving hag-children left along the ledge. When she'd cleared them all, she huffed as she faced us. Her feet stomped heavily as she closed the distance. I held out my hand as if trying to tame a lion.

"Luna," I called out. "It's Buck. We're on your side, kid."

Luna sniffed at us and then dropped the silver watch smoking in her hand. She fell over, gripping her charred palm. Her fur retracted and her body shrunk until it was the Luna that I knew and loved. I watched as she curled into a near-nude ball and whimpered.

"Keep an eye on her." I pulled the final bullet into Old Lilith's chamber. "The Mad Knight is still out there." Dillinger removed his coat and crouched next to Luna, blanketing her.

I approached the ledge where Rosita hung for dear life. I hadn't noticed before, but her nose was busted, and her lip was swollen. Her broken fingers trembled as they held on to the wet cement. The sonic waves continued to shrill from above. I stuck the barrel inches from Rosita's face.

"I was arrogant, Buck," Rosita admitted in her lifeless voice as if she weren't hanging on a ledge for dear life. "I see that now."

"Well, pride before the fall."

"I'm guessing 'please' won't help?"

"Nope."

"Is there *no* chance of convincing you that I could still help?"

"How?"

"Buck, all I ever wanted was to retake Chicago. There are others that are plotting much more nefarious endeavors. I could assist Death in stopping them."

I thought about it. So many had died already. Maybe the comfort of having Luna back played a part, but I ignored the voice inside screaming for revenge. It was a good thing I did, because suddenly the sonic shrieks from above stopped. I glanced on top of the hole. Selena and Ardicus were fidgeting with the LRAD device, which was now smoking. I lowered the rifle.

"Any funny stuff and you're dead," I cautioned.

"Naturally, Buck."

"Call off your children." I ordered before hesitantly extending a hand. Rosita reached out with her free arm. I couldn't see her other hand pressed below the sill, but by the time I did, it was too late. She had a six-inch feathered pin dripping with an inky substance that she pricked through my glove into my palm. My body tensed up as my muscles began to lock. I struggled to lift the rifle. It weighed a thousand pounds. Sweat leaked from my heating forehead. Just as I raised the barrel to her face, my body fixed in an aimed position as if I were made of stone. Rosita smiled at the barrel in her face then tried to tug herself up.

Buck, you should have killed this witch with a B a long time ago.

A sounding pop and flash came from over my shoulder. The Mad Knight reached over my back with his arms, grabbed onto my hand, and forced me to pull the trigger. A blue flash caused a splash of gore to splatter on our faces. The Mad Knight kissed my cheek as he slid off me.

"I told you I liked you, Danny Boy," he whispered in my ear. There was a flare of lightning from above. I could feel static raise the hairs along my neck. Dillinger reached where I stood and studied me. His eyes fixated on the pin still in my hand and plucked it out. Ectoplasm steamed out of the hole. I could feel my numb body come to life.

"You got her." He patted me on my back. I could hardly turn my neck but managed to creak it toward him. I sucked up a spittle of drool covered in the corner of my lip.

"I didn't do it."

"Who did?"

"Didn't you see—never mind."

I looked to the carnage beneath me. The hundreds of hag-children made it to their feet and stared at their dead mother. Like groves of ants, they kicked into a run. Hideous children in striped vintage swim costumes clamored a few floors under my feet, snarling while climbing up the first and second levels. Dillinger elbowed me and then hurried to Luna.

"Make tracks," he barked.

I forced my stiff legs to move, tramping like a robot. Dillinger lifted Luna just as the hag-children reached our level, flinging her over his shoulder while horse collaring my coat and pulling me with him. We weren't moving fast enough to lose the hoard filling up our entire balcony ring. Dillinger slung my back onto the nearby wall, handed me Thing One, and helped me point it forward. He stretched out Thing Two and pointed it out into the charging line of hag-children, his lips pursed.

"This ain't good, Abercrombie," he stammered over the gargling hisses in front of us.

"You think?"

"Any regrets?"

"Yeah, not killing you."

"Don't worry too much," he said while the front row of demon-kids fell into whispering distance. "I think they'll do the job."

24

A batting ram of rebar and concrete cleared the children three at a time. Adam and grasshopper leapt up to our level to save us. After several more swings of his makeshift fly swatter, he broke it into pieces on the back of a hag-boy in a monkey costume. The horn from Adam's semi-truck blared above. Selena and Ardicus were now in the cab, smothered by hag-children scratching at the glass. They turned the wipers on and flashed the headlights in a panic.

"*Mein Freund*, what the hell is taking Jumbo so long?" Adam snapped a hag-child's back like a chicken over his knee.

"Damn it." Dillinger unloaded the rest of Thing Two's clip into the conga line of hag- children. Where one fell, another two replaced it. "I almost forgot. I'm supposed to text him. Hold onto your wigs, I'll dial him up now and he can activate—" Dillinger froze, his free hand in his coat. I watched his nostrils flare. "Oh, no. You have to be kidding me."

"What?" I fired Thing One's last bullet into a hag-child before holstering her. My legs and arms weren't getting the feeling back in them soon enough. I closed my eyes, held my breath, and tried to concentrate. I thought about the cold feel of ectoplasm that usually worked on its own, trying to beckon it. I could feel little pinpricks in my arms and legs. I opened them. A cotton like smoke steamed from my wrists and shins.

"No freaking way," I mumbled, arm held out like a hand model.

"My phone," Dillinger sizzled, ignoring me. "I must have dropped it when I was wrestling with that clown."

"Dillinger," I fizzed while a hag-child with a safari suit tried to corner me. I crescent kicked the hag-boy, dropping him to his knees. "Every time you say something, I get a fierce desire to tell you to shut up again. We're all going to die trying to get that phone."

Dillinger delivered a lightning-fast set of jabs before upper cutting a girl in a strawberry bonnet. She collapsed into a heap. He flashed Adam a look.

"It's true." Adam knocked over two hag-kids with one swing. "It's getting too hot down there. I wasn't so much as rescuing you all as much as I was retreating."

Dillinger's arm flashed at the speed of awesome into a hag-child, cracking its teeth with a haymaker before he adjusted Luna on his shoulder. "Well then, we need to pull out. Go back to the truck. We'll have to fight 'em off us until we're safe."

The three of us stared at the path between ourselves and Adam's truck. It was covered in kids that were awake way past their bedtime. We wouldn't get but twenty feet before they smothered us. I stared at Luna's sleeping body slung over Dillinger.

"Luna first," I reminded everyone. "I'll run the distraction. Once you see an opening, go."

"No, Abercrombie." Dillinger shook his head. "You're not going to sacrifice yourself too. If we run fast enough, we can, gah—" A low crawling hag-child bit into Dillinger's calf. Dillinger's fangs protruded and his eyes flickered gold. I saw the monster beneath Dillinger's skin. He grabbed at the hag-child, pulled it up to his own mouth, and bit its throat, tearing out a chunk. After dropping the wriggling body to the ground, he corrected. "Okay, fine. Let's stop bumping gums and get out of here. Buck, do whatever it is you're about to do."

I kissed Luna on her forehead and readied for the stupidest last-minute plan I've ever come up with. "Get me to the ledge."

Adam didn't hesitate. He made like a rhinoceros and charged through a flock of hag-children. I followed behind, then put my feet on the hole's edge. This was going to be a leap of faith. I raised the rifle over my head and cleared my throat.

"Listen up, old-timers," I cried out. "I killed your evil mommy and daddy. Now, unless you want to join them, I suggest you return to your *Murder She Wrote*. By the way, thanks for ruining social security."

A thousand beady eyes stared up at me. I think they understood. All at once, hundreds of tapping feet clinked along the construction site's cement. They were coming for me, and they wanted blood.

I stretched my arms up and closed my eyes. What the hell was I doing? This was stupid, illogical and suicidal.

Then again, that summed up my life. I imagined being covered in webs of cloudy ectoplasm, acting as a conduit to the strange haunting residue. I breathed and willed it out of me. With my eyes still closed, I leaned my body forward to fall from the ledge.

The roller coaster feeling pulled at my insides. I continued to imagine the threads of ectoplasm all around me. A chill ran along my skin, a burden of heavy sadness like when I'd entered Death's doorway, and then a tug. Suddenly, my body jerked upwards. I felt weightless. Melancholy chilled my bones.

An image of Death filled my mind's eye. I could see his flowing robes, arched skeletal hands and lanky body standing in the midst of a cloud of endless fog. He pointed to me, lurched forward, and eight sets of wings ripped from Death's back. At once he lifted to the sky. He fluttered in place for a moment before the thought faded away.

I opened my eyes again. My body hovered arms reach above angry children, cloaked in a cape of grey vapors. A mask of ectoplasm tendrils shaped like a skull hovered over my face. I'd taken a cloudy form of Death. *Sweet.* The hag-children leapt from their tippy toes, nearly clipping my feet. I focused my conscience to soar higher above the ledge. I rose up. I looked to Dillinger, Adam holding sleeping Luna, who stared in astonishment.

"You see this shit?" I laughed.

"You're doing it, Peter Pan." Dillinger adjusted Luna on his shoulder. "You're learning to fly."

"Get out of here." I wobbled in the air. "I don't know how long I can keep this up." Dillinger gave a half-salute with his free hand. With Luna on his shoulder, he and Adam fought their way toward the main ladder up to the surface. The hag-children hissed under me. I searched downward near the crates. Sure enough, Dillinger's cell phone lay near his original ambush point. Several hag-children nearly stood on it. I landed on the perch of the fourth-floor balcony and waited for the children to stampede their way to me. They clambered on walls, ran along the Spiral's floor, and anything else they could do to come get me. I egged them on.

"Ha! I killed Dub. I killed Rosita. Daddy and mommy are gone."

I waited patiently, watching them climb over one another to get me.

"Hey, maybe when I'm done here, I'll go find out where you play bingo and burn it down."

Once the front line was so close they could claw me, I pushed off the ledge and directed myself to the phone. The strange ectoplasm pull whirled me past the ladder. Devil-kids leapt from the balcony, missing and plunging below. I slung the rifle back on my back, aimed my body in the direction of the phone, and focused on darting to its location.

My body cannonballed toward the crates at alarming speeds. Midway through flight, however, the sheer magnitude of what I was doing startled me. I started losing focus. The drape of ectoplasm misted back into me. Gravity began to follow up on its responsibilities. I fell two stories and twenty feet shy of the phone. I could hear my knees pop as I tried to land feet first. The pain was unbearable, but the army of little feet rerouting their charge toward my direction told me that I didn't have much time. I stood up, limping to the phone.

Smash.

A hag-child leapt on my back and bit into my shoulder. The sting caused me to reflexively grab at its head and pry it off me, taking some of my clamped flesh along with it. A second hag-child clung to my leg, ripping into my tendons with its mouth. I twirled to kick the dead weight off my leg, only to take in a wall of hag-children within fifteen yards from me. The distance between me and the phone was too great. I wasn't going to make it.

I kicked the kid off, screamed with everything I had to fight through the pain, and broke into a harrowing sprint. The agony nearly made me pass out. I leapt on the phone just as another hag-child clamped onto my back. I bit off my leather glove and activated the phone's interface as another hag-child crashed on me, followed by yet another. Before long they were piled all over, taking bits and pieces from any part exposed. I looked at the screen with an eye freshly jabbed by a finger.

Enter your six-digit code.

"Dillinger," I roared as something bit off my ear. "Did you forget to tell me something before I left?" There was no reply. What the hell could Dillinger's code be. My arm snapped from the weight of the piling hag-children. I took a wild guess as a pink tutu clawed my temples.

"Here goes nothing."

07-22-34.

The phone released. Dillinger had used his date of death. I head butted the girl trying to eat my brains, tugged my hand away from a boy with elephant patterned pajamas, and chose *Wheels* from the contact list.

"Yo, dude," Jumbo greeted. "You ready?"

"Jumbo, do it!"

"Roger that, man."

I heard a click from the other side of the receiver. Suddenly, the weight on top of me convulsed in all directions. I looked about as every hag-child standing over me fell to the ground, grabbing their hearts or heads as they dropped dead. Jumbo was worried that the plan wouldn't work, but apparently he'd figured out how to use his Death program in order to kill the hag- children. I was saved!

Well, kind of.

My body collapsed lifelessly for a moment, letting the rattling monsters atop me pass. I could feel blood flow from my body. All of my wounds hemorrhaged. I started to get cold, and my vision tunneled. I'd done this dance before. My body was dying. As my limbs went cold, my neck went slack, and everything faded into the blackness. Death had become me.

WHEN I WOKE UP AGAIN, everything was still. My body was worn. My mind was tired. My claustrophobia that I didn't know I had was in full gear. Translucent threads steamed from under my arched body. The ectoplasm was patching me up but not as quickly as I'd like it to. I heard shouting not too far away.

"Buck," Adam's thick accent called out. I could see from under a claw slung on top of my head that Adam was picking up corpses and flinging them over his shoulder. "Buck, where are you, my friend?"

Wow, friend. Life was perking up.

I heard Dillinger's voice, then Selena's, and Ardicus' too. They were all calling out for me. I blew strings of hair that looked like they belonged on the top of dirty mop out of my mouth.

"Wrong haystack," I moaned.

"Buck," Adam celebrated, crunching his way to me. I could hear the smashing of bodies beneath Adam's boots before he reached me. He lifted the carcasses on top. "Buck, you idiot." He dragged me up.

"Ow," I screamed in agony, my bones still mending. "Why don't you stop touching me and go slip into something more comfortable." I grimaced as my ribs throbbed. "Preferably a coma."

Adam roared with laughter as the group caught up. John was covered in hag-muck while Selena and Ardicus helped carry Luna. She wore a cheap rain poncho that was far too big for her. She gave a weak smile from under her wet hood.

"Hey, Selena Gomez, Ken Doll," I spoke up. "Do me a favor and put the kid next to me please."

"That's not who I was named after," Selena defended.

"Yeah, sure." I cringed while muscles readjusted under my skin. "Just put the kid down, would you?" The dynamic duo placed Luna down beside me. Luna went to lean in but stopped when she saw the gore all over me. I smiled at her hesitation, then dug in for a cigarette. The group stared as I put the stick in my mouth. "What? I earned it. Now, please, give us a moment."

Dillinger nodded. "Okay, everyone. Let's get to work. There's a lot of cleaning up to do. Ardicus, get us a room. The closer the better. Selena, put DuSable on the phone. We're going to need to get this all removed before authorities come. Adam, did you have to leave the headlights on in the truck? We don't want to draw any more attention than we already have. Come on, people."

I waited for Dillinger's orders to fade from ear shot before facing Luna. Her face went blank as a cirrus of pearly ectoplasm spewed out from a bite mark, weaving my skin back together, before dipping back into my arm.

"Yeah, I'm getting used to it, too." I puffed my freshly lit cigarette. "Hey, I just wanted to say that I'm sorry I left you alone in the apartment. *That*," I shook my head and wafted out secondhand smoke. "That was dumb. Can you forgive me?"

Luna's face turned scarlet. She rubbed at her arm and her forehead creased. After a second, she looked up at me and punched my arm playfully.

"Thanks, kid. You're as tough as they come. On that note, I also wanted to tell you that I'll never leave you alone again. That is, if you wanted that."

Luna's brow curled as she pressed together her lips. She looked puzzled.

"I mean, I know that you're a werewolf and I'm working for the Grim Reaper, so there'll be a lot of challenges, but I," I stuttered. I was having trouble trying to tell Luna what I really wanted. I finally spit out, "Did you want to live with me, maybe?"

Luna blinked several times, just as I thought it couldn't get any more awkward, she began to laugh. It was the first time I'd heard true vocals that weren't screaming or sobbing from the girl. She covered her smile, holding onto her stomach as she continued.

"So," I hummed. "Does that mean yes or no?"

Luna lifted her head, still laughing. She nodded and punched me in the arm again. Watching her giggle stirred a chuckle in my own gut. My belly tickled, and soon enough the pair of us sounded like a pack of hyenas.

"By the way," I chuckled. "I think you have some hag-hair in between your teeth. We're really going to need to get you to a dentist with those eating habits." Luna and I continued to tear up from self-amusement and relief at the bottom of that hole.

I'll tell you what, life can be brutal. Life can be strange. Hell, sometimes, there's just no way to describe it.

That night I learned two things though.

One, I wasn't the guy I thought I was anymore. I'd changed for the better this last week. I'm pretty sure of it.

And two, sometimes a good laugh fixes everything.

25

L una curled herself in a hotel towel alongside me while shoving a peanut butter sandwich in her mouth. She'd already downed a soft pretzel, chicken quesadilla, and the rest my flat iron steak. The girl must have burned off some serious calories. Once she'd licked the peanut butter goodness from her fingers, she scoured the tray for anything else that was edible. Only Jumbo's turkey club remained.

"Holy crap, dudette," Jumbo laughed from his scooter. He was watching in amazement. "You eat like a pothead on four-twenty. Maybe we should have gone to a buffet." Luna wagged her eyes between Jumbo and the turkey club. "Go on with your bad self, little one." Luna shoved the meal into her mouth.

We'd retired to the Congress Hotel for a post rescue mission debriefing. The establishment had been a favorite of Dillinger's in life. The room had an elegant antique look to it and was far nicer than anything I'd ever lived in. We sat within the drawing room of our Lakefront Suite and discussed the aftermath. Dillinger stared out of the window as he spoke to DuSable over the phone. He was arranging for a cleanup crew to round up the hundreds of hag-children from the Chicago Spiral's pit. Luckily, the late hour and downpour gave us time.

"They're called the Forgotten." Adam sat on a sofa. "They are the poor souls left behind in retirement homes and hospitals. A witch or warlock offers them a dark contract in order to extend their life, warping their elderly minds and bodies in the process. Rosita's master, Collin, perfected the process and has been collecting anyone foolish enough to take his deal. Rosita and Dub had a barge full of these creatures hiding along the riverbank."

"There you have it, dudes and dudettes," Jumbo sighed. "Another reason why we need to improve the healthcare system for elderly. That is some sick shit."

"Don't you kill old people all day through a computer program?" I challenged.

"So," he shrugged. "Also man, the program lays them to rest. I just designed it. I don't corrupt their souls or anything."

"Right," I said with a blank stare. "Anyhow, so like I said. If Dub, Rosita, and their freaky family of children are all dead, that only leaves The Mad Knight."

"You're saying the dude helped you shoot Rosita?" Jumbo probed. "It just doesn't make sense, man."

"I'm with you," I agreed. "Like I said before though, the guy is *crazy*. He offered me a counter alliance moments after his brother left my damn front room. That should be testament to his endless unpredictability."

Dillinger placed his hand over his phone's receiver. "I highly doubt he will return any time soon. The Undead Union is already getting reports from Canada's Post Mortem Federation of a green haired man, or maybe woman, teleporting across their borders. I think he's going to lick his wounds."

"Especially after you stabbed him in the knee, dude," Jumbo whistled. "Where the hell did you get a Mayan dagger from anyhow?"

"Let's get back to Luna." I culled a soddened cigarette from my crushed pack. Luna slurped her soda, eyes focused on my smoke. "You're telling me you can make moves in the mortal world so that I have custody of her? Because if so, I'd kill whoever you want."

"That's easy, dude," Jumbo pulled open his laptop. "Seeing that none of us, even her captors, have a record of her, I'll just create a new identity and insert it into the right departments. That is unless you want to tell us who you are, sweetie?"

Luna took another sip of her soda and then burped. The room looked at me as if I were going to step in to coax out her name, or at least an excuse me, from her. I shrugged.

"I think that's a no." I winked at Luna. She smiled back.

Jumbo typed rapidly at his computer. "I'm on the site now. I can just make up a name with a few clicks." He peeked over his laptop. "Or I can put her in a federal database that protects kids. We could find her a good home?"

I leaned in to Luna. "What do you say, kid, federal institution sounds mighty tempting."

Luna wiped her lips with the blanket and then

grunted. She took her index finger and poked it hard onto my chest. *It kind of hurts.*

What happened next, I never could have expected. She opened her mouth.

"You," she cooed with a voice as soft as prayer. I looked down and gave her a hug. She tolerated it. It felt good. When the moment reared its awkward point, I let her go, removed my lighter, and lit up my cigarette.

"Alright," Jumbo concurred. "One social security number for a Luna Palasinski."

"So you're saying I'll have supernatural sanctions in Chicago as well." I puffed smoke that filled the room. Adam frowned, Jumbo coughed, and Selena covered her mouth. Even Luna gave a little hand wave over her nose. "Sorry, you guys don't mind if I smoke?"

Dillinger wished goodbye into his phone's receiver and then clicked the off button. "Like I said," he corrected while rolling up the sleeves of his dress shirt. "I'll see what I can do. DuSable and I can handle the Negative One Union, but they're only a piece of the community. There's aberrations, sidhe, fiends, and other monstrosities. We'll have to dance around a lot of red tape."

"How are you going to do that?" I leaned on the sectional sofa.

"I'm going to check in with the self-appointed protector of Chicago," Dillinger answered.

"He's a fallen angel gone straight. Use to be a corruptor. Stole souls for Satan."

"Guy sounds like an asshole." I puffed more tobacco.

"He kind of is," Dillinger concurred, "but his intentions are righteous so we let him have a sheriff badge."

"You supernatural types are complicated." I puffed another plume of smoke.

"Man," Jumbo hissed. "I'm not giving you custody of Luna if you can't control your smoking. Not all of us are immune to lung cancer, dude."

I looked to Luna. She had her arms crossed and nose crinkled. I smashed the cigarette in the last of my mashed potatoes and moved the plate next to the no smoking sign along a side table.

"There," I exhaled. "It's a smoker free environment. You win. Now can we get back to Luna."

"Luna will be fine, man," Jumbo concurred. "Dillinger is the man. He'll work it out on the supernatural side."

Dillinger shrugged.

"Besides," Jumbo typed rapidly onto his laptop's keyboard. "We have more pressing matters to talk about."

"You mean lying to Death," I said frankly.

"There's no lying to him," Jumbo amended. "Trust me, I've tried. However, what I have here is a legal document I've been working on that gives Dillinger amnesty from Mr. Grim's Unmentionables operations so long as he cooperates with proper authorities. It's a tit for tat sort of thing."

"You think Death is going to give protection to a near century old vampire?" I asked.

"I think our friend may see it in his best interests to offer impunity so long as I cooperate in giving up other..." Dillinger hesitated. "Less earnest undead."

I gave Dillinger a flat look. "You do know that he would send me to stop these less than earnest undead should I not be let go from my internship? What kind of undead do you plan on giving him?"

"*Should* Death continue your employment." Dillinger

put a heavy emphasis on the word 'should.' "You would only need to continue slaying the most horrific undead. Those who abuse or pervert their status as immortal for malevolent gain. The true monsters that don't deserve a second chance."

"True monsters, as in those that murder people and drink their blood," I jabbed.

"I told you I have donors," Dillinger defended. I shook my head. "It's not going to work."

"It will," Jumbo volleyed. "I'll see to it. Death and I are boys. I'll get him to understand where we are coming from." Jumbo pivoted his scooter and drove it closer to me until I could smell the fruit gum on his breath. "Besides, as Dillinger said, you need to worry more about your status as an intern."

I swallowed the lump in my throat.

The rain let up just a step before dawn. Dillinger walked us out to Michigan Avenue while a valet retrieved the van I'd driven over. Luna had fallen asleep up in the room and continued to snuffle as I picked her up and carried her outside. The pair of us sat out in the chilled air for a moment without saying anything. Sometimes you didn't need to say anything after you just fought an army of evil. Finally Luna let out a sleepy snort and we both smiled.

"She's a doll," Dillinger complimented. "Hold her tight." He combed his fingers through his greased hair. "It can all go by so quickly. Trust me on this one."

"I do."

"By the way, this is yours." He handed over the watch Denise had given me. I placed the metal band over my wrist and clasped it on. The reflection gleamed.

"How did you know that Luna would transform when she did?"

"I'm a businessman. It's my job to know things."

"Seriously, out with it."

"I've had a few close encounters with lycanthropes. The wolf is always looking for reasons to unleash itself. Full moons, threatened pack members, and their allergy to silver are all triggers. I didn't want to, but knew that we could use that to our advantage should the situation call for it." Dillinger winked. "On that note, you may want to give your house a once over for any unnecessary silverware. It could do a number on your home decor."

"Don't think I have the money for silverware or home decor."

A confused and shaky bellman in a red soldier's coat hurried over to us, comparing a briefcase's claim ticket to the one between Dillinger's fingers. "Mr. Hellman," the young man's voice squeaked. "Here's the briefcase you requested, sir." Dillinger nodded, handed the kid a fifty and removed the case from his hands.

"Thank you, young man." He nudged his nose for the kid to go away. The bellman scurried behind his desk, eying his crisp fifty. "On that note, tough guy, this is for you," Dillinger pushed the briefcase in my hand.

"Whatever it is, I don't want it."

"Nonsense. It's not much, but it should get you through the month. If I were you, I wouldn't be too eager to ask Death for a salary, but you might want to start thinking up a line."

"I'm two steps ahead of you. How does, '*Sir, I'm the backbone of this organization. I need a raise now or I quit,*' sound as an opening?"

"I'd work on your curtain raiser a bit more before you give it to him."

The van grumbled up along the curb and a valet leapt out. Dillinger waved the woman over and handed her a crisp hundred-dollar bill. The girl smiled and hurried into the lobby.

"Why a hundred?" I questioned as I stuffed Luna into the passenger seat.

"What do you mean?"

"Why a hundred for her, and only fifty for the bellman?"

"You kidding? She's a woman. They're going to rule this world one day."

I looked to Luna as I buckled her in and crossed my fingers. After shutting the door, I walked over to the driver side, stopping before I hopped in.

"John," I called out as he began to walk back inside. He looked over his shoulder. "I hope I don't have to kill you, but I will if it comes to it."

"I'd expect nothing less." Dillinger smirked.

I drove down Congress listening to Tom Waits' *Blood Money* album. It had been a funny sort of day and I thought Luna and I deserved to sleep in until next Christmas. I wondered how I was going to get us something to eat on my salary. Maybe I'd take a loan out or ask one of the gamers for a few bucks until I figured something out. I always did.

I stared at the briefcase between Luna and I at a light just before the 290 onramp. Since red lights in Chicago define a minute as an undisclosed stretch of eternity, I figured I would take a little peak. I flipped the clasps and opened up the top. Smiling at me were bricks of Benjamin

Franklins stacked on top of each other like a cheerleading pyramid. There had to be at least a hundred-thousand dollars. I knew what Dillinger might be doing, coaxing me with hard cash, but decided to allow it. As the light turned green, my poor money management skills decided that Luna and I should get breakfast before returning home.

26

I fluffed the stupid pillows on my sofa at least ten times. *"How to speak German"* played on the speaker in the background. Our new place was a vast improvement from the hole in the wall I'd been tolerating the last few years. Luna and I each had our own room. Also, the leasing office guaranteed that the gym wouldn't give me tetanus, and that the warm water lasted longer than a commercial jingle. The place made me feel like the Monopoly guy.

I lit the strawberry-vanilla fusion candle that Luna insisted on buying at the supermarket and breathed in its fruity fragrance. My palms were sweaty, and my legs wouldn't stop twitching. Death would be here any minute. Everything had to be perfect. *Man, I wish I hadn't quit smoking just yet.*

Luna came out in her favorite Wolverine t-shirt, Harry the doll tucked under her arm. She stared at me as I scrubbed the pretend stain from the kitchen counter again. Today I'd finally know if I'd done enough to make Death happy. Jumbo warned me that he was a perfectionist. If I messed this up, I'd likely be sent to the bowels of Hell. That didn't sit well with me. I liked Earth, maybe now more than ever. The doorbell buzzed.

"Man oh man," I stuttered. Luna shoved me to the side. I went to get the door. She pressed the intercom and made a clucking noise with her tongue.

"Hello," Bethany greeted. "It's your friendly neighborhood babysitter."

"Shew," I exhaled, stress hanging from my shoulders. Luna buzzed Bethany in. I continued the breathing techniques I'd watched online, trying to ignore the call of chemical dependence. "Three deep breaths a day," I recalled the mantra. "Keeps the tobacco away." There were footsteps in the hall followed by the click of the door handle. Bethany sauntered in with her Disney smile and a suspicious bag from the toy store.

"Wow," she exclaimed. "Place looks great. Is that strawberry-vanilla I smell?"

"How do you know that?"

"I know all, Buck. Now, are you ready for the big interview?"

"Uh," I stuttered. "I think so."

"Come on, that's not the attitude that gets you anywhere."

"Heck yes, I am. When you think workforce, look no further. Buck Palasinski is your

MAN."

"Better. Oh, Buck, you're going to do great." Bethany straightened my collar. "What was the position again? Waste Management?"

"Waste Management Coordinator. I coordinate the waste, lady." Bethany giggled.

Luna collected her Star Wars backpack packed with babysitting provisions and took Bethany's hand. Luna knew what was really happening and did me a favor by shuffling Bethany out before Death literally reared his ugly head.

"Oh, looks like Luna is ready to go." Bethany waved. "See you tonight."

"Yes, see you around dinner." I hurried over for a hug. Luna gave the one-armed cool girl hug and then pulled Bethany into the hall. I shut the door. The apartment was too quiet. I needed to keep myself occupied, quick. I ran to get the booklet and pulled it out of the protective plastic cover with a pair of grill tongs. I turned the pages of the 1987 Second Series Punisher issue one I'd bought back from Denny and relaxed. Frank Castle's quest for murder kept me calm. I was halfway through when the door buzzed again.

For whom the bell tolls.

I straightened my tie and walked over to the front door. I checked myself in the mirror as it buzzed again. My reflection was as good as it got. I took one last breath and then opened it up. Jumbo sat in his original electrical throne, Death beside him. Jumbo, donned in a t-shirt that read "*Life is Good with Tacos,*" looked me up and down and laughed.

"What?" I sputtered.

"Why are you dressed up, man?" Jumbo asked. "You look ridiculous."

"Hey, it's a job interview, isn't it?" I massaged the back of my neck.

"Um, can we come in?" Death tilted his hooded, faceless head.

"Oh, yeah, definitely." I took a step backwards. "Please, enter, my friends." I bowed.

Jumbo shook his head. I stood up.

"So," Death said with his uninterested voice. "This is home, huh?"

"Yeah." I shut the door behind them. "It's not much, but –"

"No, it's not," Death cut in.

Oh man, this was not the way I wanted things to start.

I waved over to the table and pulled out a chair. "Would you like a seat?"

"Funny." Jumbo's face went sober.

"Oh, no." I pulled a chair out and moved it to the side. "I mean, I'll make a handicap spot for you."

"What?" Jumbo spat.

"I mean a spot for your wheelchair," I corrected.

Death pulled one of the freshly assembled Swedish chairs from under the table and sat down. He folded his skeletal fingers together over the counter while tapping his foot impatiently. I waited for the pair to settle.

"Coffee, anyone?" I offered.

"Finally," Death said in a vanilla inflection. "I thought you would never ask."

"Sorry," I apologized. "Coming right up."

I hurried to the kitchen and removed the coffee decanter from the heating plate. I poured two cups and brought out creamer with the sugar I'd just purchased. I was lock, stock, and barrel in coffee essentials. I balanced it all on a ridiculous looking tray with flower designs and laid out the spread. Death pushed the creamer and sugar to the side and sipped his cup.

Apparently Death takes his coffee black.

Death sipped his coffee before removing a set of note cards from his cloak's sleeve. He straightened them on the table and cleared his throat. "Buck, thank you for coming to this interview."

"We came here, dude," Jumbo interjected. Death stared at Jumbo for a long moment.

"Sorry. I'll shut up."

"As I was saying," Death rebounded. "Thank you for taking the time to interview with us. It appears that a lot has occurred while I was on vacation."

"How'd your vacation go anyway?" I tried to make small talk.

"Well enough," he acknowledged.

"Where'd you go?" I planted myself in the chair across from him. "Fiji, Bermuda, Thailand?"

"San Diego Comic-Con," he retorted.

"Oh." I stopped in my tracks. "Was it cool?"

"Uh, yeah. Except I won *Best Cosplay*."

"Oh." I gave a small clap. "What's wrong with that?"

"I didn't dress up," he concluded. "Buck, can we please get back to the cards."

"Yes." I motioned to his note cards. "Of course."

Death flipped to a white paper card with pink lines. He traced his place with his index finger. "I've reviewed your performance report. As said before, I see that you were very busy during your internship." I nodded but held my tongue. "That's good. You need to see how rigmarole matters can be. No one is just going to give you a pass in the afterlife business.

With that being said, Buck." He paused, leaned down as if he was struggling to read his own handwriting, then continued. "What accomplishments this quarter are you most proud of?"

"It was just a week," Jumbo rectified.

"Silencio, Jumbo." Death slapped his boney palm on the table. "Buck, can you just answer the question."

"Yeah," I dove in. "No worries. I'd say that I'm most proud of unveiling the plot to steal your scythe, which is safely secured in my bedroom mind you, and slaying the powerful swindlers that tried to take it."

"Yes." Death flipped to a new card, his voice monotone. "I guess you could say that was neat. Let's move on. Buck, which goals do you feel you fell snort on?"

"Snort?" I asked, perplexed.

Death pulled the note card inches from his faceless hole. "Short, not snort. Which goals do you feel you fell short on?"

"Eek." I cracked my fingers nervously. "That's a great question."

"Why?" Death accused. "Did you fall short on a lot of your goals?"

"No," I objected. "Not at all. In fact, I feel like I did a great job overall. However, if I had to pick one thing I'd have liked to do better, I'd say that I wish I could have resolved matters quicker. I mean, it took me nearly a week, and then I learned that Dillinger wasn't exactly the guy we wanted to slay."

"Ah, yes," Death jeered. "Jumbo has also updated me on the relationship built with Dillinger. He tells me you both came to a collective decision to *not* kill Dillinger as I'd instructed?"

"Dude," Jumbo cut in. "We went over this."

Death held up his hand at Jumbo. "Ah, ah. Let Buck answer."

I tried to stop my leg from bouncing nervously under the table. "Yeah." I took a breath. "You see, Dillinger was paramount in unveiling the conspiracy within your domain, and we learned later that the only reason he was your target was because fake Jumbo wanted him dead. It was an unsanctioned death ordered by fake I.T. So ultimately, we made Dillinger a business partner."

"I'd hardly call this a conspiracy," Death argued. "But I think I may understand what you're struggling to communicate."

"Uh, okay. So as I was saying." I tried to repair the derailment. "Not only did we put an end to the plot, but Dillinger is going to help weed out future Unmentionables, making this organization's workload that much more manageable."

"Yes, yes." Death knocked his paper notes on the tabletop. "Buck, I'm going to cut straight to the chase. There're a lot of people who would love this job. What makes you think you could be an agent of Death? Why are you an asset above the rest?"

Here it was, the knockout punch. The question of all questions. What makes me important? Answer wrong and I was done for. Nail it, and I might just stand a chance. I focused on the watch Denise gave me, cleared my thoughts, and then breathed out.

Here goes nothing.

"Mr. Grim Reaper, sir," I opened up. "I highly respect your millennia of hard work and service. I could only dream of being as devoted as you. I also know I may have come off as uncouth in our early encounters, but I'm hoping you can look past that. You see, I've always wanted a career that I could be proud of, but I lacked opportunity. Within my time in the service and later as a hitman, I realized that I had a real talent for researching, locating, and disposing of targets. Much like yourself, I became obsessed with my work and never stopped until the job was done. I think given that, and with my modern skill set, I may prove to be a valuable resource to this organization. Finally, I am willing to learn, always wish to grow, and am humbled by the idea that I can be trained by the greatest professional hitman in existence. For these reasons, Mr. Grim Reaper, I feel that I could be a valuable employee for your institution."

There was a moment of silence. Jumbo stared out from behind his saucer, his eyes bouncing back and forth between Death and me. I half expected my seat to burst into flame as it dragged me to Hell. The optimist in me hoped he'd at least warn me first. Death took the cup to his hood hole and tipped it until he'd finished the coffee. He pushed his chair out, stood up and hovered over me. His shadow alone cooled the air around me.

"Buck," he declared ominously. "Stand up."

I winced, then moved to my feet. Death reached out his arm...and extended his hand.

"We expect a lot out of you, Buck," Death cautioned. "Welcome to the team."

My eyes welled up. I shook it off because, well, I'm tough, and macho, and coolheaded. I reached out to grab his hand, but Death quickly withdrew.

"Ah," Death laughed. "I'm joking. You can't shake my hand, man. It'll kill you. Jumbo." Death turned to Jumbo with a chuckle, to which Jumbo joined in. "You sure about this guy? He almost let me kill 'im.'"

"Test failed," Jumbo snorted. Death patted his leg while Jumbo held his stomach. "Buck, man, you almost went from six figures to six feet under." Jumbo's laugh volume increased.

I stood there in the dining room, shoulders slumped, waiting for the rabid monkeys to stop their comedy act. Ten minutes and thirty bad jokes later, it finally ended. When they were done, Jumbo gave me a packet complete with ectoplasm training, occult studies, and yearly expectations. The pair jabbed and jested between it all, but I just took it. With all that I've endured, I was used to it, plus the joy of not burning in Hell really softened each blow. By the time they left, I had to hurry to get Luna.

Beth's condo was in Logan Square. I swaggered uncontrollably as I walked to pick Luna up, drunk with new job high. I could see from the door's window that Luna and Beth were playing violins in tandem. Beth strummed her professional instrument while Luna played with a toy one that must have been a surprise. I played the voyeur and ogled the pair, all Ebenezer Scrooge about life post-Christmas Spirits.

Sure, I was a hitman working for the Grim Reaper, but a part of me felt normal again. I'd been given a second chance, and I was going to try and make my life as fulfilling as possible this time around. No more blaming my past or locking myself up in a cell of self-doubt. I didn't care how I came to be anymore. I was just happy that I *was*. So, as sentiment and promise made my heart patter, I lifted my knuckles and rapped on the door.

Later that evening, I'd find myself at *Gamer's Pair-of-Dice*. I made nice with Darren, which earned Luna an official store t-shirt. Luna wore it while eating her healthy cheeseburger dinner at my side at the role-playing table. No one asked about Freddy; as much as it guilted me, I didn't press the matter. Together with Nicolai's barbarian, Karen's cleric, Atari's rogue, Beth's bard, and the mighty wizard, Sarsicus, we stopped Nolan's undead onslaught known as the Mere of Deadmen. For some reason, slaying vampires, zombies, and other undead should have bothered me, but it didn't. No, I was far too busy having fun with friends and family to look back or too far into the future.

There you have it—story over. It's a dime store novel, really. I'm Buchanan Palasinski, but you can call me Buck. I'm a foster dad, war veteran, tabletop gamer...

Oh yeah, and Death's hitman.

EPILOGUE

"**D**on't you just love the smell of fresh cookies?" Azazel slipped on a pair of oven mitts with prints of Nicholas Cage's heads on his hands. He opened the stove's mouth. Smoke rose. "I'm still getting use to Canadian temperatures. It's Celsius, right? I can never get it right."

The bald man in the chair blinked his eyes, breathing hard through his nose.

Azazel removed the tray of blackened cookies. "Oh look, some in the middle survived. Those will be mine." One by one, he exchanged cookies from their tray to a wax papered plate using a spatula. The bald man's eyes wandered between the kitchen's chartreuse countertops, mushroom shaped spice jars, and red checkered curtains. An antique radio played accordion in the background. His blindfold had just slipped from his eyes, and he needed to work fast. He spotted a backdoor. The bald man wiggled his hands and legs in an attempt to soften his bindings. Unfortunately, while pressing to free himself, the wood chair he'd been taped to scraped the kitchen floor.

"Gethin." Azazel removed his baker's smock, revealing a Black Sabbath t-shirt. "You're not trying to escape, are you? You just got here." Azazel sauntered to the microwave and removed a roll of duct tape resting atop. He did a little walk-dance to the polka music and stretched the silver adhesive from its reel. Azazel applied tape generously to Gethin's wrists and ankles. "Oh, Gethin. Believe me, buddy, I get it. All you want is to be left alone, but no one cuts you any slack. This is your second time being captured, isn't it?"

Gethin blew air from his nose.

"Yikes, two times in a row. It must be very frustrating. However, until you tell us how to open up that gate, I just can't let you go." Azazel stepped back and took a look at his work. Gethin was nearly all silver now. "That should keep you."

A crash in the sitting room followed by random swearing perked Azazel's ears. He looked to Gethin and forced a smile. Seconds later, Azazel's twin walked in the kitchen. The pair were nearly identical except that Azazel's double wore his hair slicked back and donned a salmon dress shirt complete with matching skinny tie. The suited twin had three scorch marks across his smoking shirt.

"Armen." Azazel put the tape back on the microwave. "How's the thing with the thing going?"

Armen took a cookie from the plate and bit in. He spit the treat back out. "Azazel, *gross*, these are burnt."

Azazel's jaw tightened. There was a moment of exchanged glances, as if a wordless discussion was being had. Azazel spun around with a wide smile of a serial killer.

"Sorry, friend." Azazel clapped to Gethin. "It looks like

I'm going to have make another batch. Don't worry, we'll feed you eventually. Now, as I was saying, what're your thoughts on telling us how to open the gate? We just can't seem to get the dang key to work."

Armen tucked the tails of his shirt into his dress pants, kneeled down to Gethin's level, and frowned. "Now, Gethin," he needled slowly. "I don't know what my brother told you, but if you don't inform us how to open up said portal, we're going to have to give you over to Satan. Now I don't want to, and I'm sure you don't want to go back to him, especially after your nasty breakup, so let's just work together. What do you say, buddy?"

Gethin gave a muffled curse.

"I'm hoping you're saying *so true*," Armen deadpanned. "Though I highly doubt it."

Just then the screech of tires shrilled from the backyard driveway. A glossy black sports bike pulled up with a rider in a sleek helmet and tight leathers in front of the canary garage. The ternion of devils stared out the kitchen window. A curvy figure removed her helmet, letting a curtain of lavender hair air out. She had dimpled cheeks, sun freckles along her nose, and puffy lips curled in a lazy smile.

Armen shook his head. "Damn succubus," he chastised before leaving for the sitting room.

The backdoor Gethin had been eyeing opened up and the succubus entered.

"Hey, Sasha." Azazel straightened out the fifteen bags of chocolate chips on the counter. "Did you bring back vanilla extract?"

Sasha shoved a tiny paper bag into Azazel's chest, drawing a pained cough.

"Oh no," he exclaimed in a pitch two octanes higher. "This is Madagascar Vanilla. I wanted Mexican Vanilla." Sasha wound up her fist. "No, no, Madagascar is fine. Rich and creamy."

Armen used a sponge to scrub his scorched shirt marks. "How'd your little trip go? Find your sweetheart?" Sasha cracked her knuckles. "Ah, ah, not me darling. Back it up."

Sasha shook her head before biting the tips of her leather gloves, undressing her hands one at a time. When her fingers were free, she drew a kitchen stool under the island in front of Gethin. Sasha perched on top, tucking a perfect strand of temple hair behind her rounded ear.

Azazel caught his breath. "Still no progress."

"Gethin," Sasha pled in a voice sweet as apple pie. "It's only a matter of time before we find Thomas. Once we do," she said, voice soothing, "we're going to pick him apart like kids with a bug." Gethin narrowed his eyes. "Now, let's go over this again. We have your ex's pitchfork. We have a fairy army and soon Dothur will return with Death's scythe. All we need is for you to tell us how to use Satan's little farming tool and we can leave you alone. It's the trilogy we want, not a lovestruck angel. Help us help you."

Gethin rolled his eyes, then pointed to his right hand with his Mirren nose. Sasha looked down at his taped hand and noticed he was giving her the finger.

"Why couldn't I be an Incubus?" Sasha looked up at the ceiling. "This would all be over." She adjusted her weight. "Okay then, Gethin, how about you tell us where Nedonius is?" Gethin stayed quiet.

Azazel measured vanilla extract in a wood measuring spoon. "Think Dothur will be able to break him?"

Armen reentered the room with Satan's pitchfork. He
held it to the kitchen light as if there were a secret button.
The over-the-top trident looked ridiculous in the business-
devil's hands. It had an iron handle charred black with
silver sequins stippled up the stem. The neck of the pitchfork had been decorated in boa of flamingo feathers, and
the crimson pointed tips were shaped like barbed hearts.

"Think Dothur will know how to work this, too?"
Armen canvassed the room. "Say, where is that guy
anyhow?"

——————

THE GREYING tailor stretched measuring tape along a pair
of strapping arms. He marked the strip's number with his
thumb before stepping to a small table in order to scribble
details on paper. The tailor's handsome customer kept his
hand stretched as he balanced himself on a stool in front
of a half circle of mirrors. His raven hair was sculpted into
a sheen pompadour that crowed over his strong brow. He
smiled at his reflection, causing his chiseled jaw to tauten
along his cleft chin. The tailor snuck a peak from behind
his station, licking his lips.

The bell from the contemporary store's entrance
called. The tailor pushed his blue framed glasses to the
bridge of his nose.

"That's peculiar," he propounded with Parisian accent.
"I locked the door."

The man on the stool winked. "Better check it out. I
wouldn't want you losing a customer over little old me."

The tailor smiled, straightened out his trendy vest and
pants, then ambled through the white walls of what

looked more like a spaceship than clothing store. He pushed the swinging door with a gold octopus emblem on its face.

"Going shopping, Danny Boy?" A raspy man's voice grated from a nearby suit wrack. The gaunt figure shuffled through sets of million-dollar suits. His epicene face had a mane of green spiraled hair and yellow cat's eyes. He wore a red Napoleonic soldier's suit with silver high heels.

"Dothur," The man on the stool kept locked on his own reflection. "How are my idiots doing?"

"Don't know." The Mad Knight wrenched his shoulders. "I came here first."

The man on the stool's lips unfolded into a dapper smile. "How's Canada treating you?"

"Not nearly as fun as the States. Too bad about the orange fat man by the way."

"No worries. His offspring aren't going anywhere. They're twice as awful."

"The trio of fools have been toying with your pitchfork ever since I gave it over. They feel as if they're on the cusp of understanding it."

"Ha, that's fun. You said they had Gethin?"

"Aye, they did *that* while I was away."

"Resourceful."

"The twins couldn't pour piss out of a boot if there were instructions on the heel." The Mad Knight held a blouse to his chest. "The succubus is a clever lass. She may be persuaded to help you."

"What about you?"

"Me?" The Mad Knight pressed his spidery fingers to his chest. "Body by Fisher, brains by Mattel."

"It's not what I meant."

"I know what you meant, laddie."

"And?"

The Mad Knight gave his hundred-toothed smile. "Better the Devil you know than the devil you don't."

"Well said."

The Mad Knight limped closer to the set of half mirrors and leaned on one.

"What happened to you?" The handsome man asked.

"Love bite. I'll be fine." The Mad Knight winced as he massaged his knee. "Anyhow, Queen Aveline has her forces in Chicago. All I need is to give the word and they'll strike."

"How can I trust you, Dothur? I trusted your mother once, and it didn't turn out well for me."

"Sounds like you had quite the happy ending," The Mad Knight said plainly. The man on the stool dropped his arms, fixing an unamused expression onto The Mad Knight through the mirror. Dothur nodded. "Truth is, I can't even trust myself."

"True chaos."

"Yes."

"You know what they say about gambling with the devil?"

"No higher stakes. I'll deliver, though. I just don't want to share the bounty with an entire pantheon of morons."

The man in the mirror puffed out his chest and winked at his reflection. "I'll finally get one over on..." he paused. "*Him*." The lights above flickered. The pair stared up until the electric returned to its perpetual state. There was a short intermission. The Mad Knight watched as the man in the mirror dressed himself in his custom-fit suit. "You did retrieve the scythe, yes?"

"About that." The Mad Knight tucked his hands in his pocket and pushed up on his tippy- toes. "What if I told you that instead of *just* getting the scythe, I retrieved the weapon along with Death's best personal agent?"

The handsome man turned to Dothur. "I'd say that's fucking fantastic."

BUCK STILL NEEDS YOU

Did you enjoy A Dead-End Job? *Reviews keep books alive ...*
Buck needs your help!

Help him by leaving your review on either
GoodReads or the digital storefront of your choosing. He
thanks you!

ACKNOWLEDGMENTS

"I am here to create greatness, not in living legacy, but memories for thereafter... and then I must go."

When I first started writing "A Dead End Job" in 2019, it was nothing more than an agglomeration of daydreams. The idea of a hard-boiled hitman working for a comical Grim Reaper burrowed a hole in my brain, so I put it down on paper and sent it out. The amazing Parliament House Press contracted the book (No, I'm legally obligated to say that — Why would think that?) and we hit the ground running with edits. However, life delivered a shot to the kisser during the book-butchering phase. I moved across the country, had my second child and then the pandemic hit. I discovered a bovarism in myself, and the world around me, that I didn't like. I would always still be the dick-joke toting writer, but some very serious allegories weaved themselves into the story while I edited. I want to acknowledge those who helped me recognize these issues.

Thanks to Johnny "A Pair of Dice" Mecha. My best friend since second grade served in the 10th Mountain

Infantry Division. His and his army buddies stories helped me not only flesh out crazy ideas like Buck's nightly rocket attacks, but it also drew my attention to the way we treat soldiers after they've served. Veterans have some of the best, darkest sense of humors I've ever witnessed, but it's sometimes a reaction to what they've suffered through. It's time to stop throwing their treatment into the political blender and help them get any treatment they deserve.

Here's to the fight against racial injustice. My Father was a Chicago born Latino in a time when it cost you your livelihood. He navigated a world unkind to minorities in order to get work, sacrificing his own pride in the process. He shouldn't have, but he did it for us. Racism stultifies all progress. Let's address it.

Finally, I wanted to acknowledge all the weirdos, nerds and grim humored readers out there who pick up my books. When I write, it's so utterly selfish and yet, somehow, wholeheartedly forged for you. Once I type *The End*, the story is bequeathed to the reader. Thanks for the substantial support, and please drop me a message on my website if you ever have questions, comments or just feel like reaching out.